THE
STONE
SERPENT

NICHOLAS
KAUFMANN

Dark, oily movement on the bathroom wall caught her eye. A snake oozed in through the open window. Its scaled, rippling body was thick and heavy, with dark brown crossbands and peculiar red stripes along its sides. It had the big triangular, unmarked head of a copperhead, but there was something frighteningly wrong with its eyes. They were an iridescent white. Colors shifted deep within them as the light hit them from different angles. The vertical slits of the snake's pupils studied her with inhuman iciness.

Meredith scrambled out of the tub, spilling water across the tiled floor. She yanked her bathrobe off the hook and quickly shrugged it on as she ran for the door. Her feet slipped on the wet floor and skidded out from under her. She fell painfully onto the hard tile, but she didn't dare look back at the window. She didn't want to see if the snake was any closer. She launched herself at the door, grabbed the handle, and pulled.

It didn't budge.

She forgot she'd locked it. She clawed at the sliding lock, shrieking in terror, but her wet fingers couldn't find a grip. Now, trapped in the bathroom, she chanced a look behind her. Her blood went cold as she saw the snake drop to the floor with a heavy slap. A forked tongue flicked out of its mouth, tasting the air, searching for her.

A second snake started to slither through the window behind it.

A Macabre Ink Production — Macabre Ink is an imprint of Crossroad Press.

First Edition

Praise for *The Hungry Earth*:

"Kaufmann drops you right into the psilocybin-fueled action and doesn't hold back when describing the manic and monstrous details of this nature-strikes-back horror yarn."

—*Fangoria*

"*The Hungry Earth* is a pulse-pounding Horror novel with a terrifyingly plausible premise and puts a fresh spin on familiar tropes."

—*Ink Heist*

"Jack Finney meets Michael Crichton meets 21st century spores. Nicholas Kaufmann's *The Hungry Earth* is a fast-paced thrill ride through a scarily plausible fungal nightmare."

—Paul Tremblay, bestselling author of *Survivor Song* and *The Cabin at the End of the World*

"Nicholas Kaufmann's *The Hungry Earth* is required reading for anyone who loves tightly plotted horror. It's a gleeful throwback to the best body horror of the '80s, updated with a modern premise. His best work to date. Devour it, before it devours you!"

—Sarah Langan, bestselling author of *Good Neighbors*

"If you're like me, *The Hungry Earth* will make you squirm out of your skin. Nicholas Kaufmann offers up an unputdownable blend of gruesome body horror and fast-paced suspense that will have you looking suspiciously at mushrooms for a long time to come."

—Ray Garton, author of *Live Girls* and *Ravenous*

"Kaufmann's *The Hungry Earth* is eco-horror at its finest. With vividly drawn characters and a protagonist you'll want to follow through additional books, the plight of Sakima and its denizens resounds with emotional intensity and accelerates with the verve of the best medical thrillers. Visceral, detailed, impeccably researched. And all too real for comfort."

—John Hornor Jacobs, author of *A Lush and Seething Hell: Two Tales of Cosmic Horror*

For Alexa, always.

"There is poison in the fang of the serpent, in the mouth of the fly and in the sting of a scorpion; but the wicked man is saturated with it."

— Chanakya, *Chanakaya Neeti*

1

Malachai Applewhite was halfway to Sakima when he started to turn to stone.

It began with his left leg, radiating outward from a sharp pain in his ankle. The leg was numb now. When he touched it, it wasn't flesh he felt under the material of his pants. What he felt was hard and unyielding. What he felt was stone.

His right leg remained unchanged, at least for now. He could still work his car's accelerator and brakes. Thank God for small miracles.

The irony made him smirk behind the steering wheel. Here he was, thanking God when in so many ways it was God he was running from. No, who was he kidding? It was his *father* he was running from. The man had kept Malachai under his heel his whole life. He'd finally had enough. This morning, before anyone was awake, he sneaked out of his family's house. With a pang of regret, he thought of Meredith, the little sister he'd left behind. He knew she wanted to leave with him, but she was just fourteen, still a kid. He didn't know if he would be able to take care of her when he got to Sakima. He hoped she would forgive him for leaving without her, but he doubted it. He knew if the tables were turned, he wouldn't forgive her.

As he'd gotten into his car, he felt a sharp, stabbing pain in his left ankle out of nowhere. That was the start of it.

For all his left leg's numbness, there was an excruciating, burning pain r the edge of it. Whatever was happening to him, it was spreading, moving up his leg and into his groin, transforming flesh into stone. The very idea of it was impossible, and yet, somehow, it was happening to him. What part of him would change next? His stomach? His chest? He was hot with a fever. He wiped the sweat from his forehead, but it was drenched again a moment later. He fought to concentrate on the road. He had to get to Sakima.

Elijah's burning chariot, pulled by fiery horses, moved through the clouds above him.

It's not real, he told himself. *It's a delusion from the fever.*

Was any of this real? How could a man turn to stone?

As he turned onto the exit for Sakima, his sweaty hands slipped on the steering wheel. The car lurched to one side. Car horns blared all around him, followed by one loud blast from a passing semi. He grabbed the steering wheel again and quickly brought the car under control. A woman with big hair and sunglasses drove by in a BMW and flipped him the bird.

Pain crawled across Malachai's gut. He put his hand inside his shirt and felt rough, hard stone. The indentation of his belly button was still there, solid as marble, like sticking his finger into the navel of Michelangelo's *David*. More pain flared, this time in his right leg. Soon, it too would turn to stone, and then he would lose control of the car altogether.

He had to reach Sakima before that happened. His friend Sam Templeton was waiting for him there with an offer of a safe place to stay while he set up a new life away from his father. Malachai wiped feverish sweat from his brow. The pain was worse now. He wanted to double over in the driver's seat, curl up like he used to do when he was a kid with a stomach ache, but he forced himself to concentrate on the road. He had to keep driving.

The burning chariot peeked out from behind a cloud like a fiery celestial body, a second sun blazing in the morning sky. It was following him.

It's not real!

He closed his eyes for a second. When he opened them again, it was gone. He was losing his mind.

Or maybe he was dying and the chariot had come for him. That was what had been drilled into his head all his life, wasn't it? That his soul would be carried up to heaven as long as he lived a pious life? Did he believe that anymore? Had he ever?

Malachai pulled out the phone he'd bought in secret. No

one knew he had it, not Meredith and certainly not his father. His father would have destroyed it if he found it. Keeping one hand on the wheel, Malachai tried to dial Sam's number. He had to let Sam know what was happening to him. Sam would send help. The car bounced over a pothole, and the phone fell to the floor. He swerved into the next lane. Amid an orchestra of angry car horns, he gripped the wheel tightly with both hands and steered back into his own lane.

Was he being punished? Was that what this was? Was God so angry with him for leaving that He decided to turn Malachai to stone like he'd turned Lot's wife to salt? Her sin had been to look back when she fled Sodom. Malachai had left home without looking back. It wasn't fair.

Following the directions Sam had given him, Malachai turned onto MacLeod Avenue, once the busy main thoroughfare of downtown Sakima but now mostly a graveyard of closed shops and restaurants. Everywhere, there were boarded-up windows and FOR RENT signs. Some of the buildings were still blackened from the fires last year. Even in the isolation of his own village, Malachai had heard what happened here. Mass hysteria, or maybe it'd been some kind of virus. He was hazy on the details, but he seemed to remember the CDC was called in.

The burning pain moved up his torso. It was getting harder to breathe by the moment. His lungs were turning to stone inside him. He struggled to suck in air.

His field of vision darkened around the edges. He felt the car wobble beneath him as his hands slipped off the wheel. Car horns blasted a warning, but they sounded a thousand miles away. Malachai was only dimly aware that he'd crossed the double yellow lines in the middle of the road and was speeding toward the sidewalk. The smell of burning rubber came to him through the windows. He heard screeching tires and saw people dash out of his way, but it was like he was watching it unfold on a distant TV screen. No more than a mild curiosity.

He could no longer breathe. Too much of his body had turned to stone, and it was still spreading. He wished he had more time. He would have liked to know what life was like away from his father. He would have liked to know what freedom felt like. He'd been so close.

The tires spat and crunched as his car mounted the sidewalk. It crashed to a stop at the base of a streetlamp. More car horns blared, including his own. But to Malachai, who watched with stone eyes as the fiery chariot came down to collect him, those horns were the trumpets of God calling him home.

2

Dr. Laura Powell approached the large glass case hesitantly. Inside, hanging off a thick iron hook, was a human ribcage. It reminded her of something out of a horror movie, the grisly trophy found in the lair of a serial killer. What it didn't look like was art, although that was precisely what it was meant to be. To Laura's trained medical eye, she could tell the ribcage wasn't real. It was fashioned from 3D-printed plastic, but it still left her feeling unsettled. She looked down at the gallery catalog in her hands. Printed in big letters across the cover was THE LUMINOUS FLESH: THE CONSTRUCTION AND DISSEMINATION OF THE HUMAN BODY BY THE NEW YORK ART COLLECTIVE STUDIO L.P. KELNER.

Booker Coates's reflection appeared in the glass as he came up behind her. Broad-shouldered and a good half-foot taller, he dwarfed her own reflection. The overhead lights cast a glare on the rich brown skin of his bald head.

"Thanks for bringing me here," he said, brushing a hand over his tightly trimmed goatee. "I'm definitely going to have nightmares tonight."

She grinned at him, though she knew he was only half joking. Booker was no stranger to nightmares. He'd been having them on and off for a year now, ever since the spores of a mutant fungus had infected the people of Sakima. Under the fungus's thrall, friends and neighbors turned violent, hunting them like animals, determined to infect them as well. Booker had nearly died in a car crash that left one of his legs wrecked. These days, it wasn't unusual for him to moan and thrash in his sleep, tortured by the memories. When it happened, she did her best to calm him, but she wasn't immune to nightmares herself. Unlike Booker, she *had* been infected by the fungus, which she'd come to know as the God of Dirt. Occasionally, she would wake up in terror, convinced she could still hear the God of Dirt calling to her from the depths of Dradin Park. On those occasions, she would lie still in bed, holding her breath and listening, but there was only ever silence. The quiet outside—and the quiet in her head—was proof that the God of Dirt really was gone.

She took Booker's hand and pulled him closer to the glass case. It was his first week of summer break as Sakima, New York's newest high school science teacher, and Laura was determined to find fun things for them to do together so they could make better memories to replace the bad ones. A day trip to the Storm King Arts Center in New Windsor sounded like just the thing, only she hadn't expected to find the Museum Building's gallery filled with glass cases containing replica human bones like something out of a state fair's haunted house.

She looped her free arm through his and nodded at the large stainless-steel dial at the bottom of the glass case. "Would you like to do the honors?"

He shrugged. "Sure. What's the worst that could happen? It's already horrifying."

Booker turned the dial slowly to the right. According to the instructions, the dial increased the humidity level inside the case, which was supposed to stimulate the formation of crystals.

Sure enough, as he turned the dial, milky white crystals formed like frost along the bones of the ribcage. Sharp and glistening, they built outward in a fractal pattern, growing larger, filling the spaces between ribs and reaching toward each other like lovers yearning to be joined. Booker turned the dial farther, and the crystal growth accelerated until it formed a latticework that filled the entire ribcage, giving the bones the semblance of a body again, albeit a crystalline one that twinkled and gleamed.

Fed by the humidity, the crystals continued growing, spiking outward, expanding past the ribcage into the empty air around it like cellular growth gone mad, turning the makeshift body into something alarmingly alien and misshapen.

Booker turned the dial all the way to the left, back to its starting point. Fans sucked the humidity out of the glass case, and the crystals began to retreat. Laura watched them shrink and let go of each other, returning the shape in the glass case to a simple human ribcage.

"It's beautiful, in a way," she said.

"That's one word for it." He took the catalog from her and read aloud. "'Each growth pattern is different. It is the viewer's interaction with the installation, in terms of how much or how little humidity they permit, that creates its own crystallization process. A unique structure of luminous flesh. A new and different human form given life with one turn of a dial, and returned to a state of death with another.' Huh. Charming."

Laura took the catalog back from him and tucked it under one arm. The small gallery was crowded with visitors examining the contents of multiple glass cases positioned around the room. Nearby, a young girl of about ten watched in awe as her mother turned a dial and a skeletal arm grew fuzzy with white crystals.

"Do you want to try one of the others?" Laura asked.

"I'd rather get some air," Booker said.

He led the way out. He still walked with a limp. It was more prominent in cold, damp weather. On a beautiful June day like today, Laura was certain no one would notice it but her.

Outside, the sky was a perfect cloudless blue. The wind blew warm and gentle, and brought with it the smell of freshly cut grass. The Museum Building was the only enclosed space in Storm King's open-air art center. It stood atop a hill that overlooked the 500-acre grounds, offering a spectacular view of the large-scale sculptures that dotted the landscape, gigantic pieces of modern art fashioned from iron and steel, built to weather the elements.

Booker put his arm around her as they took in the view. "Victor would have loved it here."

Victor Cunningham had been like a father to Booker ever since Booker was a child. He died trying to save them from the fungus. In his will, he left Booker his house, a rustic wooden split-level deep in the woods on the edge of town. It had come as a surprise, almost as much of a surprise as an angry old recluse like Victor having a will at all. Booker still didn't know if he was going to keep the property or sell it. For sentiment's sake, she hoped he would keep it. Victor would have hated to see it fall into anyone else's hands.

"Even in a place this beautiful," she said, "I'm sure Victor would have found something to complain about."

Booker grinned. "Complaining was one of the few things that made Victor happy." He paused. "That and the drugs."

Laura laughed, but was interrupted by her phone ringing in her purse. She pulled it out and saw Elena Morales's name on the screen. The smile faded from Laura's face. Booker noticed the shift in her mood and gave her a quizzical look. She answered the call.

"How are you, Chief Morales?"

"Dr. Powell, I need you to come in and perform an autopsy right away." Sakima's new chief of police wasn't one for pleasantries.

Laura bristled. The previous chief, her good friend Ralph Gorney, used to *request* her help. Morales *ordered* it. Still, as Sakima's part-time medical examiner, Laura didn't have much choice in the matter. There wasn't a lot of crime in their little portion of the Hudson Valley, especially not violent crime, but every once in a while, duty called. When it did, it rarely chose a convenient time.

"I can be there in an hour." She saw the resignation in Booker's face that their outing had been cut short. She squeezed his hand by way of apology. "Can you tell me what happened?"

"A car accident on MacLeod Avenue," Chief Morales said. "Thankfully, there was only one casualty. The driver."

"I take it you need a tox screen to see if they were drunk or under the influence?"

"No, it's not that. There's...something else."

She didn't like how that sounded. "What is it?"

"It's better if you see for yourself, Dr. Powell," Chief Morales said. "I'll expect you in one hour. Don't be late."

3

True to her word, Chief Morales was waiting for Laura when she arrived at the morgue an hour later. A black body bag lay on the stainless-steel autopsy table. Its zipper was secured with a police seal to show that no one had tampered with the body inside after its removal from the scene of the accident.

"Dr. Powell," Morales said with a curt nod. At five-foot-three, she was a shorter than Laura but carried her diminutive size with the confidence of a bulldog. Every one of her forty-nine years showed in the lines of her face. She had the sharp, probing eyes of someone who didn't take shit from anyone. She glanced at her wristwatch, as if to check that Laura hadn't taken one minute longer than the hour she'd promised.

To say that Laura didn't like Chief Morales was an understatement. The first time they'd met, workmen had still been in the process of removing Ralph Gorney's name from his office door and replacing it with Morales's. The pain of Ralph's loss was still raw then, just a few weeks out from his death, and the sight of his name being sanded off the door only made it worse. Still, walking into that room, Laura had done her best to maintain her professional composure. She needn't have bothered. Morales was cold and standoffish from the start, giving her little more than a quick, cursory glance from behind the desk. No *Nice to meet you*, no *I'm looking forward to working with you*, nothing. She didn't even offer her condolences on Ralph's death. Just a quick handshake with half her attention on the papers in front of her. It was only when Laura made the mistake of calling her Elena that she got the woman's full attention. *You are to address me as Chief Morales*, she said. Things hadn't gotten any warmer since.

"Is this the crash victim?" Laura asked, looking over the body bag. It bulged curiously at the sides.

"Direct from the crash site," Chief Morales confirmed. "The responding officers apprised me of the victim's unusual condition, but I haven't seen it for myself yet."

"Condition?"

Morales only nodded, offering no further details. Laura took that as her cue to get to work. In the adjoining bathroom, she put on her scrubs, a fluid-resistant lab coat, a surgical mask, safety glasses, a hair net, and a pair of nitrile gloves. Back in the morgue, she broke the police seal on the body bag and pulled down the heavy nylon zipper. The bright LED overheads shone down on the protruding shoulder of a male body. He was lying on his side, curled in the fetal position, which explained the odd bulges in the sides of the bag. If lifted upright, he would have looked like he was still sitting behind the steering wheel of his car. Strange. It was standard procedure to position the bodies lying supine, face up. Why had the EMTs bagged him like this instead?

She pushed the heavy folds of the bag away to get a better look. The face of the dead man was oddly discolored, a grayish brown, the color of rock. Laura touched his cheek with her gloved finger, but the skin didn't dimple no matter how hard she pressed. It didn't even feel like skin. It was as hard as stone.

"What on Earth?" she muttered.

Chief Morales moved closer for a better look. "When they told me, I had trouble believing it. I wanted to see for myself."

"This has got to be a hoax," Laura said. "This man wasn't driving a car this morning. I would guess he's been dead for years. It's why he's stuck in this one position. Judging by the lack of decomposition, I'd say he was kept somewhere with the right environmental conditions to preserve the body."

Chief Morales consulted a field interview notebook she had with her. "According to the officers at the scene, there were a dozen witnesses who all said the same thing. Only seconds passed between the crash and the discovery of the body. If it's a hoax, someone would have had to get out of the car and put this corpse behind the wheel without being seen, either while the car was moving or right after the crash. No one saw anything like that."

Laura shook her head. "It doesn't make sense. This man is a fossil."

She examined the body's stony, discolored face. He still had hair on top of his head—a buzz cut, short enough that she'd almost overlooked it. She touched the hair gently. Even through her glove, it felt soft. Real. It still had pigmentation, too; a dark brown. Fossils were rarely found with hair, let alone hair that was still soft and retained its color. The keratin made it too difficult to preserve. Strike one for her theory.

Then there was the matter of his eyes. If he really had been dead for as long a time as his condition seemed to indicate, his eyes would have sunk into the sockets. Though his eyelids were closed, she could tell from their rounded shapes that the eyeballs were still present underneath. That was strike two. She didn't need a third to know something else was going on here.

"My first thought would be metastatic calcification," Laura said. "If he had a condition like primary hyperparathyroidism—a tumor in the parathyroid gland—it's possible elevated levels of calcium in his blood serum could cause calcium salts to be deposited in otherwise normal tissue, which would result in hardening. The only problem is that metastatic calcification usually occurs in blood vessels or organs like the kidneys, the lungs, or the stomach. I've never seen it on a scale like this. It's his *entire* body."

She took a scalpel off the instrument tray, bent over the body, and scratched the blade's flat end across the hardened skin of his cheek. It sounded so much like scraping stone that she was half convinced again that this had to be an elaborate hoax.

"Then there's dystrophic calcification," she continued. "Deposits of calcium salts can occur in dead tissue, usually caused by the presence of hematomas, blood clots, or fat necrosis following acute pancreatitis. Only, the same problem applies. It just doesn't seem possible on this big a scale."

"Then what *could* cause it on this big a scale?" Morales asked.

Laura forced out a breath. "Maybe fibrodysplasia ossificans progressiva, sometimes known as FOP or Münchmeyer disease?

It's an extremely rare genetic disorder that affects the body's repair mechanism. If any of the fibrous connective tissues like muscles, tendons, and ligaments is damaged, instead of repairing the tissue, the body replaces it with new bone growth. Sometimes it can even happen spontaneously. Joints can become permanently fused. Patients can form entire secondary skeletons, which leads to them losing the ability to move altogether. It's the only known medical condition where one organ system changes into another. There's no cure or treatment. Even if you try to remove the extra bone growth surgically, it's just replaced by more bone. It's awful."

"Do you think that's what he had?"

"Right now, I'm not so sure," Laura said. "First of all, it would be too painful to sit behind the wheel of a car with Münchmeyer disease. Second, the new bones form *inside* the body, not outside. Third..." She paused and scraped his cheek with the scalpel again. "I don't think this hardened tissue *is* bone. Who was he?"

"According to the ID in his wallet, his name was Malachai Applewhite," Morales said. "He wasn't from Sakima. His home address was in Valley Grove."

Laura knew the name. A small village just east of Sakima, Valley Grove was home to a fundamentalist religious sect known as the Church of the Divine Chariot. Back when she was in high school, a man from Valley Grove gave a guest sermon at the church she and her mother used to attend. His sermon was all fire and brimstone, warnings about a wrathful God, and how a man's role was pious leadership while a woman's role was total submission. Bored, Laura tuned it out, but her mother was furious. Afterward, she told their minister if he ever had that man or anyone else from the Church of the Divine Chariot back again, it would be the last time she and her daughter attended services there.

As it turned out, they stopped attending soon after anyway, when Laura's mother went off her meds and her depression sent her spiraling. It was a common cycle for her, starting her meds and stopping them, until finally, while Laura was away at college, her mother took her own life. That long-ago Sunday at church with her mother was only a hazy memory now, but there was one thing Laura definitely remembered about the man from Valley Grove. He wore a crisp white polo shirt identical to the one on the dead body in front of her.

"You can see why I wanted an autopsy," Morales said. "I don't think the car crash is what killed him."

"I don't either." Laura took his jaw lightly in one hand and tried to move his head to the side. It wouldn't budge. She might as well have tried to turn the head of a statue. "I'll get started. I should have a report for you in an hour. Should I bring it to your office?"

"No need," Morales said. "I'm staying right here."

Laura turned to her. "I prefer to do autopsies alone."

"Not this time," Morales told her. "This is a high-profile case, Dr. Powell. The crash happened downtown on a busy street. It'll be all over the news by tonight. I want to make sure everything goes smoothly."

Smoothly? Laura had been Sakima's medical examiner for nearly five years now. She didn't need to be observed like some first-year med student.

"Have you ever seen an autopsy, Chief?" she asked, trying to keep the anger out of her voice. "It's more than most people can handle."

"Proceed, Dr. Powell," Morales said impatiently. The bulldog was showing her teeth.

"Fine."

Laura lowered the blinds over the observation window that looked in from the hallway.

"What's that for?" Morales asked.

"An autopsy is an intimate procedure," Laura explained. "The deceased deserves some privacy."

Morales was unmoved by her compassion for the dead. "We're wasting time, Dr. Powell. Let's get on with it."

Laura bit her tongue before she said something she would regret. Morales stepped up to the autopsy table, hovering over the body as if she could force it to give up its mysteries if she glared at it hard enough.

"If you're going to observe, you'll have to move back," Laura told her. "I also need you to put on a mask and a hair net. I don't want you contaminating the body."

Inwardly, she winced. She meant to say she didn't want *anything* contaminating the body, but her anger got the better of her. Morales stepped back and put on the protective equipment without comment. Laura smiled to herself. At least the chief listened to her *sometimes*. She would take that as a win.

Laura unzipped the body bag the rest of the way and photographed Malachai Applewhite's curled body inside. An external examination revealed some light damage to his clothing, presumably from the crash. A scuff here, some torn cloth there. Aside from the white polo shirt, he wore crisply pressed black slacks, dark socks, and black dress shoes. She examined the exposed skin of his face, neck, and arms for bruises and lacerations from the crash, but if there were any, they were camouflaged by the discoloration and stonelike texture of his flesh.

From the corner of her eye, she noticed Morales glance at her watch.

If you have somewhere to be, Chief, don't let me stop you, she thought.

Unfortunately, Morales stayed put, watching intently as Laura cut the clothing off Malachai Applewhite's body and put everything in an evidence bag. Like the hair on his head, his chest hair and pubic hair remained intact, sprouting from the hardened skin like normal. Did that mean the follicles underneath were still intact? Why hadn't they fossilized along with the rest of him?

She filled out the exam form as she inspected the body: race (Caucasian), sex (male), hair color and length (brown, short), height: (five feet, eight inches), age (Morales informed her the birthdate on his ID made him twenty-seven), and whether he had any identifying features like tattoos (none), scars (none), or birthmarks (impossible to tell with the skin discoloration).

She needed to record his eye color to make sure it matched his ID, but when she tried to lift the eyelid, she couldn't. It was fixed in place, as unyielding as the rest of him. She tried cutting it open, but the tip of her scalpel wouldn't penetrate the hardened skin no matter how much pressure she exerted. It was like trying to cut into granite. She felt the weight of Chief

Morales's gaze on her the entire time, judging her, waiting for her to slip up.

"Is there a problem, Dr. Powell?" she asked finally.

"I can't make an incision in the skin," Laura said. "It's too hard for the tools I've got here."

"If you can't cut into the body, how will you perform the autopsy?"

"I would need something stronger, like a mechanized saw, but I would be hesitant to use one. It could damage the body too much."

"This is unacceptable," Morales said. "I need to know what happened to this man."

Facing away from her, Laura closed her eyes and took a deep breath to keep herself from exploding. Morales was insufferable. Laura didn't think it was possible to miss Ralph more than she already did.

"I want answers as much as you do, Chief," she said. "I'll just have to think of another way to get them."

"Make it quick."

Morales looked at her watch again. Laura took another deep breath, but it didn't calm her much this time. Why did it feel like her job was on the line?

She closed her eyes. She needed to stop worrying about Morales and focus on the autopsy. If she didn't have the tools on hand to open up the body, there had to be something else available to her. Some other way to look inside him.

Her eyes popped open. "The X-ray machine."

"You have one?" Morales asked.

"No, but the forensics lab does."

Laura picked up the phone on the wall and dialed the proper extension.

"Forensics lab," a male voice said. "Dae-jung speaking."

Park Dae-jung was the new lab tech Sakima PD had hired after Sofia Hernandez's death. He seemed nice enough and was good at his job, but so far Laura had kept him at arm's length. She'd grown close to Sofia and wasn't ready to form a friendship with her replacement. She was still mourning so many lost friends, it felt like she didn't have room for any new ones.

"Dae-jung, it's Laura," she said. "If you're not using it at the moment, I'd like to borrow the portable X-ray machine."

"Is this for the stone man?" he asked.

"How did you hear about that?"

"I went to the scene with the responding officers. I saw the body myself. Guy looks like he had a run-in with Medusa."

"Not quite," Laura said. "His tissue has hardened, but it's not stone. I don't know what it is yet. An autopsy would help, but I'm having trouble opening him up."

"Ah, hence the need for the X-ray machine. Got it," Dae-jung said. "I'll wheel it over. I'd like to see what's going on inside that body, too, if you don't mind."

"I don't mind. Thanks." She hung up and turned back to Morales. "The machine is on its way. The forensics lab is just down the hall, so it won't be long."

Morales nodded and looked at her watch again.

"If you don't mind my asking," Laura ventured, "is there somewhere you need to be? You've been checking your watch a lot."

Morales looked up at her sharply. "Where I *ought* to be, Dr. Powell, is City Hall, briefing Mayor Sutherland on why a car almost plowed into a crowd on a busy sidewalk this morning, and why, exactly, the driver of said car looks like a goddamn statue. Except I can't give him the report he needs until you perform your autopsy."

The morgue door swung open not a moment too soon. Dae-jung backed into the room, wearing a lead apron over his clothes and rolling the portable X-ray machine on its wheeled base. It looked almost like a miniature crane, four and a half feet tall with a three-foot-long articulated arm. At the end of the arm was a rotating head that housed the X-ray tube. A control panel and digital monitor console were attached to the base.

"One portable X-ray machine, as requested," Dae-jung said. A Korean man in his late twenties, he looked as clean-shaven and fresh faced as someone half that age. His round, wire-rimmed glasses didn't do much to shatter the illusion.

"Thanks, Dae-jung," Laura said. "Can you set it up over by the table?"

He paused to put on a surgical mask and hair net, then rolled the portable X-ray machine up to the autopsy table. He looked over the body.

"This is some serious *Clash of the Titans* shit. Do you think he knew what was happening to him? Do you think he felt it?"

"It's hard to say," Laura said. "We don't know yet if the condition occurred posthumously or..."

"Or if it's what killed him," Dae-jung finished for her.

"Let's get this machine working," Chief Morales said impatiently.

"No problem, Chief." Dae-jung put on a pair of nitrile gloves and removed a black, square object from a sleeve on the back of the machine. "Where do you want me to set up the detector panel?"

Laura decided they might as well start at the top, with Malachai Applewhite's head. Grunting with effort, Dae-jung lifted the head with one gloved hand, tilting the whole body stiffly upward, and with his other hand he positioned the detector panel beneath it. Made of carbon fiber and aluminum alloy with a rubber insulated frame, the panel was big, eighteen inches on each side. Laura was sure it was heavier than it looked. Dae-jung pushed the sides of the body bag as far away from the body as he could. Then he extended the machine's arm over Malachai's head.

"This model uses a much lower dose of radiation than the older ones did," he said, "but I'm still going to need you both to step back as far as you can."

Laura retreated to the morgue door. Morales followed her with a heavy sigh, as if this were already taking too long.

"How long will we have to wait?" Morales asked.

"The imaging is instantaneous," Dae-jung explained, adjusting some numbers on the operation panel to select the kilovoltage and exposure time. "The detector panel sends the X-ray image back to the monitor the moment it's captured. Much faster than the bad old days when you had to wait to develop the X-ray film."

To demonstrate, Dae-jung removed the push-button switch from its holster on the console and pressed the button with his thumb. Instantly, an X-ray image of Malachai Applewhite's head appeared on the monitor.

Dae-jung waved them over. The digital image on the monitor was a crystal-clear X-ray of Malachai Applewhite's head in profile. Most people thought bones showed up on X-ray images because of their density, but that wasn't the case. The X-rays were blocked and reflected by the calcium in the bones, which made the bones appear white in the imaging, while the X-rays passed right through soft tissue, which appeared much darker. Laura saw right away that this X-ray image wasn't right. A normal image would show the outline of the skull in a hard, bold white. The cranial cavity, auditory canals, sinuses, and orbits of the eyes would all be much darker. In this image, however, it was all white, as though the skull had been filled with cement.

"It's not just his skin that's fossilized," she said. "Everything inside the cranium has, too. His eyes, his brain, everything."

"What are those?" Chief Morales pointed to spots on the teeth that were a brighter white than the rest of them.

"Fillings," Dae-jung replied. "Modern composite resin fillings from the look of it. They add metallic compounds containing barium or zirconium to composite fillings these days to make them more radiopaque."

Morales gave him a quizzical look.

"To make them show up better on X-rays," he clarified.

"Modern fillings." Morales said. "So much for your theory that he's been dead for years, Dr. Powell."

Laura was certain Morales was purposely needling her, but she held her tongue. She wasn't going to give Morales the satisfaction of losing her temper.

"Did you find anything when you were at the scene?" Morales asked Dae-jung.

"I examined the tread marks on the road," he said. "The car was driving steadily until just before it swerved onto the sidewalk. No stops, nothing suspicious. Whatever happened to this man happened inside the car."

"Which I take it you examined thoroughly?" Morales said.

"I did," he said. "I didn't find anything unusual."

"Let's continue," Laura said. "I'd like to X-ray his chest cavity next."

Dae-jung moved the detector panel to underneath Malachai's torso. The image showed similar results. The ribcage and spine showed up in bright, thick white. The lungs, which should have appeared so dark as to be almost black on a normal X-ray image, were as white as the bones. It reminded Laura of the exhibit at Storm King, complex crystals forming inside the ribcage. In the art piece, the crystals had responded to the humidity inside the glass case. What had Malachai Applewhite's internal organs responded to? What could have caused this?

She'd seen enough to know further X-rays would only show the same throughout his body. All the soft tissue—the organs, the blood vessels, the subcutaneous fat—had fossilized, just like his skin.

"I'm sorry, Chief Morales, but there's no way I can perform an autopsy on this body," she said. "Even if I could cut him open, I wouldn't be able to determine if there was a toxin in his bloodstream, or if there was an infection. All his internal organs have been compromised."

Morales looked like she was going to explode. "Unacceptable, Dr. Powell."

"There's still one thing we can do," Dae-jung said. "The organs may be affected, but as far as we can tell from the X-rays, the bones haven't been." He pointed to the ribcage on the screen. "If we're lucky, the marrow might still be intact inside the bone. If I can examine it, I might be able to figure out if there was a disease or toxin involved in this man's death, particularly if it was bloodborne. The marrow can't tell us everything, but it's a start."

"How soon can you begin?" Morales asked.

"Not before tomorrow."

Morales pinched the bridge of her nose in annoyance. "And why is that?"

"Sorry, Chief, but I need special tools to extract the marrow, and unfortunately I don't have them in the lab." He turned to Laura. "With your permission, of course. You're the M.E. The body's under your jurisdiction."

"Just do it," Morales interrupted. "We don't need any more delays."

Laura's anger hit a rolling boil. It was her decision to make, not Morales's. Dae-jung, to his credit, waited for her to give him a nod before continuing.

"Okay, tomorrow it is," he said. "I'll be on it first thing."

"Well, I'm glad this wasn't a complete waste of time," Morales said.

Was she deliberately trying to get under Laura's skin? Laura struggled to keep her cool. Dae-jung must have noticed the anger in her eyes, because he broke the tension by offering to help her move the body into the morgue refrigerator. Grateful for his help, Laura started to zip up the body bag again, then paused.

"Hold on a minute."

She bent to look closer at Malachai's feet. In the course of her full-body examination, she'd missed something on his left ankle. A mark of some kind. Laura grabbed a magnifying glass for a closer look. There was a small hole between the Achilles tendon and the lateral malleolus bone.

"Did you find something?" Chief Morales demanded, her impatience for answers surfacing again.

"Some kind of puncture wound on his ankle," she said. "It might not be anything, but it's worth noting." She added it to the exam form.

"And you're only just seeing it now?" Morales pressed.

"It's very small, easy to miss, especially with the skin discoloration."

Morales shook her head disdainfully. "Sloppy work, Dr. Powell. I expect better from you."

If Laura had been holding a scalpel at that moment, there was no telling what she might have done. Instead, she ignored the remark and zipped up the body bag. She opened one of the refrigerator doors and pulled out the stainless-steel body tray while Dae-jung rolled the portable X-ray machine away from the autopsy table to give them room. Then, together, they strained to lift the heavy body bag off the table by its handles and carry him to the refrigerator. They laid him down on the body tray.

Because of the position his body was stuck in, he just barely fit. She slid the tray into the refrigerator and closed the door.

Morales started to leave the morgue without thanking either of them, which Laura had to admit was on-brand for her.

"Wait, Chief," she called. "I'd like to assist with the investigation. I think I can be helpful—"

"I've got it from here, Dr. Powell," she interrupted. "I'll call you if I need you."

With that, Chief Morales blew out of the morgue like a cold wind.

4

"There's no way Morales is going to let me help with the investigation," Laura said. "You should have seen her today, looking over my shoulder like I don't know how to do my job."

"I'm sorry," Booker said. He cleared the plates off the dining room table and brought them into the kitchen.

She was spending the night at his place again, as she'd done most nights this week. Booker was one of the lucky ones whose house had survived the fires last year. Laura's own house across town had survived as well, and although she found herself staying at Booker's more often these days, she wasn't ready to give it up yet. It wasn't about their relationship. Laura knew she and Booker were in it for the long haul. The real reason—the only reason—was that she'd worked so hard at her medical practice to be able to afford her own house that she was reluctant to sell it. To his credit, Booker never pressured her about moving in with him, though she could tell he wanted that. Among other things, it was why he kept cooking amazing dinners for her.

"Maybe Chief Morales is still trying to find her footing," he said from the kitchen. He rinsed off the plates and put them in the dishwasher. The scent of roasted chicken with pancetta and olives lingered in the air.

"I doubt it. She's been chief for a year," she said. "I think she just doesn't like me. I know I sound like a child, but I'm convinced it's true."

Booker came back into the dining room holding an open bottle of red and two wine glasses. He put the glasses on the table and poured.

"You read my mind," Laura said.

"I figured this was the kind of conversation that required wine."

Laura lifted her glass to her lips. The wine had a rich claret color and tasted of dark cherries and plums. It was a sipping wine, but she was angry enough to seriously consider emptying the whole glass in a single gulp.

"Not that I'm defending Chief Morales," Booker said, taking his seat again, "but it *is* unusual for the M.E. to help with an investigation, isn't it?"

"Ralph always welcomed my help."

"She's not Ralph."

"That's for sure." This time, she did empty her glass. She quickly refilled it from the bottle. "There's something about this case, Booker. I've never seen anything like it. I've never even *heard* of anything like it. How can someone fossilize so quickly?"

"He was petrified," Booker said. "Not fossilized."

She raised an eyebrow. "Is there a difference?"

"There is in my field," he said. "A fossil is any evidence of life that's been preserved in rock—droppings, eggs, footprints. It doesn't have to be an actual organism. Petrifaction, on the other hand, is the process by which organisms become fossils. Over time, the organic tissue is replaced by minerals."

"Like petrified wood," Laura said.

"Exactly." Having finished his glass of wine, Booker poured himself another. "You get petrified wood when fallen trees are buried under layers of river mud. If there's enough mud, it forms an airtight seal that prevents oxygen from reaching the dead tree. Without oxygen, it can't decay. The wood's organic tissue breaks down extremely slowly, and the resulting voids in the wood are filled with minerals. Over millions of years, those minerals crystallize within the wood's cellular structure. Of course, by that point, the wood isn't even really wood anymore. It's closer to stone."

His eyes twinkled the way they always did when his mind was revving like an engine, focusing on a topic he found fascinating.

"The really cool thing about petrified wood is that it takes on different colors, depending on which minerals have replaced the wood's cells. Green and blue petrified wood has copper or cobalt inside it. Pink has manganese. Imagine that. Wood goes under the mud and comes out millions of years later as a totally different thing, a hybrid of sorts between what it used to be and what it has become, and when it finally emerges, it wears the colors of the minerals that transformed it."

It wasn't hard to imagine Booker standing in front of his science class at the high school, imparting the same information to his students with the same joyful ebullience. The thought made her smile, something she hadn't done since her miserable experience with Morales earlier.

Laura picked up her wine glass and carried it into the living room. She sat down on the couch and tucked her bare feet under her. Booker sat down next to her.

"The man in the morgue was named Malachai Applewhite," she said. "This didn't happen to him over the course of millions of years. It happened to him while he was driving. It must have been quick."

"I take it he wasn't found buried in river mud, either," Booker said.

"I'm starting to wish he had been. At least that would make sense." Laura took another sip of wine. She was feeling a little better now. Talking it out with Booker helped. "Without the mud, and without millions of years passing, have you heard of any other ways for someone or something to become petrified like that?"

Booker swirled the dark red wine in his glass as he thought it over. "Have you ever heard of Stuckie the dog?"

"Stuckie?" She chuckled and put her glass down on the coffee table.

"It's a nickname, but it's not a happy one," he said. "Back in the Eighties, some loggers in Georgia cut down a chestnut oak tree. They discovered it was hollow, and inside the trunk was the perfectly preserved, mummified body of a dog."

"Oh no!" Laura immediately regretted having laughed. "What happened?"

"They think he was a hunting dog from the Sixties who chased something small like a squirrel into the tree," Booker said. "The dog followed it up the hollow tree trunk, but the higher he climbed, the narrower the space became until finally he got stuck. Most likely, he died of dehydration."

Laura put one hand over her mouth. The thought of that poor dog wedging himself into a tight space and not being able to turn around or get out was heartbreaking.

"But here's the interesting part," Booker said. "Because the dog died inside the tree, the carcass was protected. Other animals couldn't get to him, and the dry environment inside the tree dehydrated the carcass. But that's not what preserved it. The chestnut oak contains natural tannins, which seeped into the dog's body and prevented it from decaying. It preserved Stuckie the dog for all those years."

"That poor dog. They gave him a terrible nickname." Laura finished the wine in her glass, then got up and took the bottle off the dining room table. She returned to the living room with it, sat down, and refilled both her and Booker's glasses. "It still doesn't sound like the same thing. The dog in the tree was essentially mummified, but Malachai... I really wish you could have seen him, Booker. Dae-jung said it looked like he was turned to stone."

"Petrifaction and mummification are both forms of preservation, and they can both be caused by environmental conditions," Booker said. "So, what environmental conditions would be necessary for Malachai to become naturally preserved?"

Laura held her wine glass in both palms and leaned against the couch cushion. Some couples spent the evening watching television or streaming movies; she and Booker talked about dead bodies and scientific oddities.

Take that, Cosmopolitan *magazine!* she thought.

"Okay, there are three conditions I can think of," she said. "The first would be extreme cold. Permafrost ice can preserve bodies almost perfectly. Even the clothing. They found graves in the Canadian Arctic from the 1845 Franklin expedition, and the bodies inside were nearly pristine. But right now, the evidence says whatever happened to Malachai happened in his car, so it can't be the cold."

"That would be one hell of an air-conditioning system."

Booker pursed his lips and swirled the wine in his glass. "What's number two?"

"A lack of oxygen, like with petrified wood." She chewed her bottom lip, deep in thought. "Preserved bodies have been found buried in peat bogs. The sphagnum moss that forms over the bogs keeps out oxygen from the air and turns the bog acidic enough to be inhospitable to bacteria. Together, those factors cause organic material to decompose at an incredibly slow rate. In Denmark, they found a bog body they called Tollund Man, whose death dated back to the fourth century B.C. He was so well preserved they found stubble on his face. But again, it's the same problem."

"The location of his death," Booker said. "Even if you could somehow remove every bit of oxygen from inside the car, he would suffocate, not petrify."

"Right." She groaned, annoyed that the answer was still eluding her.

"Let's keep going," Booker said. "What's the third option?"

"Extremely arid conditions," she said. "Bodies found buried in the desert are naturally mummified, presuming scavengers don't find them. Bodies lose their moisture in those conditions, the skin becomes dry, papery, and tight to the bone. That's not what happened to Malachai. He doesn't look dried out, only discolored and with all his soft tissue now as hard as stone. I couldn't even cut into him with a scalpel."

"If he didn't dry out, what happened to all the liquid in his body?" Booker asked. "You said he was petrified all the way through."

"His blood, the moisture in his skin, even the vitreous humor in his eyes, everything must have crystallized," she said. She thought again about the art installation at Storm King, *The Luminous Flesh*. Crystals growing between the bones. Filling the empty spaces.

She put her empty wine glass down on the coffee table. It felt like she was going round and round in circles, only to bump up against the same problem: the timing of Malachai Applewhite's death. There was a petrified man in her morgue, except there hadn't been enough time for the body to petrify naturally. As much as she wanted to, she wasn't going to solve this tonight by drinking wine and bouncing ideas off of Booker. What she needed was more information, but it was clear she wouldn't get any if Morales had her way.

Frustrated, she lay down and rested her head in Booker's lap. He put down his glass and stroked her hair, brushing one long, chestnut-colored strand out of her eyes.

"I'm sorry," he said. "I know how much you can't stand not knowing the answer."

"It's not just that," she said. "Malachai Applewhite came from Valley Grove. I never told you this, I never told *anyone* this, but that's where my aunt Gwen lives. My mother's sister."

"She lives in Valley Grove?" Booker asked. "Does that mean she's part of the Church of the Divine Chariot?"

"Yes," Laura said. "She was devastated after my mother's suicide. My way of coping was to throw myself into my studies. Her way of coping was to throw herself into religion. She moved to Valley Grove and joined the Church of the Divine Chariot. I didn't understand it then, and I guess I still don't. We stayed in touch for a while, writing letters back and forth, until one day I got a letter from her saying goodbye."

Laura took a deep breath. She wished she still had some wine in her glass. This wasn't a story she ever thought she would tell.

"In the letter, Gwen told me that even though I was her niece, I was an outsider, and as a member of the Church of the Divine Chariot, she had to keep herself separate from the secular world or 'risk being corrupted by its depravities.' I couldn't believe it. My pride told me if my crazy religious zealot of an aunt didn't want anything to do with me, then so be it, good riddance. I never wrote back. I never even tried to reach her again. That's why I don't talk about her, because what she said in that letter hurt me. But the truth is, I always regretted not being in touch with her for all those years. She was my last living relative, not counting my father, but of course he stopped counting the day he left. And now this. If what happened to Malachai Applewhite was caused by an environmental factor in Valley Grove, Gwen could be in danger."

"Maybe you should check in with her. Do you have her phone number?"

"No, I never had a number for her, just an address." She sat up and leaned against him. "Ugh, I can't think about this right now. It's too much."

He put his arm around her. She turned her head and kissed him. His lips were flavored with wine, and for a while, she let herself forget her worries.

It didn't last long. Upstairs in the bedroom, Laura couldn't fall asleep. The mystery of Malachai Applewhite's petrified corpse ricocheted through her mind like a pinball, bouncing off explanations that ranged from the absurd to the impossible. Beside her, Booker moaned and twitched in his sleep. Another nightmare. She ran a hand over his brow and whispered that he was okay, everything was okay, until he quieted. His naked body gave off a heat she clung to. She pressed her own bare body against his back, hoping it would help her relax enough to sleep, but it didn't work. She slipped out of bed, careful not to wake him now that he was finally sleeping peacefully. She put on a fresh pair of underwear and a t-shirt from the drawer Booker had given her in his dresser, then made her way downstairs.

She found Booker's laptop on the breakfast table in the kitchen. She opened it and pulled up a search engine. Was there a chance Malachai Applewhite's petrifaction wasn't the result of external environmental factors, but something *internal* instead? That would certainly make her less worried about Aunt Gwen, but what could transform tissue on such a grand scale? For that matter, what could crystalize all the fluids in his body? She knew proteins could crystalize, like the natural crystalline arrays of aquaporin in the lens of the eye. Crystals could form when there was a medical condition like gout, when too much uric acid in the body caused urate crystals to accumulate in the joints. But every ounce of liquid in a human body? It seemed impossible, and yet the corpse in her morgue was clear evidence it wasn't.

She typed the words *petrified bodies* into the search field, but the results that came back were things she already knew. The victims of Mount Vesuvius's eruption in Pompeii in 79 A.D. Bog mummies like Tollund Man, Koelbjerg Man, and Röst Girl. Ötzi the Iceman, whose frozen corpse was found in the Alps in 1991, skin and organs intact despite dating back to 3300 B.C. All of them were the consequences of extreme external factors. None of them were helpful.

She kept looking, determined not to give up. On the third page of search results, something finally caught her eye. An article in a magazine called *Corpus Delicti: The Journal of Death Studies* told the story of scientists in nineteenth-century Italy who routinely petrified cadavers by replacing their biologic liquids with chemical preservatives through intravascular injections as a way to preserve and study them. It allowed the scientists to maintain the deceased's features and preserve their tissue and internal organs in a state of stone hardness.

Those last five words caught her attention. If she were to describe Malachai's condition, *a state of stone hardness* definitely fit the bill. Why had he come to Sakima from Valley Grove? Where was he going? Was it the crash that killed him, or had he already died behind the wheel and *that* was why he lost control of the car? She wished she could have performed an autopsy on the body. It would answer so many questions. As it was, she was stuck bumping up against the same wall again and again.

By all accounts, Malachai was alone in the car. The body was recovered right after the crash, already petrified. There was no time for anyone to inject it with chemical preservatives like the Italian scientists of old.

Everything was pointing to an environmental cause, but she was no closer to an answer.

She exited the search engine and considered going back to bed, but her curiosity got the better of her and she launched it again. She typed in the words *Stuckie the dog*. The first article that came up related the same sad story Booker had told her earlier. However, she was not prepared for the pictures.

She was not prepared to see the dog.

It stared back at her from within the ragged, black hollow at the center of the tree trunk, a grisly horror with one paw thrust forward as though it were still trying to climb. Its skin was a brownish gray, like Malachai's, but its eyes were gone, leaving only dark sockets in their place. For a moment, she had the sense it could still see her through the laptop screen, that it was staring at her across the distant reaches of time and space, life and death.

Laura exited the search engine again and closed the laptop. She shouldn't have looked. She climbed up the stairs and got back under the covers beside Booker, but sleep still didn't come. Every time she closed her eyes, she saw the pictures of Stuckie again. Her mind focused on a single haunting detail, one thing in particular that had crept under her skin and stayed with her.

The withered flesh of the dog's face was drawn back from its snout to reveal sharp teeth locked in a ferocious snarl. Even to her normally rational mind, it struck her as a warning. Death comes for us all, Stuckie seemed to be saying, and when it does, it isn't always peaceful.

5

When morning came, Laura left Booker's house and crossed the street to Dradin Park. It was still closed to the public, its entrance blocked off with metal police barricades and plywood. Months ago, someone had spray-painted Fuck mushrooms! across the plywood panels in big black letters. No one had removed it. No one wanted to. Inside the park, the community garden that had once been the heart and soul of Sakima was gone. It had been dug up and the earth salted to keep the mutant fungus from returning. Half the homes that burned in last year's chaos had been rebuilt, but no one knew if or when Dradin Park would reopen. There was talk about getting a new community garden started in another location, but so far it was only talk.

Erected next to the park entrance was a memorial to the people Sakima had lost, two towering slabs of polished granite etched with the names of the dead. Victor Cunningham's name was there, and so were Ralph Gorney's, Sofia Hernandez's, and over a hundred others who'd perished.

After Ralph's death, she and Booker had taken care of his wife Debra as best they could. They brought over food, looked after her baby Darius when Debra needed time to herself, and tackled the lion's share of the paperwork required by the city, the state, the bank, the police union, and the life-insurance company. Time passed, but Debra never quite recovered. *Everywhere I look, there are memories of Ralph,* she told Laura one day. *Sometimes I hear footsteps behind me, and I turn around thinking it's him, but there's no one there, or it's a stranger minding their own business. Of course it's not him. Why would it be? Just because my life feels like a bad dream doesn't mean it is one.* In the end, she decided to take Darius back to Baltimore to be closer to her family. As much as Laura supported the decision, she still missed her friend.

She traced Ralph's name in the smooth stone with her finger, wishing she could ask for his advice one last time. Chief Morales had made it clear she didn't want her involved in the investigation, but she couldn't shake the case from her thoughts. It was just the way she was. Even as far back as medical school, if there was something she didn't understand, she would work at it obsessively until she had the answer. This was no different. She wanted—*needed*—to know what happened to Malachai Applewhite.

But that wasn't the whole truth. Something *was* different this time, in a very big way. Her aunt was in Valley Grove, and she could be in danger.

What would Ralph say if he were still here? He would tell her nothing was more important than family, and he would be right. Maybe Gwen had cut off contact with her, but it didn't mean Gwen wasn't family anymore. Gwen was her aunt, and Laura's last connection to the mother she lost. That had to mean something, even now.

With her mind made up, she drove to the central police station in City Square and parked in the official lot. She hung a placard on her rearview mirror that announced she was here on official business, and then marched into the station. She found the door to Morales's office closed, but the light coming through the frosted window told her Morales was inside.

Because it was how she'd always done things with Ralph, Laura opened the door out of habit and walked right in. The chief's office was a big, square room with multiple chairs for meetings and a view of the Hudson River from the window. The photos Ralph used to keep on the desk had been replaced with piles of papers and books on procedure. Morales sat at the desk, but she wasn't alone. A dark-haired man in his late twenties sat across from her. He wore a crisp navy-blue shirt and a gray tie loose around his neck like a man who had to dress professionally but didn't enjoy it.

Morales glared at Laura from the desk. "Can I help you with

something, Dr. Powell?" Her tone of voice couldn't have been colder if it came out of the morgue freezer.

Shit.

Morales had every right to be annoyed at the interruption. Ralph might have always had an open-door policy with her, but as Morales had already made clear to her, she wasn't Ralph. Laura had come to plead her case, but now she looked like a buffoon, barging clumsily into a closed-door meeting. She'd shot herself in the foot before she even got a word out.

Before she could make her apologies and back out of the office with what she hoped was her last shred of dignity intact, the young man rose from his chair.

"Wait, you're Dr. Powell? Dr. *Laura* Powell?" he asked.

"Yes, I am," she said. "Have we met?"

"No, but I've heard about you. You saved a lot of lives last year, including mine. I'd only just moved to Sakima when... everything happened." He extended his hand. "I'm Sam Templeton."

"Nice to meet you, Sam," she said, shaking his hand. "I didn't mean to interrupt. I can come back later."

"That would be for the best, Dr. Powell," Morales said flatly.

"Wait, but...you're the medical examiner, right?" Sam asked. "Did you perform the autopsy on Malachai Applewhite?"

"I tried to," Laura said. "Unfortunately, the condition of the body didn't allow it."

The color drained out of Sam's face. "Condition? What—what happened to him?"

"That's what I was getting at before we were interrupted." Morales stood up, glaring at Laura. "Dr. Powell, Mr. Templeton is a friend of the deceased."

"Please, can you tell me what happened to him?" Sam pleaded. "I thought it was a car accident."

"There *was* an accident," Morales told him. "However, once his body was recovered, there was an unexpected problem. Dr. Powell can explain it."

"A problem?" Sam's eyes brimmed with tears. "Please, just tell me what happened to my friend."

"Something affected his body," Laura explained. "All his

soft tissue has petrified, including his skin. It prevented us from performing a full autopsy."

Sam gaped at her, tears rolling down his cheeks. "Petrified?"

"I'm so sorry, Sam. I know it's a lot to take in. We're still trying to figure out how it happened."

"Do you have any ideas, Mr. Templeton?" Morales asked.

"No," Sam said, pulling himself together, "but I wouldn't be surprised if it had something to do with his father."

"Why his father?" Morales asked.

Sam sat down. "Malachai belonged to the Church of the Divine Chariot in Valley Grove. They're a fundamentalist Christian sect."

"I'm familiar with them," Morales said.

"I—I used to be part of the sect," Sam said. "I was born into it, just like Malachai was. I left a little over a year ago."

"Why?" Morales asked.

"Why?" Sam repeated as though he didn't understand the question. "You don't know what it's like living with religious zealots. They're more like a cult. You're not allowed to question authority. You're not allowed to think for yourself, or to think differently from everyone else. You're told what to do every hour of every day, whether it's what you want or not. But maybe worst of all, you're told when you'll get married and to whom. That's how it works there. You don't get to choose your own wife or husband. The Shepherd, the head of the Church, decides for you. When I turned twenty-seven, it was decided for me that I would marry the daughter of one of our neighbors. Her name was Miriam. She was..." He paused, cringing, on the verge of tears again. "She was twelve years old. That's how it works there, too. It was the last straw. I couldn't stay there. I ran away and never looked back."

Laura felt sick. She wasn't naïve. She knew there were thousands of forced marriages involving minors every year in the United States, almost all of them involving young girls married off to older men. Remembering what she'd been like at that age—sensitive, introverted, socially awkward—the idea that she could have been married off to a man twice her age, or more, put a knot in her stomach. More often than not, religious custom was to blame, which was why so many elected officials were too cowardly to do the right thing and legislate against it. They were afraid of being pegged as anti-religion by their rivals and possibly losing elections because of it. Apparently, re-election was more important to them than what was happening to those girls. It infuriated her.

"Malachai ran away from the Church of the Divine Chariot just like I did," Sam continued, wiping the tears from his face. "He was coming here to stay with me, until he could find work and someplace to live."

"Why did you say you thought his death had something to do with his father?" Morales pressed.

"Malachai's father is Eliezer Applewhite." He paused as though he expected Laura and Chief Morales to recognize the name. When it was clear they didn't, he said, "*Shepherd* Eliezer. He's the head of the Church of the Divine Chariot. His word is law. He's not to be questioned. He doesn't care about anything except holding on to his power. It's like a drug to him. Everyone knows it, but no one would dare say a word. They're too scared of him. Now imagine how it would look if Shepherd Eliezer's own son, his firstborn child, turned his back on the Church and ran away. He must be terrified that the Elders are talking behind his back, wondering if he's still worthy of being Shepherd. They're the only ones who can take away his power."

"You think that would be enough for him to kill his own son?" Morales asked.

"I don't know," Sam said. "If he felt like his power was being threatened, I wouldn't put it past him."

"Thank you for coming in, Mr. Templeton," Morales said. She took down Sam's contact information and asked him to call her if he thought of anything else that might be helpful.

"Malachai was a good person," he said. "He didn't deserve to end up the way he did. Dr. Powell, I know you'll help him the way you helped me and so many others last year."

She shook his hand. "I promise you, I'll do everything I can to find out what happened to him."

Sam nodded solemnly, his eyes downcast. She didn't envy

what he was going through. She knew what it was like to lose a close friend, knew the grief and anger all too well. She watched him walk out of the office. His steps slow and careful, as if he didn't trust the ground under his own feet anymore.

Morales gestured for Laura to close the door. She sat down at her desk and began jotting notes in a file.

"You have quite the fan club here in Sakima, don't you, Dr. Powell?" Morales asked. It wasn't a friendly question.

"The city went through something terrible," Laura said. "Whatever I did to help, I didn't do it alone. There are a lot of people who deserve more praise than me."

Morales nodded, still writing in her file. "And what was so important you had to barge into my office in the middle of an interview?"

Morales was obviously angry with her, but Laura soldiered on. She had to. If she wanted to be part of the investigation, it was now or never, and that meant coming clean.

Laura took a deep breath. "I wasn't entirely honest with you yesterday," she said.

Morales finally looked up at her. Of course she did. Laura was admitting a fault, and that, more than anything else, got Morales's undivided attention. If Laura wanted clear evidence that Morales hated her, here it was.

"One of the reasons I want to help investigate Malachai Applewhite's death is because I have a personal connection to Valley Grove," she said.

Morales raised a surprised eyebrow but didn't interrupt.

"My aunt moved there about fifteen years ago." She didn't have to mention Gwen had joined the Church of the Divine Chariot. It was implied. People didn't move to Valley Grove for any other reason. "If what happened to Malachai is environmental in nature, something in the water or the food they grow, it could be affecting other people there, including my aunt. I owe it to her as much as to Malachai to find out what's happening and how to stop it."

"I told you I'd call you if I needed you." Morales returned her attention to the file in front of her, and Laura knew she'd lost her. "Your personal connection with the victim's hometown has no bearing on the case. In fact, it could be good reason to keep you out of the investigation altogether."

"You need me, Chief Morales," Laura insisted. "What happened to that body is unique. It's not dystrophic calcification. It's not Münchmeyer disease. I can't find another case like it anywhere. You're going to need someone with medical experience, someone who can determine if his condition was brought on by toxins or—"

"It's not up for debate," Morales interrupted. "We're done here, Dr. Powell. Be sure to close the door on your way out."

Laura's mouth hung open in anger, but anything she said now would only endanger her continued employment with the Sakima Police Department. She left Morales's office, resisting the urge to slam the door behind her.

When she got back to her car, she called Booker.

"Hey, how'd it go?" he asked.

"I got a lead," she said. "Malachai Applewhite's father is the head of the Church of the Divine Chariot. A friend of Malachai's thinks he might be involved somehow. I'm driving to Valley Grove today to check in on Gwen, but I'm going to look around, too. Maybe talk to some people."

"So Chief Morales finally came to her senses and brought you in, huh?"

"No, she didn't," Laura said. "She brushed me off again, but I'm going anyway."

"Of course you are. I forgot who I was talking to."

"Morales can't stop me from paying a visit to a family member."

"Laura, this is dangerous."

"Not really. The worst she can do is fire me, right?"

"No, I mean going to Valley Grove on your own is dangerous," he said. "They're not exactly welcoming to outsiders, and if someone there is responsible for Malachai's death…"

"I can handle myself," she said.

"I know you can, but at least let me come with you," he said. "I have a faculty meeting at the high school, but I'll be out by one and I can go with you then."

"I can't wait that long, Booker, I'll go out of my mind. I need to see Gwen. I'll be fine."

"I'm not thrilled about this," he said. "Just promise me you'll be careful."

"I will," she said. "I'll check in with you later."

She ended the call and sat a moment behind the steering wheel, thinking. This wasn't going to be easy. Aside from being hardcore fundamentalists, the Church of the Divine Chariot were separatists. They wanted nothing to do with the outside world. Gwen's final letter had made that clear. It would be hard enough to get them to talk to an outsider, but considering the sect's rigid gender roles, it would be even harder to get them to talk to a woman.

She bit her fingernail, a nervous habit she fell back on whenever something worried her. This sudden need to see her aunt—was she fooling herself by thinking Gwen would talk to her? Booker once said she had a habit of jumping in with both feet without being sure there was water in the pool first. Was that what she was doing now?

She'd made a promise the day she became a doctor that she would never give up on anyone. It meant never ceasing to look for answers until she knew exactly what ailed them and what to do about it. It meant when she knew something had to be done, she did it, whether it was for a living person like Aunt Gwen or a body in her morgue like Malachai Applewhite.

Laura started the car, pulled out of the police lot, and drove back to her house. Before she made the drive to Valley Grove, there was something she needed to pick up.

6

Laura drove east out of Sakima, avoiding the traffic on Interstate 84 and sticking to local roads on the way to Valley Grove. The radio was tuned to the Classic Rock station. R.E.M.'s Michael Stipe sang about losing his religion, and though she knew the song wasn't literally about religion, it struck her as apt considering where she was going.

This visit would go a lot more smoothly if her aunt knew she were coming, but when she tried to look up Gwen's phone number, it wasn't listed. She suspected none of the numbers in Valley Grove were. Laura glanced at her purse in the passenger seat. The edge of an old, wrinkled envelope stuck out from a pocket in the side—the last letter Gwen sent her. She didn't know why she'd kept it all these years, tucked in the back of a drawer. She'd been angry enough to throw it away the day it arrived. She was glad she hadn't. The return address in the upper-left corner, written in her aunt's neat cursive handwriting, was all she had to go on.

"I just hope you still live there, Aunt Gwen," Laura muttered.

The letter was still nestled inside the envelope, slightly yellowed with age. Its edges were frayed and its corners crumpled from all the times Laura had read it in the past. She was tempted to pull over and read it again now, if only in the hope of better understanding why Gwen did what she did, but she remembered how her heart had broken each time she'd read it years ago. It would only break again now.

Even if Gwen *was* still at the same address, would she talk to Laura now, after all this time?

She will, Laura thought. *If I show up at her doorstep, she'll have to talk to me.*

On the radio, Duran Duran proclaimed the union of the snake was on the climb. The jagged shadows of tree branches played across her windshield. Outside, houses passed by, nestled in green yards, shaded by colossal oaks and maples.

What if Gwen didn't recognize her anymore? Or worse, what if she did and slammed the door in her face?

The houses along the sides of the road thinned out and were replaced by a thick forest. The trees were set so closely together that the woods looked dark, like stray pockets of night that defied the sun. Following the GPS instructions, she turned onto a road that cut through the forest. It felt like she was passing through a barrier between worlds. In a way, she was. When she emerged on the other side of the woods, she was in Valley Grove, home of the Church of the Divine Chariot. People on the sidewalks paused to watch her car go by, intrigued by—or suspicious of—a vehicle they didn't recognize. They were all dressed the same—the men in white collared shirts and black slacks, the women in long, embroidered prairie dresses that covered them from neck to ankle.

On the radio, Blue Oyster Cult told her not to fear the reaper. She thought of Stuckie's death snarl, frozen in time, and switched it off.

The houses in Valley Grove were different from the ones she'd passed on the way there. Each house was identical, a modest ranch house with pristine white siding to match the white picket fences. The lawns were immaculate, neatly trimmed and a vibrant green. Not a single piece of litter marred the sidewalks or road. She was almost jealous of how clean and tidy everything was, until she remembered *why* it was so neat. The women of Valley Grove weren't allowed to hold jobs or positions of power within the Church, so their days were taken up with prayer, raising their children, and tending to their homes, including keeping everything looking just so.

Very few of the men held paying jobs either. They ran the Church and its religious schools full-time, which meant most of the households relied on public assistance to get by. It struck her as deeply ironic that the Church of the Divine Chariot was financially dependent on the very same outsiders they were so contemptuous of.

Valley Grove bordered on a wide lake. Like the thick forest she'd passed through, the lake acted as a natural barrier that kept the village isolated. On the far shore, Laura thought she saw a large, gleaming building of glass and steel, and then the view was lost behind more houses.

At last, she pulled into the driveway of a house whose address matched the return address on Gwen's letter. Stenciled on the plain black mailbox was the name Ponder. Laura sat in the car a moment, staring at the house. She tried to imagine her aunt's life here. Was she truly happy? It was hard to imagine a fulfilling life if you weren't allowed to do anything except pray and keep your house clean. And yet Laura supposed Gwen must be happy if it meant enough to her to cut off contact. She steeled herself, got out of the car, and walked up to the house. It looked just like the others in every respect, right down to the neatly trimmed lawn and the flowers growing along the base of the house. Gwen's handiwork, she figured. Her aunt always had a green thumb.

Laura took a deep, steadying breath and knocked on the door. In the silence that followed, she remembered visiting Gwen as a teenager. Her aunt was always so happy to see her, greeting her at the door with a big, rib-crunching hug. There was always a pot of herbal tea ready to pour, and the two of them would sit at the kitchen table, sipping from their cups while Laura filled Gwen in on all the drama of her high school life. Could it ever be like that again? Would Gwen open the door, hug her tearfully, and invite her inside for tea like no time had passed? Was that what Laura wanted? There was a part of her that yearned to have that connection again, to be connected to *family* again, no matter how unlikely or unrealistic it was.

The door opened. A fourteen-year-old girl in a floral-printed prairie dress stood staring at her. "Yes?"

"I'm sorry to bother you," Laura said. "I'm looking for Gwen Davies—or rather, her name would be Gwen Ponder now. I think she lives at this address."

The girl cocked her head, her blue eyes studying Laura for

a moment. Her dark hair, tied into a ponytail, rested on one shoulder of her dress. Finally, she turned and walked into the house, shouting, "Father! Someone is here asking about Mother!"

Laura gasped out loud. Gwen had a daughter?

The girl's father appeared in the doorway. Gwen's husband. The uncle Laura had never met, only heard about in letters. She was dumbstruck. He was tall and in his fifties, with dark hair that edged into silver at his temples. Like all the men she'd seen in Valley Grove, he was clean-shaven and wore a white shirt with dark slacks. He looked at her in confusion, clearly not expecting to see a stranger on his doorstep.

"I'm Francis Ponder," he said. "What can I do for you?"

"I'm—I'm looking for my Aunt Gwen."

"Gwen's your aunt?" Francis asked. There was a kindness in his voice that caught her off guard.

"My name is Laura Powell. Gwen is my mother's sister."

Francis shook his head sadly. "I'm so sorry, Laura. Gwen was called home a few years back."

"Called home?" Laura asked. "I don't understand…"

"Called home to God," Francis explained.

The air went out of her lungs. Whatever connection she'd hoped to rebuild, she was too late. Gwen was dead.

7

Beth Richter ran through the woods of Valley Grove toward the lakeshore, gripping the long skirt of her prairie dress in both hands so she wouldn't trip on the hem. The summer sun was too hot to run in, but there was no time to waste. Her mother would come looking for her soon. It was very nearly time for her midday chores, and if Mother found her gone from the house, she'd be in a world of trouble. Beth was fifteen years old—would be sixteen in another month and a half—but she wasn't too old to be punished for disobedience. Father had already given her the switch once before. The stick he'd used was no wider than the width of his index finger, as dictated by Church law, but it stung something awful and left ugly red marks on her back even through the fabric of her dress. It wasn't something she wanted to repeat.

Beth was still unmarried, which at her age practically made her an old maid in Valley Grove, but she didn't mind the freedom it gave her. She knew the Shepherd would match her with someone soon enough. She prayed he chose someone handsome. If she was lucky, maybe it would be Eddie Gordon, the young man who'd already caught her eye. In fact, Eddie was the reason she was hurrying through the woods this morning in the first place.

She and Eddie had sneaked away together yesterday between afternoon prayers and dinner, a time when they knew both their parents would be busy, and ventured deep into the woods so they could have some privacy. When they reached the edge of the water, they lay down together in the grass and kissed for a while. It wasn't their first time sneaking away. It was, however, the first time they'd almost done more than kiss.

Eddie tried to convince her that it was okay to do things over the clothes. It wasn't a sin because they wouldn't actually be touching each other skin to skin. He called it a loophole. The stiff shape in the crotch of his trousers fascinated Beth, and the idea of touching it through the fabric gave her a strange thrill, but something held her back. The fear of going to Hell, maybe, or the fear of getting the switch again if her parents found out. Sensing her hesitation, Eddie assured her it would be no different from brushing dirt off his pants, and she could even pretend that was what she was doing if it felt too sinful. In the end, she decided against it. Eddie was upset, and they walked out of the woods in awkward silence.

She would have preferred to forget the whole thing, but in the course of rolling around in the grass, the ribbon had fallen out of her hair. She could hardly sleep that night for worry that someone would find it and know it was hers. Worse, they would know what she'd been doing in the woods. She couldn't let it stay there, waiting to be discovered.

Bushes snagged and pulled at her dress as she followed the dirt path to the lakeshore. She nudged sharp, groping branches out of her way. Had she made a mistake with Eddie yesterday? Maybe she *should* have done it. Now she would be lucky if Eddie ever spoke to her again. He'd probably go into the woods with Selma Jacobs from now on. Everyone knew Selma was the queen of over-the-clothes.

When Beth reached the water's edge, she found her pink satin ribbon in the grass. She picked it up and wrapped it tightly around one hand to make sure she wouldn't lose it again. Something rustled in the underbrush nearby. Something just on the other side of a cluster of bushes and ferns. Or perhaps some*one*. She and Eddie weren't the only ones who sneaked away to this spot. All the teenagers knew about this place. She inched closer to the bushes.

"Hello?" she called.

No one answered. Why would they? No one wanted to get caught out here. If word got back to their parents, it wouldn't just be bad for them, it would be bad for *everyone* who tried to sneak away in the future. Their parents would patrol the woods morning, noon, and night.

She was struck with the sudden certainty that it was Selma hiding behind those bushes with a boy. She smirked, but her smugness passed quickly. *Please don't be Eddie,* she thought, but she already knew in her heart it was. Eddie would have gone right to Selma the moment he could, not wasting any more time before getting what he wanted, and of course Selma had agreed to go into the woods with him. She'd go into the woods with any boy. Now they'd seen Beth and were keeping quiet, hoping she'd go away. Selma's hand was probably still on the crotch of Eddie's pants. Well, Beth would give her a good scare and make her squeeze that hand so tight Eddie would shriek!

Beth leapt forward, parting the bushes. "Aha!"

Selma Jacobs wasn't there. Neither was Eddie.

Something else was.

Strange, opalescent eyes split with black, vertical pupils fixed upon her. She froze as its mouth opened to reveal frightening, hooked fangs. She had no time to run before it struck. Fast as a whip, it sank its fangs into the meat of her leg. Beth screamed, but down by the lake there was no one to hear it.

8

The cemetery stood atop a gentle hill in the middle of Valley Grove. The headstones were identical, humble slabs of stone that were nothing like the soaring monuments and gothic mausoleums Laura had seen in other cemeteries. The headstone she stood before was as plain as the others, unremarkable except that it bore the name GWEN PONDER. There was no mention of Gwen's original surname, the one she'd shared with Laura's mother, but of course there wouldn't be. She'd left that life behind a long time ago. Gwen Davies was gone long before Gwen Ponder was.

A warm wind blew through Laura's hair. She brushed it out of her eyes.

"What happened?" she asked.

Francis Ponder bowed his head beside her. "She had cancer in her ovaries. We were blessed to have Rebecca when we did, before she could no longer bear children."

The teenaged girl who'd answered the door—Rebecca—squatted to brush dead leaves from the headstone. The hem of her floral dress was already smudged green from the grass.

"The illness wasn't easy on Gwen, or on us," Francis said. "There were difficult times when it seemed like the Lord was testing us. But there were good times too, weren't there, Rebecca? Times when your mother was in good spirits."

Rebecca nodded silently, her mouth in a thoughtful frown. She straightened and brushed one last leaf off the top of the headstone. The breeze caught it and carried it off into the distance.

"I don't claim to know why the Lord would put a good woman like Gwen through such hardship. His ways are His own to understand, not ours," Francis said. "In the end, He saw fit to end her suffering and call her home to glory."

The headstone gave the date of Gwen's death as March 1, 2016. Her aunt had died six years ago and Laura never knew. She felt heavy with emotion. If only she'd tried harder, if only she could have convinced Gwen that just because she was an outsider didn't mean she was a threat to her aunt's beliefs, but she'd been too hurt by Gwen's letter for that. Now she wished she'd swallowed her pride and fought to keep her aunt in her life.

The rational part of her brain told her it wasn't her fault, that there was no way she could have known Gwen was sick, but it didn't matter. It would be a long time before she forgave herself.

"My mother was your aunt?" Rebecca asked.

"Yes," Laura said. "My mother and your mother were sisters. Unfortunately, they're both gone now."

Rebecca nodded thoughtfully. "I'm sorry you lost your mother, too. It's hard, isn't it?"

Laura gave a thin smile. "It was hard for me, but I was older than you when I lost mine. I can't imagine how I would have felt if I'd lost her when I was your age."

"The Lord helped me through," Rebecca said. She took Francis's hand. "And so did Father. Remember what you taught me from the Book of Matthew, Father?"

Francis smiled down at her. "Blessed are those who mourn, for they shall be comforted."

Rebecca turned her gaze back to Laura. "I never knew I had a cousin."

"Neither did I," Laura said. The understatement of the century.

"May God bless you and keep you, Cousin Laura," Rebecca said.

Laura felt an overwhelming desire to hug the girl, but she held back. This was all so new.

"Why are you here, Laura?" Francis asked. "Why come looking for Gwen after all this time?"

"I wanted to make sure she was all right."

Of course, she was six years too late for that. She couldn't protect Gwen anymore, but she could protect Gwen's family.

After all, they were her family, too.

"Has anyone in Valley Grove been feeling sick lately?" she asked. "Any strange or unusual symptoms?"

Francis shrugged. "Just the occasional common cold. I think Elder Bernard had the flu back in the spring. Nothing unusual."

That wasn't the answer she was looking for. The key to what happened to Malachai Applewhite had to be somewhere in Valley Grove. It was the only explanation that made any sense. It wasn't something in his car; Dae-jung hadn't found anything out of the ordinary. It had to be here, where Malachai started his journey to Sakima.

She turned away from Gwen's headstone and gazed down the hill at the large building that stood below. It was constructed entirely of wood and was much bigger than any of the houses.

"That's the holy sanctuary," Francis explained. "We don't call it a church. It's our belief that we, the congregation, embody the church. The building is simply where we meet for worship."

Without a steeple, the holy sanctuary looked almost like a barn, but there was no doubting its purpose. The front door and window shutters were adorned with large wooden crosses. Above the door was the carving of a chariot tilted upward as though flying into the sky.

"Why a chariot?" she asked.

"We're named after the chariot that took the prophet Elijah to Heaven, body and soul," Francis said. "'And it came to pass, as they still went on, and talked, that, behold, there appeared a chariot of fire, and horses of fire, and parted them both asunder; and Elijah went up by a whirlwind into heaven.' Second Kings. Elijah defended the worship of God over that of the false god of the Canaanites, Baal. We strive to achieve that same level of fealty and devotion in a modern world that, unfortunately, has its own share of false gods."

"I thought Elijah was a Jewish prophet," Laura said. "This is a Christian sect."

Francis smiled. "The New Testament doesn't erase what came before. It builds upon it. We seek to do the same."

As she watched, a crowd gathered in front of the holy sanctuary. She heard the uneasy buzz of their voices and saw them point up the hill at the cemetery. Her presence had been noticed.

"Why ask me if anyone's been sick?" Francis asked.

"Did you know Malachai Applewhite?"

"I did," Rebecca chimed in. "He was my friend Meredith's older brother. He was always nice to me."

"Everyone knew him," Francis said. "Malachai was the Shepherd's son. Shepherd Eliezer shared the sad news with us at services last night. It's a shame what happened. To die in a car accident at such a young age."

Interesting, Laura thought. No mention of the petrifaction of Malachai's body. Chief Morales must have left it out when she informed his father of the young man's death. The only reason she would have held back that information was if she was planning an investigation. Laura would have to tread lightly. Morales didn't know she was in Valley Grove.

"If I tell you something, can I trust you not to repeat it to anyone?" Laura asked.

"Of course," Francis said.

"You too, Rebecca. Can I trust you to keep a secret?"

Rebecca nodded. "You can trust me, Cousin Laura."

"I work with the police in Sakima," Laura said. "I'm the one who examined Malachai's body after the crash. I'm not convinced it was the accident that killed him."

Francis appeared surprised. "What did?"

"When I examined the body, I discovered his skin and internal organs had petrified," she said. "I don't know for sure yet, but I suspect that was the actual cause of his death."

"Petrified?" Francis repeated, trying to make sense of it. "Like he turned to stone?"

"Not stone," Laura said. "Something hardened the soft tissue of his body, to the point where his organs couldn't function properly anymore."

Rebecca looked as horrified as her father. "How can something like that happen?"

"I came here to find out," she said. "Maybe I should talk to Malachai's family. They might know more about who or what he came in contact with."

Francis scoffed. "Shepherd Eliezer won't be any more interested in talking to you than he is in talking to me."

"He won't talk to you?" Laura asked. "I thought you were a Church Elder."

"He stopped talking to me the day I petitioned the other Elders to remove him from the Shepherdom."

"And make you Shepherd in his place, Father," Rebecca added.

He smoothed the hair on top of his daughter's head. "Perhaps, if that's God's will. The most important thing is removing Eliezer. I don't think he's fit to lead, and I know I'm not alone in that."

"From what I've heard, Shepherd Eliezer isn't someone who'll let go of power willingly," Laura said.

"What choice do we have?" Francis said. "Our numbers are dwindling. Once, the Church of the Divine Chariot was a thousand strong. Now we're only two hundred. I've been trying to convince Shepherd Eliezer that our community needs to make certain changes if we're going to survive. A better relationship with the outside world. A place for women in Church leadership. Your aunt Gwen was in favor of these reforms, too. Unfortunately, Shepherd Eliezer is stuck in the old ways. The only way things are going to change is if we have a new Shepherd."

"That's why Shepherd Eliezer doesn't like us," Rebecca whispered, as if she were afraid of being overheard. "He's forbidden his daughter Meredith from being friends with me anymore. He's threatened to kick Father out of the Church, but he wouldn't dare. Not with Father being an Elder."

"That's enough, Rebecca." Francis clearly wasn't comfortable discussing these things in front of an outsider. "Is there anything else I could help you with, Laura?"

"There is one more thing." Laura pulled Gwen's letter out of her purse and handed it to Francis. "I'm surprised to hear Gwen was in favor of a better relationship with the outside world considering what she said in this letter."

Francis removed the letter from its envelope and unfolded it. Rebecca stood on tiptoes to read it over his shoulder. When he finished reading, he folded the letter and handed it back to her.

"I remember this letter," he said. "It wasn't Gwen's idea. Shepherd Eliezer told her to write it when he discovered she was still corresponding with someone outside the Church. She didn't want to, but once the Shepherd tells you to do something, you have no say in the matter. That's another thing that must change. Don't be upset with Gwen, Laura. She told me many times that she had a niece who was very important to her. I wish she were still with us so she could see you again. I think she would have liked that."

Laura slipped the letter back into her purse. That her aunt had been *forced* to cut off contact with her changed everything. Laura felt ashamed of the anger she'd held on to for so many years. Gwen didn't deserve it.

"Are you married, Cousin Laura?" Rebecca asked.

The suddenness of the question caught Laura off guard. "No, I'm not. I have a very nice boyfriend named Booker, though. I hope you can meet him one day."

"Who matched you to each other?"

"Who *matched* us?" she said. "What do you mean?"

The color drained from Rebecca's face before she could answer. The girl stared at something over Laura's shoulder. Laura turned to see an older man standing between the headstones, dressed in the familiar white shirt and black slacks of the men of Valley Grove. His close-cropped hair was white with age. She placed him in his mid- to late-sixties, but his broad shoulders announced that there was nothing frail or feeble about him. His eyes were as sharp and cunning as a wolf's, and his lips were pinched tight in an expression of disapproval. Two men stood with him, flanking him on either side. They were half his age but looked equally disapproving. One was clean-shaven. The other stood out with a thick red beard.

"Good day, Elder Francis," the older man said. His voice was as sharp and pointed as a scalpel.

"Good day, Shepherd Eliezer," Francis replied with a nod.

The Shepherd stepped forward. The two men fell in behind him like bodyguards.

"Is this one of the famous reforms you seek to enact,

Elder Francis?" Eliezer said. "Bringing outsiders to one of our community's most hallowed places?"

"We were just leaving, Shepherd," Francis said.

He held out his hand to Rebecca and the girl rushed to his side. Eliezer eyed the young girl in a way that Laura didn't like.

"If you're leaving, don't let me slow you," Eliezer said. He stepped aside to give them passage.

The message was clear. They were to exit the cemetery immediately, but Laura wasn't about to leave without asking him about Malachai.

"Shepherd, my name is Laura Powell. I'd like to speak with you about your son."

Eliezer looked shocked that an outsider—a *woman*, no less—dared speak to him. The two men behind him muscled forward as if to get between her and the Shepherd. Francis grabbed Laura by the arm and steered her away.

"Now's not the time," he hissed in her ear.

Eliezer's lips pinched tighter, his sharp eyes following her. The two younger men crossed their arms and scowled like bouncers at a bar. The one with the red beard glared at Laura with beady, animalistic eyes.

Francis pulled her with an iron grip down the path to the street at the foot of the hill. She nearly tripped trying to keep up with him. Rebecca hurried after them.

"I need to speak with him," Laura insisted.

Francis shot her an angry, frustrated look. "You don't know that man. You have no idea what he's capable of. Leave it alone, Laura."

She looked back up the hill. Shepherd Eliezer and his two men stood silhouetted at the top, glaring down at them, surrounded by graves.

9

Laura accompanied Francis and Rebecca back to their house. Once they were inside, Francis strode wordlessly down the entrance hallway as Laura stormed after him. It was a tidy, spartan corridor decorated with a single plant atop a small table and a pastel drawing of Jesus on the wall, opening his robe to reveal a heart crowned with fire and wrapped in a wreath of barbs.

"You shouldn't have pulled me away like that," she said. "I needed to talk to him."

"You need to leave," Francis replied.

She followed him into the modest, sunlit kitchen. Francis took a glass off a rack on the counter and filled it with water. He drained it in three large gulps.

"I'm not leaving until I talk to Malachai's family," she said. "They might know something that could help us figure out what happened to him."

"The Shepherd won't talk to you. I thought that was obvious," Francis said. "I'm sorry, but you need to go."

Rebecca walked past them to the kitchen table, where a couple of carboard boxes waited. She opened one of the boxes and pulled out a handful of crisp white pamphlets, stacking them neatly next to the box.

"Father made these," she said. "We're going to hand them out later. You can join us if you like, Cousin Laura."

"I don't think handing them out today is a good idea, Rebecca," Francis said. He filled the water glass again and took another gulp. "Shepherd Eliezer will be too riled up after what happened. Which is why you need to go, Laura."

"The Shepherd can't make me leave," Laura said. "I don't

answer to him, and I haven't done anything wrong."

Francis shook his head. "You're mistaken. He can have you removed from Valley Grove. Those two men you saw with him—Damien Acker and Fritz Ruggen, the one with the red beard—together they're known as the Order of the Faith. They do whatever Eliezer tells them to do, without question. On his orders, they would personally *carry* you out of Valley Grove. Of the two of them, Fritz is the worst. He's a savage. There are... rumors."

He drained the glass and filled it again. It was clear the water was keeping him calm, or at least calmer than he would be without it. A ritual, or a nervous habit. Often, they were one and the same. The run-in with Shepherd Eliezer at the cemetery had shaken him.

"Rumors of what?" Laura pressed.

"People have disappeared, or worse. All of them were people who displeased or challenged Shepherd Eliezer. I can think of a few off the top of my head who died in house fires. I don't think that's a coincidence."

"I'm not afraid of him," Laura said.

"It's not about you, Laura." He watched his daughter pull another handful of pamphlets out of the box. "Please, just leave now, before things get worse. If it were up to me, you would be welcome here, but it's not. I'm sorry about that, I truly am. If it were up to me, a *lot* of things would be different."

"That's why we have to hand these pamphlets out today, Father, like we planned," Rebecca said. "People need to hear what you have to say. I know some of the Elders are with us already, even if they're afraid to speak out, and I'm sure there are even more people in the congregation who don't like the way Shepherd Eliezer leads us. Probably more than we think. They'll stand with us, but they need to know they're not alone."

"We'll see," Francis said. He took another gulp from the glass.

"Father, we *have* to spread the word," Rebecca insisted. "Nothing will change if we're too scared to do anything about it."

Francis sighed. "She's brave, like her mother," he told Laura. She watched Rebecca neaten the piles on the table and thought she could see some of Gwen in the girl's face. They had the same way of knitting their brows when they concentrated, the same way of pursing their lips when they got worked up. Rebecca was Gwen's daughter, through and through.

Laura was putting Rebecca and Francis in danger by being here. Those men from the Order of the Faith, there was so much anger in their eyes, so much violence simmering just beneath the surface. How much would it take to coax that violence out? Probably not much, and the longer she stayed here, the worse she made it for Rebecca and Francis.

"All right, I'll go," she said. "I don't want to get you in any more trouble."

"It's for the best." Francis wrote his phone number on a slip of paper and handed it to Laura. "Take this, and stay in touch."

She folded the paper and put it in her purse. "I thought Shepherd Eliezer forbade contact with outsiders."

"Who's going to tell him?" Francis said. "Not me."

"Not me, either," Rebecca added. Then, to Laura's surprise, the girl hugged her tightly. "May the Lord take you into His heart and keep you safe until we meet again, Cousin Laura."

"I'm so glad I finally got to meet you, Rebecca."

Rebecca looked up at her. "Does that mean you'll call?"

"I promise I will."

Rebecca hugged her again before letting her go. Francis led them to the door, but before Laura left, Rebecca exclaimed, "Oh, wait! There's something I want to give you!"

She ran down the hallway and returned a moment later clutching a thin silver chain in her small fist. She held it out to Laura. Dangling from the chain was a silver heart pendant.

Laura recognized it instantly. It was Gwen's necklace, a birthday present from Laura's mother. The last time Laura had seen Gwen wear it was at her mother's funeral.

"I want you to have it," Rebecca said. "It belonged to Mother."

A lump formed in Laura's throat. "I couldn't. She would—she would want you to have it, not me. You're her daughter."

"We're not allowed to wear jewelry," Rebecca said matter-of-factly. "Sometimes, when I was little, I saw Mother take this necklace out just to hold it and look at it. I think it meant a lot to her. She wouldn't want it to sit in a drawer forever. She'd want someone to wear it, so I think you should have it."

Laura nodded, too overcome with emotion to speak, as Rebecca dropped the necklace into her hand. Laura closed her fingers around it gently. In a way, it felt like Gwen was with her again. Her mother, too. Laura had come to Valley Grove wondering if she could repair the last connection she had to her family. Now she felt foolish for thinking that connection had ever truly been broken. Her eyes filled with tears.

"Thank you," she said.

Rebecca nodded and took a step back. "Don't forget to keep your promise to call us every now and then."

"I won't forget."

Laura said goodbye to them both and walked out to her car. An air of melancholy engulfed her. She wanted to spend more time with them. She wanted to learn everything about the family she never knew she had. She sat behind the steering wheel for a moment, breathing the hot, stuffy air inside the car. Then, with a pang in her chest, she fastened Gwen's necklace around her neck. How strange to think this simple piece of jewelry had traveled through time from her mother to Gwen and now to her. The silver pendant felt cool against her skin, as comforting as finding something you didn't know you'd lost.

Her phone rang.

"How's it going?" Booker asked when she picked up. "Did Gwen talk to you?"

"It turns out Aunt Gwen died six years ago," she said. "I didn't even know."

"Laura, I'm so sorry. Are you okay?"

"It's a lot to process," she said. "I met Gwen's husband and daughter. They're good people."

"She had a family in Valley Grove?"

"I'm as surprised as you are. I'm not used to having any family. I hope you'll get to meet them someday."

"I'd like that," Booker said. "What about Malachai Applewhite? Have you found anything that could explain what happened to him?"

"I'm still no closer to an answer, but it's got to be here somewhere," she said. "I know death very well, Booker. It's part of my job. People die from bodily trauma, disease, toxins, and natural causes. Petrifaction is nowhere on the list. It's not natural."

"I wish I could be there with you," Booker said. "My faculty meeting is over. I'm going to head home and do some more research. I'll call you if I find anything useful."

Movement outside the windshield caught her eye. Farther down the street, Shepherd Eliezer entered a house. He was by himself, without the Order of the Faith flanking him, which meant the house he'd entered was likely his own.

She wouldn't have a chance like this again.

She ended the call with Booker and got out of the car. She wasn't leaving without answers from Eliezer. As she walked toward the house, her thoughts returned to Aunt Gwen. Gwen hadn't wanted to cut off contact with her. Eliezer made her do it. Because of him, Laura never knew Gwen had a daughter. She never knew Gwen was sick, or that Gwen died. She never knew any of it. Her anger flared.

When she reached the house, she banged forcefully on the door. She imagined she looked wild, her eyes burning with anger, her hair a gorgon-like tangle. She took a breath. She had to calm down. She couldn't approach the Shepherd in anger or she'd get nothing out of him.

A young woman in her twenties opened the front door. The delicate red design on her prairie dress matched the healthy ruddiness of her cheeks. Her strawberry-blonde hair was tied back with a red ribbon.

"Can I help you?" The young woman clasped her hands over the small but noticeable swell in her stomach.

Second trimester, Laura thought, *likely five months along.* People in these small religious communities started their families early.

"Hi," Laura said, replying in a pleasant voice. "I'm sorry to bother you. I'm here to talk to your father."

The young woman looked confused. "My father?"

"Shepherd Eliezer," Laura clarified. "I'd like to speak with him, please."

The young woman smiled, and Laura was struck by her youthful beauty.

"I'm sorry, there's been a mistake," the young woman said. "The Shepherd isn't my father. He's my husband."

10

Laura couldn't believe it. This young woman was Shepherd Eliezer's wife? He had to be forty years older than her. And her pregnancy—Laura thought of Sam Templeton, who'd almost been forced to marry a twelve-year-old girl before he ran away from this place.

"I'm sorry for the confusion," Laura said, doing her best to keep the shock out of her voice. "I'd appreciate it if I could speak to your husband, please."

"May I ask what this is about?" the young woman asked.

"It's about Malachai," Laura said.

"Malachai?" Her eyes widened into bright blue pools, and she stepped aside. "Please, come in. My name is Sharon Applewhite, and you are?"

"Laura Powell," she said as she entered the cool shade of the house. "I drove from Sakima. I'm looking for any information I can find about what happened to him."

"Of course, anything for Malachai."

Sharon closed the door. The entrance hallway of Eliezer's house was as austere as Francis's, with a pale, polished hardwood floor and walls painted a stark white. There was very little furniture, just a standing coat rack adorned with coats and jackets that wouldn't be worn again until the fall, and a porcelain umbrella stand painted with flowers. An ostentatiously large wooden cross hung on the wall facing the door, approximately three feet from top to bottom. Elijah's flaming chariot was etched on the center of the cross, where the beams met.

There was no doubt this was the Shepherd's house.

"Malachai's death was a tragedy," Sharon said, clasping her hands nervously in front of her swollen belly. "It came as a terrible blow to this family, and to the whole community. He was a sweet boy, even if he and his father rarely saw eye to eye."

"What didn't they see eye to eye about?" Laura asked.

"Faith. Our traditions. All of it," Sharon said. "I think maybe he didn't know where he fit in anymore. I can understand that. Everyone has felt that way at times."

"Is that what he told you?"

She shook her head, eyes downcast. "No. He never confided in me about what he was going through. I wish he had. I cared so deeply for him, but... to be honest, my relationship with both of Eliezer's children from his previous marriage hasn't been what I'd like it to be. It's something I'm still working on with Meredith. I only wish I'd had more time with Malachai. It's not easy being a new mother to those who've lost their own."

"Their mother passed away?" Laura asked.

"Cancer," Sharon said. "There's been so much of it in Valley Grove lately, so many lives lost. We've all been tested by tragedy. It's not for me to question the will of God, but I pray there will be an end to it."

"Who are you talking to, Sharon?" Eliezer's voice called from deep within the house.

"We have a visitor, Eliezer," she replied.

She motioned for Laura to follow her through another spartan, white-walled hallway. In the dining room, Eliezer sat at a rustic wooden dining table. He was hunched over an ancient-looking Bible with a worn and flaking cover, jotting notes down on a yellow pad beside it. A massive painting of the Sermon on the Mount hung on the wall behind him.

"Eliezer, this is Laura Powell. She came all the way from Sakima to talk to you about Malachai," Sharon said.

Eliezer looked up from his work. The moment he saw Laura, he turned red with fury and rose from his chair. "What is the meaning of this? You have the nerve to come here after trespassing in our cemetery? To come to my *home*? Sharon, get her out of here immediately!"

Sharon looked stricken, her eyes as wide as a frightened horse's. Her mouth quivered. Unsure what to do and worried she'd made a terrible mistake, she looked even younger, like a child awaiting punishment.

"Wait," Laura said. She put her medical examiner's business card on the dining room table and slid it toward Eliezer. She wished she had an actual badge—flashing it would have been a lot more intimidating—but they only gave badges to law enforcement officers, not M.E.s. "I'm with the Sakima Police Department. I'm here on an official investigation."

She was surprised at how easily the lie came out of her mouth. Yet it was only half a lie, wasn't it? She *did* work with the Sakima PD. Eliezer didn't have to know she was here against Chief Morales's orders.

Eliezer picked up the card and examined it. His gaze moved sharply back to Laura and he tossed the card back onto the table. "So what? The Sakima Police Department has no authority here. Valley Grove is under the legal jurisdiction of the county. Sharon, do as I say and show her out."

"I'm sorry, you have to go." Sharon moved quickly toward Laura, her face pink with humiliation. She extended one arm to usher Laura out of the room.

"Please, wait," she said.

Sharon froze again, caught between obeying her husband's command and wanting to be hospitable. Laura knew what she had to do. She hated it—this was the man who'd ordered Gwen to cut Laura out of her life—but it was the only way to get Eliezer to open up. If she played her cards right, it would take the heat off Francis and Rebecca at the same time.

"I want to apologize," she said. "You were right, I shouldn't have been in your cemetery, and I'm sorry. It's my fault, not Elder Francis's. He was just being kind and doing what I asked of him. I think you and I got off on the wrong foot, Shepherd, and I'm hoping we can start over."

Eliezer regarded her silently. Finally, with his ego assuaged, he nodded. Sharon, looking extremely relieved, retreated to stand by the door to the kitchen with her hands clasped in front of her stomach again.

Eliezer sat down once more. "As the Book of Luke teaches us, 'If your brother or sister sins against you, rebuke them; and if they repent, forgive them.' You see, Dr. Powell, I can be as forgiving as our Lord commands. Sharon, why don't you bring our guest some water? It's hot today, and she's spent far too much time outside in the sun. Haven't you, Dr. Powell?"

He was still needling her about being in the cemetery. Laura pretended she didn't pick up on it.

"Some water would be great, thanks," she said.

"Of course," Sharon said and disappeared into the kitchen.

Eliezer's gaze cut back to Laura.

"Why are you here?" he asked.

"As I said, I'm investigating your son's death," she said.

"I see." He leaned back in his chair and steepled his fingers. "Are you familiar with the Book of Acts? In it, Gamaliel the Pharisee, who was widely considered one of the greatest educators of the ancient world, teaches Jewish law to the Apostle Paul, who was then known as Saul. Gamaliel imparted much wisdom to him, including how to see past what others present as truth to the ultimate truth that hides behind it. For instance, were Paul here now, he might ask why a common car accident would necessitate an investigation that brings the police all the way out to see the victim's family. So, why don't you tell me what this is really about?"

"I'm not convinced the accident was the cause of Malachai's death."

"Of course it wasn't. I can tell you the cause of my son's death."

That was unexpected. "You can?"

"Absolutely," Eliezer said. "Malachai was willful and obstinate. He refused to obey my authority or that of the Church. Did you know when he abandoned us, he left at dawn, before any of us were awake? He sneaked out of this house like a thief. But the Lord saw him. He saw Malachai's disobedience and struck him down just as He struck down the men of Beth Shemesh when they disobeyed Him."

"Are you saying Malachai died because he left?" Laura asked.

Eliezer leaned forward in his chair. "I'm saying the Lord struck Malachai dead for turning his back on us. It was *divine retribution.*"

A gasp came from the kitchen doorway, followed by the sound of breaking glass. Sharon stood there, mouth agape, balancing two glasses of water in her hands. The third had fallen and shattered on the dining room floor.

Sharon let out a despondent moan. "I—I'm so sorry! I'll clean this up right away!"

She rushed to put the two glasses she was holding down on the table, then ran back into the kitchen for paper towels.

Through it all, Shepherd Eliezer didn't take his eyes off Laura.

"And how do you feel about God striking down your son?" Laura pressed.

Eliezer shrugged as if she'd asked his opinion of a bland meal. "God gave His only begotten son to save mankind from sin, and now He has taken mine to save our community from doubt and disobedience. Perhaps I should be honored to be in such illustrious company."

His son had been a problem, and now he wasn't anymore. His lack of grief or conscience was chilling. No doubt he'd been just as cold-blooded the day he ordered Gwen to cut Laura out of her life.

Sharon returned with a roll of paper towels. She struggled to her knees, one hand cradling her swollen belly. She wiped at the spill with a paper towel and carefully collected shards of broken glass.

"Here, let me help," Laura said, kneeling beside her and reaching for the roll of paper towels. "I don't want you to put any undue strain on your stomach. How many months along are you now?"

"Leave her," Eliezer interrupted. "She needs to learn to be more careful. Those glasses cost money."

"She's pregnant," Laura snapped. "With your child, I assume. I would think you wouldn't want her exerting herself unnecessarily."

"Of *course* the child is mine!" Eliezer roared indignantly. "I am her husband!"

"It's okay," Sharon said. "I'll be fine. Just let me clean this. It's my fault. I'm so clumsy."

Laura stood up again. It wasn't clumsiness that had made Sharon drop the glass. The timing of it told the full story. Sharon had heard Eliezer refer to Malachai's death as divine retribution. It had upset and shocked her enough to allow the glass to slip from her hand. Sharon wouldn't admit it, of course, or take Eliezer to task for his words. This wasn't a community where women stood up to their husbands, no matter what awful things they said. Laura found it heartbreaking and infuriating in equal measure.

Footsteps sounded in the hallway, and a young redheaded girl of about fourteen entered the dining room. "I heard something break. What happened?"

The girl paused when she saw Laura.

"Everything is all right, child," Eliezer told her. "Dr. Powell, this is my daughter Meredith."

"It's nice to meet you, Meredith," she said. "My name is Laura. I'm from the Sakima police department and had a few questions for your father about Malachai."

Meredith nodded shyly. Like all the other girls and women in Valley Grove, she wore a white prairie dress with a floral print, red flowers that matched her own frizzy, coppery hair. A spray of freckles covered the bridge of her small, upturned nose. Her brown eyes were big and curious as she regarded Laura.

"And now *I* have a question for *you*, Dr. Powell," Eliezer said, rising from his chair. "When will my son's body be returned to us? Our traditions demand that there be no unnecessary delays before burial."

"That's up to Chief of Police Morales," Laura told him. "I'm just looking into what happened to him. Do you know if Malachai had any health conditions? Or was he acting strangely at all?"

Eliezer didn't answer. Francis had warned her the Shepherd wouldn't talk to an outsider about any of this. She wished she had the authority to compel him to talk, but she didn't. Sharon held her peace too, although that was no surprise. If her husband wasn't going to speak, she wouldn't either. Instead, Sharon finished cleaning up the spill, gathered up the wet paper towels into a ball, and went back into the kitchen to throw them away.

Meredith continued to stare at Laura. Her gaze wasn't hostile or frightened, just curious, as if she were intrigued to see a woman wearing something other than a prairie dress and speaking to her father like an equal.

"Did Malachai have any enemies that you know of?" Laura pressed. "Someone who might try to hurt him?"

Again, no answer from Eliezer.

"He didn't have any enemies," Meredith said.

Laura was surprised to hear her speak up. So was Sharon, who returned from the kitchen and went right to the girl as if to quiet her.

"Everyone liked my brother and was sad when he left," Meredith said.

"What about angry?" Laura asked her. "Was anyone angry that he left?"

"Meredith, let me handle this," Eliezer said. "Go help your mother fix lunch. We're late to eat as it is."

Meredith darkened and stared at the floor. "She's not my mother."

Eliezer raised his voice. "What was that, child?"

Meredith flinched.

Sharon took the girl's hand and gently ushered her toward the kitchen, unfazed by the girl's outburst. "Come, Meredith, you can help me chop the greens."

"You've asked enough questions, Dr. Powell," Eliezer said. "It's time for you to leave."

Before Laura could protest, they were interrupted by angry, raised voices from outside. She went to the dining room window. Eliezer rose from the table to look as well. Outside, Francis had set up a table on the street, and he and Rebecca were handing out the pamphlets they'd made. The two men who comprised the Order of the Faith were there too, confronting them, yelling and trying to grab the pamphlets out of their hands.

"Sharon, you and Meredith stay here," Eliezer growled. He thumped angrily out of the dining room toward the front door.

"Shit," Laura muttered and hurried after him.

11

Shepherd Eliezer reached Francis's pamphlet table before Laura did, moving remarkably quickly for a man of his age and pushing his way through the crowd that had gathered. Fritz, the red-bearded member of the Order of the Faith, grabbed fistfuls of pamphlets off the table and tore them to pieces. The other, Damien, snatched pamphlets out of Francis's hands.

"What is this nonsense, Elder Francis?" Eliezer raged. "Remove this filth immediately!"

The spectacle of the confrontation caused the crowd around the table to grow. They formed a tight human wall, keeping Laura on the outside. She stood on her toes and saw Fritz push Francis roughly aside, then grab two big handfuls of pamphlets and crumple them into balls. Rebecca tried to gather up other pamphlets to save them from the same fate. Damien grabbed Rebecca roughly by the arm and yanked her away from the table. Furious, Laura began to force her way through the crowd.

"People have a right to know there are other ways of doing things," Francis insisted. "There can be a role for women in the Church. The community is interested in this idea, Shepherd Eliezer. Look!"

He pointed at the crowd. Many of them dropped the pamphlets they were holding, afraid of the Shepherd's wrath.

"The Devil has filled your mind with folly, Elder Francis," Eliezer said, speaking loudly so everyone could hear him. "When the Lord chose his Apostles, he chose twelve *men*. That's why Church leadership is reserved for men alone. We follow His example, just as we live His word."

Laura broke through the crowd and stormed up to Damien,

who held Rebecca roughly by the arm. Rebecca squirmed, trying to free herself.

"Let go of her!" Laura said.

Damien turned his head toward her. His features were as sharp and angular as a weasel's. His slate-gray eyes were full of animosity. "You're not welcome here. Why don't you go home where you belong?"

She could tell from the confidence his voice and his easy, unconcerned stance that he was accustomed to telling women what to do. He'd probably done it all his life. If he expected Laura to obey, he would be sorely disappointed.

"I said let go of her."

"Laura, don't," Rebecca warned her.

Damien's eyes narrowed. "Didn't you hear me? Leave, or I'll drag you to your car myself."

"Try it," Laura said. "See how far you get."

He glared at her, but she didn't back down. Slowly, doubt crept into his eyes. She guessed he'd never been defied by a woman before. Finally, he let go of Rebecca's arm.

"You're not worth the trouble," he sneered, trying to save face before oozing back into the crowd to join Fritz and Eliezer.

Laura put her hand on Rebecca's shoulder. "Are you okay?"

The girl rubbed her arm and nodded. "You shouldn't have done that, Cousin Laura. You're going to get in trouble."

"I'm already in trouble."

"Me, too." Rebecca grinned slyly. Laura saw Aunt Gwen so clearly in the girl's features that she could have been looking at a younger version of her. "I thought you left, Cousin Laura."

"Not yet. I have more to do."

"I'm glad you're still here. Excuse me, please." Rebecca hurried back to the table and snatched up any pamphlets within reach.

"The word of the Lord is not to be questioned, Elder Francis," Eliezer said, his voice raised as loud as a carnival barker to make sure everyone heard him. "The old ways are best. These modern ideas have no place here. Nor does anyone who adheres to them, which is why it's so laughable that you wish to replace me as Shepherd!"

Rebecca glared at him, holding the pamphlets protectively to her chest so they couldn't be taken from her. "The old ways aren't the best ways, Shepherd Eliezer, they're just *your* ways!"

A shocked gasp rippled through the crowd. Everyone, even Francis, froze, wondering how Eliezer would react. But he only smiled patiently and reached out with an age-spotted hand. Rebecca backed away from his touch.

"Poor child. Your misguided father has filled your head with his foolishness." Then, louder, he said, "'Wives, submit yourselves unto your own husbands, as unto the Lord. For the husband is the head of the wife, even as Christ is the head of the church.' Ephesians 5:22."

"I believe the women among us can be so much more," Francis said. "My *daughter* can be so much more. All our daughters can."

Eliezer only bellowed to the crowd again, "'Let the woman learn in silence with all subjection. But I suffer not a woman to teach, nor to usurp authority over the man, but to be in silence. For Adam was first formed, *then* Eve.' First Timothy 2:11."

The more Laura saw of Shepherd Eliezer, the more she leaned toward the possibility that he was responsible for Malachai's death. There were rat poisons that calcified the soft tissue of rats; a similar poison used on Malachai could have done the same to him, although on a much grander scale. Sam Templeton said everything Shepherd Eliezer did was about holding on to power within the Church of the Divine Chariot. For a man like him, the public humiliation of a wayward son could be reason enough to murder his own flesh and blood.

A girl's voice rang out suddenly. "Rebecca!"

Laura saw a blur of copper hair as Meredith ran up to the table.

"Meredith!" Rebecca said. The two girls beamed and hugged each other. "I haven't seen you in so long!"

Sharon came running after Meredith, one hand on her swollen stomach as if to keep it steady. "I'm sorry, Eliezer, she got away from me."

"Get her out of here!" Eliezer raged. "Who knows what lunacy Elder Francis will fill my daughter's head with?"

"That's not fair—" Francis began, but Fritz and Damien

grabbed more pamphlets and his attention was drawn away. "Stop! Put those down!"

The crowd grew larger as things became more chaotic. More bodies clustered in front of Laura, keeping her from helping Francis.

"Meredith, come!" Sharon ordered.

She pulled the girl away from Rebecca. Meredith slipped out of Sharon's hands and ran back to her. The girls hugged again, laughing, and Sharon pulled Rebecca away once more—although not before Laura saw Meredith pass something small into Rebecca's hand.

"*Now,* Meredith!" Sharon dragged the girl back toward the house.

"You are sorely testing my patience, Elder Francis," Eliezer said. "Pack up these papers at once and return to your home, or I'll have the Order of the Faith do it for you."

"This isn't right," Francis protested.

"You'll do as a I say. I'm still your Shepherd, Elder Francis."

"For now," Francis said. He knew he'd lost this round. He and Rebecca began shoving pamphlets back into the box.

The crowd thinned as people realized the drama was over. Laura looked back at Eliezer's house and saw Sharon usher Meredith through the door. Sharon wouldn't talk to her without Eliezer's permission, which he was never going to give, but what about Meredith? The girl seemed strong-willed. Laura might have better luck getting answers from her than from Eliezer. While the Shepherd and the Order of the Faith supervised Francis and Rebecca as they packed up their pamphlets, Laura made her way back to the house.

She would have to do it before Eliezer returned. He wouldn't like her talking to his daughter. Laura knocked on the door. When no one answered, she tried the knob and found it unlocked. She stepped into the empty entrance hallway.

"Sharon? Meredith?" she called.

Raised voices came from deeper in the house. Meredith and Sharon were arguing. She followed the sound of it through the dining room and kitchen and into an angled hallway that led to the bedrooms. She heard a door slam. As Laura rounded the corner, she almost collided with Sharon coming toward her.

Sharon gasped and put a hand to her chest. "Oh!"

"Sharon, I'm so sorry, I didn't mean to startle you," Laura said. "I just wanted to make sure you and Meredith were okay."

"We're fine, thank you," Sharon said. Her hands went protectively to her stomach. "You really should go. When Eliezer gets back, he'll be in a foul mood."

"I was hoping I could talk to Meredith. Just for a moment."

"I don't know." Sharon folded her arms, and her gaze darted back down the hall to a white-painted wooden door. Meredith's bedroom. Sharon had a terrible poker face. "She's in a foul mood, too. She takes after her father that way. But I'm sorry, I don't think it's a good idea. Eliezer wouldn't approve."

"I know he wouldn't," Laura said, taking a risk. "That's why I was hoping to talk to her before he comes back."

Sharon's eyebrows lifted in surprise. "If you know my husband wouldn't allow it, why would you think I would?"

"Because I saw how you reacted when your husband said God struck Malachai dead as divine retribution," she said. "I know you cared deeply about Malachai, and I know you want to know the truth about what happened to him as much as I do. Eliezer won't tell me anything because I'm an outsider—and also because I'm a woman. I'm right, aren't I?"

Sharon nodded, eyes downcast. Her pink cheeks turned darker. Laura got the sense Sharon already felt like she was betraying her husband just by talking to her.

"Meredith knew Malachai better than anyone," Laura continued. "He was her big brother. They spent every day together. If anyone can help me figure out what happened, she can. Please, let me talk to her. Even just for a moment."

Sharon glanced at Meredith's bedroom door again, then sighed and nodded. "Very well. For Malachai's sake. But I can only give you a few minutes. If Eliezer finds you here…"

"I know," Laura said. "I'll be as quick as I can."

Sharon led her to the door and knocked softly. "Meredith?"

"Go away," Meredith sulked from inside.

"Laura would like to talk to you," Sharon said. "Will you let her come in?"

"Laura?" There was a pause. "Okay."

Sharon gave Laura a nod. "Remember, you need to be gone before Eliezer gets back," she said, retreating down the hall.

Laura gently opened the door. Meredith's bedroom was as spartan as the rest of the house, with none of the posters, pillows, and stuffed animals she expected to see in a fourteen-year-old girl's room. There was a single pine chest of drawers, a plain wooden armoire, and a narrow bed with an equally plain wooden frame. One white wall was adorned with a cross, another with a small framed painting of Jesus tending to a flock of sheep while gingerly cradling a lamb in one arm. Meredith was lying face-down on the bed where she'd thrown herself during her tantrum. She sat up quickly when Laura entered, straightening her wrinkled prairie dress. Her frizzy red hair looked as wild as tumbleweed.

Laura closed the door behind her. "I'm sorry about what happened with Rebecca out there. She's a nice girl."

It didn't feel safe to mention that she and the Ponders were family, not even to Meredith. She didn't want any more attention to fall on them than she'd already brought.

"It's not fair that we can't be friends just because our fathers don't get along," Meredith said. She lowered her voice to a whisper. "But it's okay. We have secret ways to talk."

"You passed her a note outside, didn't you?"

Meredith looked worried. "You saw?"

"Yes, but it's okay, I don't think anyone else did," Laura reassured her. "May I sit?"

Meredith moved over on the bed to make room for her.

"I have an important question to ask you, but it's also a difficult one," Laura said, sitting down.

"That's okay. What is it?"

"Would your father ever do anything to hurt Malachai?"

"You mean punish him?" Meredith asked. "Some of the other kids get the switch from their parents when they misbehave, but Father never did that to Mal. When he wanted to punish Mal, he put him in the Penitence Room."

Laura didn't like the sound of that. "What's the Penitence Room?"

"It's where Father puts you if you talk back or disobey. You sit in the dark and the cold, with no light at all, and no food or water, and you're supposed to take that time to ask God for forgiveness. Sometimes Father leaves you there for hours. It's awful."

"Meredith," Laura said, "did he ever put you in the Penitence Room?"

She nodded gravely. "Now can I ask you a question, Laura?"

"Sure."

Meredith bit her lower lip as though she were afraid to ask what was on her mind. "What's it like where you live?"

"It's nice. It's quiet, usually. Most of the people are friendly. It's very small, though, only about three thousand people."

Meredith's eyes went big. Laura realized three thousand people wouldn't sound small to Meredith at all, not when there were only about two hundred in Valley Grove.

"I work as a family doctor in Sakima," she went on. "Sometimes I help the police department with their investigations. My boyfriend Booker teaches science at the high school."

"You have a boyfriend?" Meredith asked.

Laura smiled. "Yes, I do. Would you like to see a picture of him?"

Meredith nodded, and Laura pulled up a photo of Booker on her phone. Meredith's eyes went big again.

"He's *huge*," she said.

"It's true, Booker is pretty tall."

"He's not just tall, he's…" She flexed her arm muscles.

Laura put her phone away. "Yes, that too."

"Do you and Booker…?" Meredith paused and lowered her voice to a whisper. "Do you *do* stuff?"

"What do you mean?" Laura asked, although she had a definite idea what Meredith meant.

The girl turned away from her, embarrassed. "Can I tell you something, Laura?"

"Of course. Anything."

"And you can't tell Sharon. Or my father," she said. "Definitely not my father."

"I promise," Laura said.

"When Mal left, I was jealous. I wanted to go, too. I wanted to leave with him."

"You don't like it here?"

"I *hate* it here," she said. "I think about running away all the time, but I don't want to leave Rebecca behind. Maybe I could get her to run away with me. Or maybe I won't leave at all. I'll have to make up my mind soon. I don't have a lot of time left."

"Why do you say that?"

Meredith's face darkened. Her mouth tightened into a frown. "I'm supposed to get married next month."

Laura felt like somebody punched her in the stomach. "Married?"

"I've been matched to Elder Bernard," Meredith said. "I don't even know him, except that he's one of the Church Elders. I think he and my father made some kind of deal. Elder Francis wants to replace Father as Shepherd, and Father is worried it might happen. He got Elder Bernard to promise to back him if it comes down to a vote. And in return ..."

"In return, he gave you to Elder Bernard." Laura could hardly keep the disgust out of her voice.

Meredith got off the bed and opened the armoire. She pulled out a white, lacy, beaded dress on a hanger. A wedding dress. It was so small Laura's heart broke at the sight of it.

"My mother made this," Meredith said, admiring the elaborate beadwork on the bodice. "My *real* mother. She started when I was little. When she got sick, her only wish was to live long enough to see my wedding day. She didn't. Part of me wants to go through with it for her sake. It was all she ever wanted for me, but..."

"But it's not what *you* want."

"I'm not interested in it." Meredith hung the dress in the armoire again.

"Getting married to an older man?" Laura said. "If I were your age, I wouldn't be interested in it, either."

"No," Meredith said. She sat on the bed again and lowered her voice. "I'm not interested in *it*. You know." She looked down at her hands folded in her lap. "I know I'm supposed to be. It's all the other kids talk about when there are no parents around. They all run off into the woods together to *do* things. Everyone except me. I don't want to. I don't even care about it. But if I marry Elder Bernard, I'm supposed to give him babies. I'm not dumb, I know where babies come from."

Laura's heart sank. The poor girl. "Meredith..."

"It's not like I don't want a boyfriend or even to get married one day, if it's someone I choose for myself," Meredith said. "I just don't want to do *that*. I never have, and I never will. But Elder Bernard won't care. He already has five children from his first wife. All of them are older than me. But I know he wants more."

Laura didn't know what to say. She wanted to take Meredith away from here, bring her back to Sakima where she wouldn't be forced to marry someone. Forced to have his children.

"Maybe there's something wrong with me," Meredith said. "I'm supposed to want to do it, aren't I? Especially if it's with someone I like. But... I just don't. Does that make me a freak?"

"No, there's nothing wrong with you, and you're not a freak," Laura said. "There are other people who feel the same way you do."

"I doubt that."

"It's true. I had a friend in school who felt the same. We didn't have a word for it back then, but we do now—asexual. People who are asexual make up about one percent of the population. I know that may not sound like a lot, but one percent of the world's population is still over 77 million people. You're not alone."

"It doesn't matter," Meredith said. "There's no one else like that *here*. I haven't told anyone. They wouldn't understand, especially not my father. Please, please, please, don't tell him."

"I won't," Laura said. "And I promise to help if I can. Is there anyone I can talk to about stopping the wedding?"

Meredith shook her head. "My father is the Shepherd. There's no one above him to talk to. This is what he's decided for me, which means it's what's going to happen. That's why I wanted Mal to take me with him, but I never worked up the nerve to ask him. And now it's too late."

"I'm so sorry about what happened to your brother," Laura said.

"Me, too," Meredith said. "Sometimes I can't believe he's dead. Like, maybe he faked it so no one could find him and force him to come back here."

"I'm so sorry," Laura said. "It's not fake."

Meredith looked down at her feet. "I know. It was just something I liked to pretend."

"I came here to find out what happened to Malachai, but your father won't tell me anything about him."

Meredith rolled her eyes. "Of course he won't tell you anything. Neither will Sharon. She's so stupid. She just does whatever he tells her to."

"That's not true," Laura said. "She's the one who let me talk to you, even though she knows your father wouldn't like it. She cares about you very much. She cared about Malachai, too."

"Mal hated her as much as I do."

"Why?"

"He and Sharon are the same age!" Meredith exclaimed. Realizing she'd raised her voice, she lowered it to a whisper again. "She keeps trying to be our mother, but she's not our mother."

They were getting off track and Laura was running out of time. Eliezer could return at any moment.

"I was hoping you could tell me something about Malachai that might help me," she said. "You mentioned before that he didn't have any enemies. What about illnesses? Was he sick at all before he left?"

"No," Meredith said. "He was happy and excited about leaving. He got into so many arguments with Father about it. Father didn't want Mal to leave, but only because of how it would look for him. He didn't like that Mal had a job outside Valley Grove. He didn't want him being around outsiders because he said their secular ideas would make him question the Church, but he had it backward. Mal was already questioning the Church. Taking the job was how he saved money to start a new life somewhere else."

"I didn't know Malachai had a job," Laura said. "What did he do?"

"He worked at Thurmond Biotech, that big building on the other side of the lake," Meredith said. "They make prescription drugs, I think. I don't know what Mal did for them, but they must have made him work really hard because he always came home tired."

She'd seen the gleaming glass building across the lake when she'd driven into Valley Grove. Malachai working at a biotech company was an interesting wrinkle. Could he have been exposed to something there that was responsible for his petrifaction? It was worth digging deeper to find out.

Laura stood up. "Thank you, Meredith. You've been a big help."

"You're welcome."

She started toward the door but stopped and turned back to Meredith. "I meant what I said before. I'll do whatever I can to help you."

Meredith smiled, but Laura knew it was only for her sake. There was no happiness in it. Laura walked back to the bed and hugged her. Meredith hugged her back, tighter than she thought the girl would.

Laura left the bedroom, closing the door gently behind her so it wouldn't make a sound, and started down the hallway back toward the kitchen. She promised herself she would find a way to get Meredith out of her predicament. There *had* to be something she could do. She couldn't let this marriage happen.

Eliezer's agitated voice bellowed from somewhere in the house. "Elder Francis thinks he can take the Shepherdom from me? He thinks he has what it takes to lead this congregation? This community? He's a fool!"

Laura froze, staying quiet. She heard Sharon's voice trying to calm Eliezer down. Laura crept silently into the kitchen. She peeked through the open doorway to the dining room and saw them both standing by the table. Eliezer had his back to her. Laura wanted to storm up to him and give him an earful about Meredith's impending marriage, but she knew the repercussions would only come down on Meredith's head. Hiding in the kitchen, she waited for a chance to make her exit.

"I had a visit from Emma Richter," Sharon told Eliezer. "She says her daughter Beth has gone missing. She went looking for her when it was time for Beth's midday chores, but she was nowhere to be found."

"She'll turn up," Eliezer said. Laura couldn't see his expression from where she hid in the kitchen, but his voice betrayed his lack of concern.

"Beth's only fifteen," Sharon pressed. "No one's seen her since this morning. Her mother is going out of her mind. I know she'd appreciate your help."

Whoever Beth Richter was, Laura couldn't help wondering if she had run away like Malachai did. Like Meredith wanted to. They couldn't be the only ones desperate to get out of Valley Grove. But there were other reasons teenage girls went missing. Darker reasons. From what she'd seen of the Church of the Divine Chariot so far, there was a sick obsession with teenaged girls among the older male population.

"Enough, Sharon. I said she'll turn up," Eliezer said. "Emma's a worrier, that's all. I'm sure the girl is fine. Now, don't disturb me with anything else."

Sharon sighed and looked away from her husband, suddenly noticing Laura in the kitchen. She froze a moment, then darted her eyes briefly to one side. It was a message, Laura realized, telling her which way to go. Nodding her gratitude, Laura doubled back and found a door in the kitchen leading to the backyard. She slipped quietly out of the house.

At the far end of the yard, standing at the head of the driveway that ran alongside the house, was a wide concrete garage. Laura made a break for it, staying low as she dashed across the yard, hoping she wouldn't be seen from the house. She darted behind the garage and into the woods in back. Picking her way through the trees as she circled back toward the main road, she wondered again about the missing girl, Beth Richter. Had Beth fled through these same woods, desperate to escape the oppressive life of the Church of the Divine Chariot, or had something else happened to her? Something worse?

12

It was a half-hour drive from Valley Grove to Thurmond Biotech. With no direct route around the lake, Laura was forced to drive through the streets of the next town over while her GPS recited directions. Occasionally, the gleaming building would show itself in the distance atop a tall, craggy cliff above the lakeshore.

Booker called. She put it through to her car's hands-free speakerphone.

"How's it going?" he asked.

"The Church of the Divine Chariot is more messed up than I thought," she said. "They're marrying off girls—*children*—to older men like it's nothing, like the only purpose these girls serve is to bear their children. One girl went missing today, and the Shepherd, the leader of the Church, doesn't give a damn. I hope she's okay. I hope she ran away from this madness and is somewhere safe."

"It sounds awful," Booker said. "How much longer are you going to be there?"

"Probably not much longer. I'm just following a lead. Malachai Applewhite had a job at a pharmaceutical company called Thurmond Biotech. The president of the company agreed to answer a few questions."

"Great. In the meantime, I found something interesting," Booker said. "It turns out spontaneous petrifaction isn't unheard of in nature. Have you ever heard of Lake Natron in Tanzania?"

Laura stopped at a red light. "No, I can't say I have."

"It has a reputation as the deadliest lake in the world," he said. "It's believed that any creature that enters its waters is instantly turned to stone. That's an exaggeration, of course, but it's not far from the truth. Lake Natron is a landlocked salt lake, so over time, as the water evaporates in the desert heat, it leaves behind a higher and higher concentration of salt, just like the Dead Sea or the Great Salt Lake in Utah. Except here, there's also an active volcano nearby that spews a dark, muddy lava that's rich in natron, which is a naturally-occurring sodium. In fact, it's the same stuff the ancient Egyptians used to dry out cadavers for mummification."

The light turned green, and Laura drove on through a sleepy neighborhood of small, two-story houses.

"The natron must make the lake even saltier than it already was," she said.

"Hotter, too," Booker said. "The natron-rich lava pours into the lake and turns the water hot enough to cause third-degree burns. All of this results in a lake that's like a caustic, preservative cauldron. Now imagine a passing bird dives into the lake, thinking it's going to get itself a nice fish to eat. The heat kills the bird almost instantly, and thanks to the natron and the high level of salt, its carcass becomes calcified into a hardened, stonelike state and sinks to the bottom. When the lake waters recede during the dry season, the shore is littered with chemically-preserved carcasses. It's like a sculpture garden of dead birds."

"You always tell me the most romantic stories," Laura said.

"That's not even the weirdest part," Booker continued. "Only three creatures are known to survive the waters of Lake Natron. One is a species of tilapia that has evolved to exist in the hypersaline environment. The second is a blue-green algae called *Spirulina*. And the third is...flamingos."

"Flamingos?" she said with a laugh. "You've got to be kidding me."

"It's true. Flamingos evolved in such a way that Lake Natron's high salinity doesn't bother them. On the contrary, it gives them a plethora of algae to eat and a chance to breed safely away from their natural predators, all of whom avoid the lake because it's deadly to them."

Laura shook her head. "The deadliest lake in the world, except to flamingos. The same big pink birds people in Florida put plastic replicas of on their lawns."

"What can I say? The natural world is full of wonders and terrors alike," he said. "Flamingos aside, Lake Natron proves spontaneous petrifaction exists."

"The dead birds in Lake Natron were petrified by the introduction of an external chemical catalyst," Laura said. "I was already thinking Malachai might have been exposed to something at Thurmond Biotech. If it was a similar chemical catalyst..."

"Bingo," he said. "Let me know what you find out. I'll keep researching."

"Thanks," she said. "I love you."

He scoffed. "You only love me when I bring you weird science facts."

"True. The rest of the time I only tolerate you."

"I tolerate you too, dear," he said. "Be careful. Call me later."

She ended the call and continued driving. According to the GPS, Thurmond Biotech wasn't much farther now. She passed an abandoned gas station on the side of the road. Its pumps were gone, but the building still there, boarded up and graffitied. An old Sunoco sign, shattered and sun-bleached, sat on top of a rusted pole. It was clear this road didn't get the traffic it used to. There were lots of old roads in the Hudson Valley like this one, all but abandoned after being replaced by newer roads and highways. Wherever this road used to lead, it only went to one place now. Thurmond Biotech reared up before her, a gleaming monolith of glass and steel that reflected the midday sun like an enormous mirror. Beyond it, the old road petered out into overgrown grass, weeds, and eventually the forest. Thurmond Biotech was the end of the line.

She turned into the driveway, which after a few yards split like a forked tongue. One side led around the side of the building to a loading dock, where several unmarked semi-trailers were parked. The other led Laura to a huge parking lot in front of the building, where she parked and got out of the car. There was no shade in the lot, and the sun beat down mercilessly as she crossed the shimmering asphalt to the entrance. In the distance, beyond the building, Laura could see the rippling water of the lake and, on the other side, Valley Grove in miniature.

The name THURMOND BIOTECH was etched into the frosted glass of the front door. The door slid open automatically for her, granting her access to a cavernous, air-conditioned lobby. Laura soaked in the cool air as the sweat evaporated on her skin. The walls and floor of the lobby were a polished white granite marbled with dark veins. The reception desk, made of the same granite, was manned by a single uniformed security guard. Standing next to the desk was the man she was here to meet—Hugh Robertson, president of the company. Wearing a crisp blue suit and a red-striped tie, he approached her with a smile and extended one hand.

"You must be Dr. Powell," he said as he shook Laura's hand. It was a salesman's handshake, firm, steady, one pump and done. His skin was the color of bronzing cream, but his hair was gray enough to be almost white. "Welcome to Thurmond Biotech."

Laura handed Hugh her business card. "Thank you for agreeing to speak with me, Mr. Robertson. I just have a few questions about Malachai Applewhite."

"I'm happy to answer any questions you have. Anything to help the police." Hugh looked at the card and furrowed his brow. "Isn't it, um, unusual for a medical examiner to interview people?"

She ignored the question. "Did you know Malachai Applewhite personally?"

He slipped the card into the inside pocket of his blazer. "Of course. I make it a policy to get to know everyone who works here. We were all shocked to hear the news about Malachai. He was a valued member of the Thurmond Biotech family."

A chime sounded from the lobby's elevator bank as one of the elevators opened. A young man stepped out, not yet thirty, with sandy-blond hair and soft features. He wore a black Dio t-shirt and pulled a vape pen out of his pocket as he went out to the parking lot for a smoke break.

"Mr. Robertson, who notified the company about Malachai's death?" Laura asked. "Was it his family?"

"Oh no, definitely not," Hugh said. "As I understand it, his family lives across the lake in Valley Grove. They're with the Church of the Divine Chariot, and so they—how should I put this?—weren't exactly supportive of Malachai's decision to work here. I'm sorry to say we received the tragic news directly from the Sakima PD. Apparently, Malachai's keycard and company ID were found in his wallet. Honestly, I'm not sure what I can tell you that I didn't already tell them on the phone."

"Let's start from the beginning," Laura said. "What was Malachai's role here?"

"He worked on the manufacturing floor downstairs. I can show you, if you'd like to see."

She told him she would like that very much, and he led her past the elevators to a door that he opened with a swipe of his key card. Beyond it was a corridor that looked much more like an average office than the highly polished stone lobby, complete with gray industrial carpeting and off-white plaster walls. The corridor let out onto a large administrative space made up of numerous cubicles and a few private offices separated by frosted glass walls. Along one wall, picture windows overlooked the sparkling waters of the lake. Men and women in business-casual attire sat talking on their desk phones or moving between enormous file cabinets the size of walls.

"This is our order fulfillment department," Hugh explained, brushing a hand through his white hair. "Forgive me for crowing, but we just closed out the best quarter in our company's history, with revenue of two-point-five billion dollars. We also just received FDA approval on a product that we estimate will increase revenue by another fifteen percent by the end of this quarter."

"That's very impressive," Laura said. "What exactly do you make here, if you don't mind my asking?"

"I don't mind at all, Dr. Powell. Thurmond Biotech originally made its name with biofuels and pest-resistant crops, but today we specialize in life-saving medicine and medical research."

His words were well practiced, as if he were giving a tour to prospective investors. She wondered how many times he'd done this before. They passed into a hallway. At the far end was a heavy-duty stainless-steel door with a keypad on the handle.

She started toward it, but he stopped her.

"That's our Research and Development Department," he said. "It's off limits, I'm afraid. This way."

He used his key card to unlock another door in the middle of the hallway. Behind it was a concrete stairwell leading down. As they descended, Hugh resumed his speech, his voice echoing off the austere concrete walls of the stairway.

"Currently, the project we're most excited about is an anti-aging remedy that enhances immune function to increase longevity. Just think of it. No more macular degeneration, no more hearing loss, no more osteoarthritis. No more atherosclerosis, cataracts, or osteoporosis. No more dementia. All thanks to one little pill. I don't have to tell you how competitive the anti-aging field is. The first company to make it to market with a pill that actually works stands to make a fortune. I intend for that company to be Thurmond Biotech."

"An anti-aging pill sounds like a dream," Laura said. "How would it work?"

"I'm afraid that's proprietary information, Dr. Powell. I'm not at liberty to share."

She nodded. "Research and development."

"Precisely. However, I can tell you this: What sets biotechnology above the pharmaceutical industries of old is that it allows us to manipulate microorganisms and certain biological substances to perform specific processes."

"Genetic modification?" Laura asked.

Hugh grinned. His teeth were as white as his hair. "Mother Nature always has the answer, Dr. Powell, but sometimes you just need to give her a little push."

He used his card to open a door at the bottom of the steps. Inside was a small locker room with private showers and changing areas. At the far end were two more doors, one labeled MANUFACTURING, the other OBSERVATION. He took Laura through the second door and into a long, narrow room with a window of thick glass along one wall. On the other side of the window was a gymnasium-sized space filled with rows of gleaming, stainless-steel machines. Workers moved back and forth between them in the harsh artificial light, covered from head to toe with protective body suits, gloves, goggles, hair nets, and respirators.

"This is the manufacturing floor," he said. "As a doctor, you're no doubt familiar with many prescription medications, but have you ever seen exactly how medications are turned into pills for consumer use?"

When she told him she never had, he took visible pride in leading her down the length of the observation room and explaining the purposes of the various machines on the floor. The medicine's active ingredient was ground into a powder mixed with a binding agent, then dried in enormous dryers operating between one hundred and one hundred and twenty degrees Fahrenheit. Heavy presses crushed and molded the dried powder into tablet form with a pressure between two and five tons. Each press could produce five thousand tablets per minute, which were then shoveled into the coating units, where the pills were sprayed with a coating solution of water and coloring pigments. Once the pills were properly coated, they were funneled down a chute to the packaging department. His description of the process was as practiced as his sales pitch. His smile remained plastered on his face the whole time.

"Malachai was stationed at the coating units," he said. "He was a good worker. Always willing to cover a shift. Never complained about being on his feet all day. The other workers liked him, but he kept to himself. I don't think I ever saw him go out for drinks after work with the guys. Of course, that might have been because of his background."

"Could Malachai have come in contact with any dangerous chemicals on the manufacturing floor?" Laura asked.

Hugh shook his head vehemently. "Absolutely not. We take our workers' safety very seriously. Our OSHA incident rate is well below average."

She watched the workers at Malachai's station attend the coating units in their heavy-duty protective suits. "If there were a tear in his suit—"

"Impossible," Hugh interrupted. "There are redundancies upon redundancies to ensure worker safety, including immediate decontamination if anyone comes in contact with something they shouldn't."

"Are there any waste materials from the manufacturing process that could be toxic—"

Hugh's permanent smile faded. "What's this about, Dr. Powell? I thought Malachai died in a car accident. Why all the questions about worker safety?"

"I can't answer that right now," she said. "Do you think I could talk to one of his co-workers?"

His smile didn't return. She'd touched a nerve. "I'm afraid not. It's imperative we stay behind the glass partition so we don't contaminate the raw materials. That's just one of our many, *many* safety protocols, Dr. Powell. Besides, I couldn't spare anyone right now. Malachai's tragic accident has left us short-handed. If you wish to speak with anyone else, or if you have any other questions about our safety procedures, you'll need to come back with the proper paperwork."

"You mean a warrant," she said.

"Sorry, but that's what our legal department requires." Hugh shrugged like he wished he could help but his hands were tied and wasn't this all just terribly silly.

She thanked him for his time and followed him back upstairs, already mentally revising her theory. As much as she loathed the man, Shepherd Eliezer didn't poison his son. It was far more likely something here did. If Malachai worked on the manufacturing floor, he could have easily become contaminated with an unknown biotechnological ingredient. A tear in his hood, or the oxygen line, or even a tiny hole in his glove would be all it took for the granulated powder to float in on an air current to be swallowed, inhaled, or absorbed through the skin, allowing any genetically manipulated microorganism or biologically engineered substance into his system. That could be the external chemical catalyst she was looking for. Malachai's own Lake Natron.

Hugh brought Laura back to the granite-walled lobby and shook her hand again. "Please let me know if there's anything else I can do to help, Dr. Powell. You have my phone number."

"And you have mine, if you remember anything," she said.

Hugh flipped back a lock of white hair that had fallen across his forehead. "Of course."

He card-swiped himself back inside through the door in the granite wall. If she were a betting person, she'd put good money on never hearing from Hugh Robertson again. Everything she'd experienced since walking into the building, including the tour of the manufacturing floor, had been an exercise in stonewalling.

Laura walked out into the oppressive heat of the parking lot. When she reached her car, the man in the black Dio t-shirt waved at her and hurried toward her across the lot. Dark sweat stains colored the armpits of his t-shirt as he continued waving frantically.

"Wait, please!" he called. When he reached her car, he squinted his eyes against the sun. "I heard you earlier, in the lobby. You were asking questions about Mal Applewhite, weren't you?"

"Who are you?" Laura asked.

"My name is Craig Hutsell." Tired of squinting, he shaded his eyes with one doughy hand. "I worked with Mal on the floor. We had the same shift most of the time, so we got to know each other. I liked him. I was probably one of the few people he talked to in this place." He looked over his shoulder in both directions. "There's something I need to tell you, but not here. Is there somewhere we can go?"

"Why can't you tell me here?"

He glanced over his shoulder at the building again. "People might hear. It's bad enough I could be seen talking to you. The company lawyers are gonna be up my ass about it. Look, I'm really sticking my neck out with this. Are you interested or not?"

"Okay," she said. "Do you know Valley Grove, across the lake?"

"Sure. Everyone around here knows about Valley Grove. That's where Mal was from."

"We can talk there," Laura said. "I know a place that should be safe."

"Okay, fine, Valley Grove it is," Craig said. "My shift is over.

I just need to get my stuff. You go ahead. I'll be right behind you. Five, ten minutes max."

She handed Craig her business card. "My number's on here, in case anything comes up."

He took the card and stuffed it in his pocket. Then, without another word, he turned and hurried back to the building.

Laura got into her car, wondering if she could trust anything Craig Hutsell told her. His paranoia didn't exactly make him sound rational, but there was no harm in hearing him out.

She drove back to Valley Grove and parked in front of Francis's house. He wouldn't be happy to see her again—he'd told her to leave Valley Grove hours ago—but she wanted to check on him and Rebecca after their altercation with Shepherd Eliezer. She got out of the car and walked toward the front door.

Someone behind her yelled, "Dr. Powell!"

Laura turned around. Chief Morales stormed across the street toward her. Even with half her face hidden behind mirrored sunglasses, she did not look happy.

"What the hell are you doing here, Dr. Powell? I told you to leave this case alone!"

"Shit," Laura muttered.

13

Chief Morales was furious, her lips pulled back in anger, flashing her teeth like a threat. It reminded Laura of Stuckie the dog and the ominous warning in his rictus snarl. Here was her demise, in the form of her angry boss.

"Imagine my surprise when I arrived to interview Malachai Applewhite's family and was informed someone from the Sakima Police Department had *already* interviewed them," Morales said. They'd moved under the shade of a tree away from Francis's house. "And then I was handed *this*."

She brandished the business card Laura had given Shepherd Eliezer like a weapon. Laura's face burned. She was busted and she knew it. There was no point in making excuses.

"I'm sorry," Laura said. "I know you told me to stay out of it, but I thought my aunt might be in danger. It turns out she died years ago and I didn't know. But I still have family here, and I had so many questions about what happened—"

"Tell me why I shouldn't fire you right this minute, Dr. Powell."

Frankly, Laura was surprised she wasn't fired the second Morales laid eyes on her. Still, she'd be a fool to think one wrong answer wouldn't tip her over the edge. She proceeded with caution.

"I might have a lead," she said. "Malachai had a job at Thurmond Biotech, a pharmaceutical company near here. He frequently worked with raw chemicals, including unknown genetically modified agents. If he was exposed to any of it without protection, it could explain the petrifaction of his body. One of Malachai's co-workers by the name of Craig Hutsell has agreed to meet me here with some information about Malachai that he thinks is important. I can't guarantee it's going to pan out. Truth be told, this guy seems a little off to me, but I'm willing to hear what he has to say."

Morales sighed and took off her mirrored sunglasses. "There's no denying that you stepped over the line, Dr. Powell. I told you to stay away and you ignored me. Make no mistake, there will be repercussions. However, I'd like to hear what Malachai's co-worker has to say. What time are you meeting him?"

Relief washed over Laura. It seemed she still had her job. For now.

"He should be coming anytime now."

She checked her watch. Craig Hutsell said he'd only be five or ten minutes behind her, but it had already been twice that. If he was delayed, why hadn't he called? Maybe he was nothing but a paranoid kook after all. If he didn't show up, she was going to look even worse in Morales's eyes.

"Once we're finished talking to Mr. Hutsell, you're going right back to Sakima. No ifs, ands, or buts. Clear?"

Laura nodded.

Morales put her sunglasses back on. "Until then, I don't want you leaving my side or talking to anyone without my permission."

"You can't be serious," Laura said.

"I assure you, I'm very serious, Dr. Powell. You have no idea how much you might have compromised the investigation. Eliezer Applewhite was furious when he found out your presence here was unauthorized. When his wife heard the news, she looked like someone had slapped her in the face."

Laura's heart sank. Sharon had trusted her. She'd gone against her husband's wishes to let Laura speak to Meredith alone. No wonder she felt so betrayed.

"As long as you're in Valley Grove, you and I are joined at the hip," Morales went on. "If I so much as lose sight of you for a minute, I'm sending you home in the back of a police car. Understood?"

"Don't you think that's a bit extreme?"

"Am I understood?" Morales repeated.

Laura sighed. "Yes."

"Excuse me! Excuse me!" someone shouted.

Laura looked up to see Shepherd Eliezer storming toward them. Another man was with him, old, bone-thin, and stooped at the shoulders. His long, scraggly gray beard was yellowed around his mouth from nicotine. He was out of breath by the time he stood before Laura and Morales, huffing and wheezing like a faulty engine.

"Chief Morales, I must ask you again to release Malachai's body to me," Eliezer insisted.

"I'm sorry, I thought I made it clear that I can't," Morales told him. "The investigation is ongoing and your son's body is evidence."

"The Church of the Divine Chariot has strict customs about burial," the skinny old man interjected. His voice was coarse and wet, as if a muddy puddle had taken up residence in his throat. "Bodies must be buried in consecrated ground within twenty-four hours of their death. That deadline has already passed. Those who have been called home to glory are not meant to remain among the living for this long."

"I'm sorry, who are you?" Morales asked.

"This is Elder Bernard," Eliezer said. "He cares for the cemetery and is in charge of the interments."

Elder Bernard? Where had Laura heard that name before?

"It is my holy duty to tend to those who have been called home," Elder Bernard continued. "There are rituals that must be attended to before the burial. Prayers. The washing and anointing of the body. It takes time."

"I'm sorry, but I'm afraid it's going to have to wait," Morales said. "My hands are tied. I can't release the body until the investigation is concluded. The law is the law."

Elder Bernard flapped his bony arms in frustration. "That is the law of *man*. Here, we follow the law of *God*."

"Understood," Morales said. "But only one of them signs my paycheck, so it's just going to have to wait."

Eliezer turned his sharp gaze on Laura. His features tightened in anger and he turned back to Morales. "Can I speak with you a moment in private, Chief Morales?"

"Of course."

He led her a few steps away. Laura could still hear him clearly. "What is *she* still doing here? You should arrest her for impersonating a member of the police department!"

"I'm not arresting anyone," Morales told him. "Technically, Dr. Powell *is* a member of the police department, she's just not a detective."

It almost sounded like Morales was sticking up for her. Almost.

Elder Bernard, upset that no one was paying attention to him, grumbled loudly, "This delay is a travesty!"

Now, finally, Laura remembered where she'd heard his name before. She looked the old man up and down—he had to be in his eighties—and felt sick to her stomach all over again.

"You're marrying Meredith Applewhite next month," Laura said.

Elder Bernard nodded, his long beard sweeping his concave chest. "That's right. The Shepherd's daughter and I have been matched. It will be a glorious union."

"Don't you think she's too young?" Laura pressed. She knew she ought to stay out of it, but she kept thinking about how much Meredith was dreading the marriage.

"Too young? No, I don't think so," Elder Bernard said. "Her father assures me she is the right age to bear children. He told me he's seen the signs."

Laura almost hesitated to ask. "What signs?"

"Hair," he said.

She turned away and fought off a wave of nausea.

Eliezer returned, storming past her to collect Elder Bernard. "Come, Elder Bernard, it's a waste of time talking to these interlopers!"

"Fine, fine," Elder Bernard said, running a hand through his greasy beard. "I have business to attend to anyway. We'll talk later, Shepherd."

Laura watched Eliezer stamp angrily back toward his house, then turned to watch Elder Bernard shuffle off in another direction. Neither of them had Meredith's best interests in mind. She was being passed off like a bribe to a man old enough to be her grandfather. It was repulsive. And yet, short of kidnapping

Meredith, what could she do? Legally, the girl was a minor, but even the law couldn't stop the wedding from taking place. It was protected under the guise of religious freedom.

A car blew past them on Valley Grove's main road. "Rainbow in the Dark" blasted out of the rolled-down windows. The car found a parking spot in front of Eliezer's house and screeched to a halt. Out stepped Craig Hutsell, still in his black Dio t-shirt.

Eliezer stopped, took one look at him, and called out sarcastically to Chief Morales, "This one must be with the Sakima Police Department, too! Such professionalism!"

Morales ignored him.

Laura leaned over to her. "That's Craig Hutsell."

"Good. Let's hope he has some answers."

They crossed the street toward him. Craig waited for them on the far sidewalk.

"Sorry I'm late," he said. "Mr. Robertson must have seen us talking because suddenly he had a lot of questions for me—"

He cried out suddenly, grabbing his left leg and falling onto the grass. Laura hurried toward him and spotted a long, brown snake slithering away through the grass.

Eliezer hefted a large, rounded stone off the ground and dropped it on the snake's head, killing it.

14

Craig Hutsell sat on the grass with both hands clasped around his ankle. He rocked back and forth, groaning in pain. Laura crouched next to him.

"I'm a doctor. Let me see."

Sucking in a sharp breath, Craig let go of his ankle. The snake had bitten him above the top edge of his sneaker. Its fangs pierced his jeans and sank into the flesh just above the lateral malleolus bone, the part of the fibula that formed the knob on the outside of the ankle. There were two distinct puncture wounds in the skin. The flesh around it was already turning red and beginning to swell.

"And the Lord God said unto the serpent, 'Thou art cursed above all cattle, and above every beast of the field,'" Eliezer intoned. "'Upon thy belly shalt thou go, and dust shalt thou eat all the days of thy life.'"

The dead snake lay at his feet, its crushed head hidden beneath the stone. Laura guessed from the snake's reddish-brown color and the darker hourglass-shaped bands across its body that it was a copperhead. They were common to the Hudson Valley and certainly had no compunctions about biting people when they felt threatened. The snake must have been hiding in the grass and lashed out when Craig came too close.

She put a reassuring hand on his shoulder. "You're going to be okay."

"What the fuck was that?" Craig said.

"A copperhead," she said. "Don't worry, their venom is the least deadly of all the venomous snakes in the country. We just need to treat it quickly."

"God, it hurts like hell." He winced and put his hands on

his ankle again. "Has anyone ever died of a copperhead bite?"

"Fatalities are extremely rare."

He blinked at her. "That's not a no!"

"You're going to be fine," Laura said. "Let's get you somewhere we can take care of it."

She and Chief Morales got their shoulders under Craig's arms and helped him to his feet. Sharon came out of the house just then, curious about the commotion.

"My goodness, what happened?"

"It's just a snake bite," Laura said.

Sharon stared at her. Laura felt her face grow hot. She wanted to apologize for misleading her, but now wasn't the time.

Sharon pushed the door open wider, her expression softening. "Bring him inside. We'll put him on the couch."

"Thank you," Laura said.

Sharon smiled and nodded. Apparently, all was forgiven in the face of an emergency.

Laura and Morales supported Craig as they made their way into the house. He moved slowly, favoring his injured leg. Sharon led the way, her hands hovering nervously over her pregnant stomach. She brought them through the house to a large, cozy sitting room where the walls were decorated with family photos and the air held the faint scent of vanilla from unlit candles on the side tables. Against the far wall was an antique wood-framed couch with several crocheted blankets draped over the back. Sharon quickly moved a pile of books off the cushions and onto the floor. Laura and Morales gently lowered Craig onto the couch. It was a three-seater, which gave him plenty of room to keep his injured leg extended. Laura made sure he sat with his back up against the armrest. Keeping the bite below the level of his heart would slow the venom's progress.

"Copperhead bites are easily treatable, Craig. You just need to stay calm and still," Laura said. "Sharon, I'm going to need some warm, soapy water."

"Of course." Sharon hurried out of the room, past Eliezer, who lurked in the doorway like a scowling shadow.

"Oh shit, it hurts," Craig said.

Eliezer grunted at the profanity.

Despite the cool air inside the house, Craig's forehead was beaded with sweat. Big sweat stains marred his t-shirt.

"What's going to happen to me?" he asked.

"Absolutely nothing, okay?" Laura said. "There might be some temporary tissue damage at the location of the bite, but that'll be the worst of it. The pain should pass soon. You might feel some nausea, maybe some tingling in your extremities. If you have trouble breathing, let me know immediately."

"Why? Is that—is that something that could happen?"

As much as she needed him to stay calm, he deserved a straight answer. "It can happen with some people who have extreme reactions to copperhead bites. Again, it's very rare. Just relax and let me take care of this."

She knelt beside the couch and pulled up the cuff of Craig's pants leg to inspect the bite again. She was surprised to see his ankle was already darkening. Infection had set in much faster than expected.

Sharon returned with a bucket of soapy water and some clean rags and put them on the floor next to Laura. Laura grabbed one of the rags, dipped it in the warm water, wrung it out, and gently dabbed it on the bite.

"Unfortunately, the wound is infected," Laura said. "Sharon, do you have any kind of topical antibacterial in the house?"

Sharon gave her a confused look.

"Neosporin? Bacitracin?" Laura pressed.

Sharon looked at Eliezer, who shook his head.

"No," she told Laura. "We have nothing like that."

Laura thought a moment. She needed something for the infection or things would get a lot worse. He would be at risk for sepsis, or even septic shock. She racked her brain trying to think of any household items that could do the job, until she remembered a trick she'd picked up in medical school.

"What about honey? Do you have any honey in the house?" she asked.

Sharon brightened. "*That* we definitely have." She hurried out of the room again.

"Honey?" Craig asked. "What's that supposed to do?"

Laura went back to cleaning the bite, wiping away the watery blood and venom that oozed out of the puncture holes. "Honey has been used to disinfect wounds since ancient Egyptian times. The high sugar content slows bacterial growth. Obviously, I'd rather have an antibacterial ointment, but we have to make do. Time is of the essence."

Craig grimaced. "I thought you said copperhead bites were no big deal."

"Normally, they're not, as long as they're treated quickly. But this infection..."

"Is it..." He paused and swallowed hard. His face was so wet with sweat he looked like he'd just stepped out of the shower. "Is it bad?"

She didn't want to answer that. He was already panicked enough. Luckily, Sharon returned just then with a jar of honey. Laura unscrewed the cap and poured some of the honey onto another rag.

"Craig, I'm going to have to take off your shoe and roll up your pants leg. Is that okay?"

Craig didn't answer. She looked up and saw he'd passed out. She moved quickly, unlacing his left sneaker and pulling it off his foot as gently as she could. She took off the sock next. Beneath it, his entire foot was discolored. The infection was spreading fast.

Wait, she thought. The color wasn't right. An infection would turn the flesh a dark red or even black. Instead, his foot had turned a grayish-brown.

The color of stone.

Above the couch, Malachai Applewhite stared down at her from a family portrait, stoic and expressionless.

"Chief Morales, take a look at this," Laura said. "Doesn't this look like...?"

"It does," Morales said. "It looks exactly like it."

Laura felt Craig's foot. Where she expected to feel soft skin giving under the pressure of her fingers, she felt an unyielding hardness. "It's petrifying."

Morales leaned closer over her shoulder. "The snake...do you think Malachai was also bitten by one?"

"It's possible," Laura said. "He did have a puncture wound on his ankle, remember?"

"But there was no snake found in the car."

"He could have been bitten before he started his drive to Sakima." Laura imaged him driving through the pain of a copperhead bite. That was how desperately he'd wanted to get away from this place. "Only, I've never heard of a snake whose bite can petrify organic matter."

"I'm sorry, are you talking about Malachai?" Sharon interrupted. "What does this have to do with him?"

Laura looked up at her. "This is what I was trying to tell your husband before, when I said the accident might not be the cause of Malachai's death. His condition was similar to what's happening to Craig now. When I examined his body, it was completely petrified."

"Impossible," Eliezer pronounced. "Such things don't happen."

"It's happening right now on your couch, Shepherd." Fed up, Laura turned back to Sharon. "I don't know how to treat this. We have to get Craig to a hospital. Can you call 911?"

"Yes, right away," Sharon said and left once more.

Sharon hurried into the kitchen, where a telephone was mounted on the wall. Eliezer chased after her, his footsteps heavy on the wooden floor. He positioned himself between her and the phone.

"Why did you invite those outsiders into our home?" he demanded.

"It was an emergency," she said. "Can't you see the man needs help?"

Eliezer's features twisted into a mask of resentment. "*I* make the decisions in this house, Sharon, not you!"

"You're being ridiculous, Eliezer."

She reached past him to pick up the phone's handset. He immediately pressed down the cradle, cutting off the dial tone.

"What are you doing?" she said.

"I don't want them here. If no ambulance comes, they will leave." Eliezer took the phone from her and hung it up. "It's just a snake bite, Sharon. It's nothing."

"You heard what Laura said. It's the same thing happened to Malachai. It might even be what killed him. That man needs to go to the hospital!"

Eliezer didn't move from his spot between her and the phone. "Trust me, just give it time. Eventually, they'll take him to the hospital in their own car, and then they'll be gone from here."

"No, Eliezer. In Romans 12:13, God tells us to contribute to the needs of His people, and to welcome strangers into our home."

"These are not God's people."

She blinked at him. She couldn't believe what her husband what saying. There was no time for this. The man on their couch needed help, and judging by what Laura said, he needed it quickly. Sharon reached for the phone again. Eliezer grabbed her sharply by the wrist.

"I said no, Sharon."

She winced as his fingers dug into her flesh. "You're hurting me, Eliezer."

"I wouldn't have to hurt you if you listened to me," he said through gritted teeth. "You know what happened to Malachai whenever he was disobedient. Don't think I won't put you in the Penitence Room, too."

He let go of her arm, shoving it roughly back at her. Sharon rubbed her sore wrist and stared at him in shock. How blind she'd been. She'd always taken Eliezer's side, because that was what a wife was supposed to do for her husband, but now she saw that everything Elder Francis said about him was true. She'd married a monster.

Laura found a sharp pair of sewing scissors in a drawer and used it to cut open the leg of Craig's jeans, from cuff to hip. The petrifaction was already spreading, creeping up Craig's calf and thigh, hardening his soft tissue as it progressed. Laura hoped the ambulance would get here soon. She felt helpless and stupid with her warm, soapy water and jar of honey. If only she knew how to stop the petrifaction from spreading. If only she knew what was causing the reaction in the first place.

"Guh."

The pained sound came from Craig's throat. His eyes opened. She put a hand on his sweat-drenched forehead. He was feverish, his system burning like a coal fire. His Adam's apple bobbed at his throat as he swallowed and gasped for air. He had to be in immense pain.

"Don't try to speak," she told him. "Help is on the way. There's an ambulance coming."

"I have to..." Craig wheezed. His voice was weak and gravelly. "I have to tell you about Malachai."

"It's okay, Craig, it can wait," Laura said.

He grabbed her hand. His palm was hot and wet.

"The cave under Thurmond Biotech," he said. "Malachai saw...saw them hiding something in the cave. Something that shouldn't be there. He—he didn't report it. He just—" Craig winced, gritting his teeth against the pain. "Just wanted to keep his head down. Make enough money to leave Valley Grove."

"Who did he see?" Laura asked.

Craig cried out again. Laura pulled up his t-shirt. The petrifaction had spread along his side and across his stomach. He didn't have much time left. As soon as the wave of petrifaction reached his lungs and heart, it would be over. Where the hell was the ambulance?

He squeezed her hand hard. "Jesus, it hurts!"

"Craig, who did Malachai see?" she asked. "What did they hide in the cave?"

He seized suddenly, his body tensing as tight as a drumskin. She pulled her hand from his grip and held his shoulders down so the tremors wouldn't knock him off the couch. It passed quickly, but she could see the line of petrifaction had moved up his torso. His kidneys and liver were shutting down. His pulmonary system would be next. It was only a matter of time. Minutes.

Eliezer came back into the room, followed by Sharon, who rubbed her wrist as if it were sore.

"Is he—will he be all right?" Sharon asked. She sounded nervous, agitated.

Laura shook her head sadly.

Sharon glared angrily at Eliezer beside her, then stormed

off. Laura didn't have time to wonder what that was about. Craig grabbed her hand again. He tried to say something, but Laura couldn't make it out. His lungs were already starting to petrify. She leaned closer.

"Basilisk," Craig wheezed in her ear.

His eyes closed and his final breath hissed out of his throat. His grip on her hand relaxed. She looked up at Chief Morales.

"He's gone," she said.

"What did he say to you?" Morales asked.

"Just one word," Laura said. "Basilisk."

"What does that mean?"

"I don't know."

She turned back to Craig's body. In a few minutes, he would look the same as Malachai in her morgue, completely petrified from head to foot.

"Isaiah 14:29," Eliezer said from the doorway. "'Rejoice not, O Philistia, all of thee, because the rod that smote thee is broken: for out of the serpent's root shall come forth a basilisk, and his fruit shall be a fiery flying serpent.'"

15

Laura covered Craig's body with one of the crocheted blankets off the back of the couch. His face was already discoloring, petrifying like the rest of him. She drew the blanket up over his head. The room was silent. She could feel the eyes of Chief Morales and Shepherd Eliezer on her back. They wanted answers. She didn't have any.

All around her, the walls of the sitting room were covered with Applewhite family photos. No matter where she looked, Malachai stared back at her as if to say, *Figure this out. Don't let it happen to anyone else.*

She didn't have a clue where to start.

Craig's last word kept playing in her mind. *Basilisk.* What was he trying to tell her? A basilisk was a mythological serpent said to have the power to petrify men with its gaze. That couldn't be a coincidence, but it was just a myth, wasn't it? Basilisks weren't real.

On the other hand, the petrifaction was very real. Whatever caused it was equally real, not mythological. The petrifaction had started with the copperhead's bite. That was where she should start, too.

"I need to see that snake again," she said.

She left the sitting room and found Meredith standing in the hallway outside, staring in horror at the shape under the blanket. How long had she been there? How much had she seen? Before either of them could speak, Sharon pulled the girl away. Meredith went with her stepmother silently, her eyes still wide with shock.

Morales followed Laura out of the house. The dead snake still lay in the grass out front. The sun sank toward the horizon, as ready to be done with this day as Laura was. The impending twilight cast a gray pall over everything, dulling the colors on the dead snake's thick, sinuous body. She rolled the stone off its head with her foot. There wasn't much left aside from a pulpy reddish mess.

She called Booker. When he answered, she put it on speakerphone so Morales could hear, too.

"Hi, Booker, I'm still in Valley Grove. Something came up."

"I figured," he said.

"What do you know about copperheads?"

"Copperheads?" He paused, thinking. "They're pretty commonplace. You can find them over most of the eastern seaboard. Why?"

"Someone got bitten."

"I'm not surprised. More people are bitten by copperheads on the East Coast than by any other venomous snake, but that's only because there are so many of them. Normally, they only bite people when they feel threatened. They're not generally aggressive. They're ambush predators. They prefer to wait for an unsuspecting meal to come by, like mice or frogs, rather than go on the hunt."

"Hold on a moment, I'm sending you a picture."

She used her phone to snap a photo of the dead snake. The brief light from the flash made it appear to twitch in the grass, giving her a momentary fright. She texted the photo to Booker.

"Is this a copperhead?" she asked.

It took him a moment to answer while he looked at the picture. "Honestly, I don't know. It's got all the markings of a typical northern copperhead, particularly the light brown body and darker brown hourglass-shaped bands across its back, but that red stripe on its side...I've never seen that on a copperhead before."

She looked at the snake again. Booker was right. There were dull red scales along the snake's sides that she hadn't noticed, stretching from head to tail like racing stripes.

"Have you seen red markings like that on any snakes before?" she asked.

"Some garter snakes have them, but on their backs, not their sides," Booker said. "I don't think I've seen that kind of snake before. Is it venomous?"

"Very," she said. "In fact, its venom may be the cause of the petrifaction. A friend of Malachai's from Thurmond Biotech got bitten, and within half an hour he was dead and petrified, just like Malachai." She paused. "I saw it happen, Booker. I *saw* him petrify. There was nothing I could do. I couldn't help him."

"I'm so sorry," he said. "Are you okay?"

"I'll feel better when I know what the hell is going on," she said. "Right now, I'm flying blind. Can you do me a favor and try to find out what kind of snake this is? Any information at all will help."

"Absolutely. What are you going to—?"

A loud scream interrupted him. Laura looked around quickly.

"What was that?" she asked.

"It came from the woods," Morales said.

"Booker, I have to go," she said into the phone. "I'll call you later."

She ended the call, and she and Morales sprinted for the woods. Another scream came, longer than the first one and full of anguish. Behind them, a crowd of men from the village came running, a bobbing sea of white shirts and dark slacks. Laura crashed through the trees and found herself on a dirt path that led down to the edge of the lake. Her shoes slipped on loose pebbles, but she pushed herself forward, running toward the source of the screams. At the foot of the path, near the shore, she saw a woman in her forties bending over a girl on the ground.

Laura slowed to a halt. The girl looked about fifteen years old, wearing a prairie dress and lying curled on her side. A pink ribbon was wrapped tightly around one of her hands. The woman collapsed on top of the girl, sobbing.

Emma Richter had found her missing daughter Beth.

Laura and Morales knelt beside the girl's body. Her skin was discolored, and when Laura touched the girl's face, she felt the same familiar stony hardness.

"She must have been bitten, too," Morales said.

Laura nodded. One victim yesterday, two today. The snake attacks were escalating.

She stepped back to let a group of men pray over Beth Richter's body. One among them intoned solemnly, "'Then it happened that suddenly a chariot of fire appeared with horses of fire, and separated the two of them; and Elijah went up by a whirlwind into heaven. And Elisha, his son, saw it, and he cried out, "My father, my father, the chariot of Israel and its horsemen!" So he saw him no more. And he took hold of his own clothes and tore them into two pieces.'"

At that, each of the men took hold of the breast pocket of his white shirt and tore it at the seam. Emma Richter tore the neck of her dress and wailed.

Someone shouted from the lakeshore, "What is that?"

Laura looked where the man was pointing. Out toward the center the lake, the water churned and splashed.

"What on Earth?" Morales said.

Laura moved to the edge of the water for a better view. A dark, formless blob undulated on the surface, accompanied by a wet, thrashing sound that grew louder as it approached.

Snakes.

Dozens of snakes, all swimming toward their side of the lake—writhing, twisting, and sidewinding through the water, their heads held above the surface like the figureheads of ships.

"Everyone, go back!" Laura yelled. "Go back to your houses and stay inside! Go! Go!"

The men started running back up the path, shouting in fear. Laura and Morales stayed at the bottom of the path and directed them, making sure nobody was left behind. In the chaos, she saw Emma Richter still clinging to the body of her daughter. The men had come when she screamed to make sure she was all right, but in their panic they'd forgotten about her. Laura ran to her and pulled her away from the body.

"We have to go!"

"No, I won't leave Beth!" The woman tried to break free, but Laura held her tight.

"You have to," Laura said. "She's gone! Your daughter is gone!"

Unable to bear the awful truth, Emma went limp, switching off like lamp. Laura got her shoulder under one of the woman's arms, but she was too heavy to carry alone. Laura looked back at the water. The snakes were drawing closer, near enough that she got a better look at them.

There was something wrong with their eyes. If she remembered correctly, copperheads had yellow or orange eyes. These snakes' eyes were white as milk.

"Chief, over here!" she called. "Help me!"

Morales ran over and took Emma's other arm. Together, they half carried and half dragged her away from the shore. They didn't move as quickly as Laura wanted. Emma was dead weight hanging between them, but their only other choice would be to leave her behind and Laura refused to do that. When they were halfway up the path, she slipped on loose pebbles again. This time, she fell to one knee, banging it against the hard-packed dirt and stones. A sharp pain radiated through her leg. She lost hold of Emma, but Morales caught the woman before she followed Laura to the ground.

Laura glanced back. What she saw made her get to her feet, jam her shoulder under Emma's arm, and drag her up the path to the village.

Below them, the writhing mass slithered out of the water and blanketed the shore, teeming over everything in their way. Stones, grass, roots, weeds, even Beth Richter's petrified body, everything disappeared under a carpet of snakes.

16

Meredith Applewhite ducked her head under the surface of the bathwater and rinsed the shampoo from her hair. The warm water was so comforting, so peaceful, that she wondered what it would be like to stay submerged in it until her lungs ran out of air and she drifted off into nothingness. She'd had thoughts like that before, fantasies of escaping Valley Grove the one way that was within her power, but she never acted on them. Fear always stopped her. Fear that maybe you really did go to Hell if you killed yourself, like they always said, or fear that her best friend Rebecca would never recover from it and be scarred forever. This time, it was a different fear—a *new* fear—that made her to lift her head out of the water and breathe again.

She'd watched a man die. It was more horrible than she imagined.

None of the people gathered in the sitting room had known she was watching from the hallway outside. She kept quiet, and they were so focused on the man on the couch that they didn't notice her. That was okay; she didn't want to be noticed, and being ignored was nothing new to her.

The man on the couch died right in front of her. Even from the hallway, she saw the fear in his face, the desperation and desire to live, and then saw his face go slack. Then he...

She wiped the soapy water from her eyes and nose, trying to piece together what she saw.

The man died and...turned into a statue? *Petrify* was the word Laura had used. Was that really what happened? It couldn't be, and yet Laura said the same thing had happened to Malachai. Her own brother, petrified like some ancient piece of wood. Meredith wouldn't have believed it if she hadn't just seen it happen to someone else.

Laura and the other woman, the short one with the stern face and a brass badge on her shirt, had talked about snakes and snake bites, but it couldn't have been a snake that killed her brother. A snake was just a reptile, one of God's creatures, neither good nor evil. If what they said was true, the culprit was a *serpent*. That word sounded much eviler. Deadlier. A serpent was the Devil in disguise.

She wrung water out of her thick red hair, but it was frizzing up already. Her hair was uncontrollable. From outside, through the bathroom window that was open to let out the steam from the hot bath, she heard a commotion of raised voices. People were shouting. She didn't know what it was, but at least it wasn't another fight between her father and Elder Francis. That was something to be grateful for. She listened for Laura's voice, wondering if she was out there, too. There was something about Laura that made Meredith feel like she could be her real self around her. Laura was the only person Meredith had ever opened up to, outside of Malachai, and she told Laura things she'd never even told her brother.

She closed her eyes as the warm bath water enveloped her and wondered what Laura's life was like in Sakima. She was so cultured, so sophisticated, and most important of all, so *free*. She had her own home, her own car, her own career. She had a boyfriend she chose for herself, not someone who was matched to her by her father as part of a deal to stay in power. Laura's world was so different from hers. Once Meredith was forced to marry Elder Bernard, all hope of having a life like Laura's would be lost. She'd spend the rest of her years squeezing out babies until she was old and used up, and then it would be too late to start her life.

"Stay here!" Her father's booming voice made her eyes open again. He was talking to Sharon somewhere in the house. A moment later, the front door slammed.

What had gotten him worked up this time? It didn't take a lot. As much as she hated Sharon, deep down Meredith wondered if she hated her father more. She was glad she'd locked herself in the bathroom, even if she wasn't supposed to lock the door in case there was an accident. She couldn't deal with either of them right now.

Dark, oily movement on the bathroom wall caught her eye. A snake oozed in through the open window. Its scaled, rippling body was thick and heavy, with dark brown crossbands and peculiar red stripes along its sides. It had the big triangular, unmarked head of a copperhead, but there was something frighteningly wrong with its eyes. They were an iridescent white. Colors shifted deep within them as the light hit them from different angles. The vertical slits of the snake's pupils studied her with inhuman iciness.

Meredith scrambled out of the tub, spilling water across the tiled floor. She yanked her bathrobe off the hook and quickly shrugged it on as she ran for the door. Her feet slipped on the wet floor and skidded out from under her. She fell painfully onto the hard tile, but she didn't dare look back at the window. She didn't want to see if the snake was any closer. She launched herself at the door, grabbed the handle, and pulled.

It didn't budge.

She forgot she'd locked it. She clawed at the sliding lock, shrieking in terror, but her wet fingers couldn't find a grip. Now, trapped in the bathroom, she chanced a look behind her. Her blood went cold as she saw the snake drop to the floor with a heavy *slap*. A forked tongue flicked out of its mouth, tasting the air, searching for her.

A second snake started to slither through the window behind it. She screamed again.

Sharon knocked on the door from the outside. "Meredith, are you all right in there?"

The first snake inched its way across the wet tiles toward her. Meredith backed away from it.

Sharon banged on the door. "Meredith, are you okay? Answer me!"

As much as she wanted to answer, Meredith couldn't find her voice other than to let out another shriek. She grabbed a towel from the rack and threw it at the snake. The towel didn't do anything except cover it, hiding it from view, which only made it worse. Its sinuous bulge wriggled underneath the towel.

The second snake dropped heavily to the bathroom floor, and Meredith finally found her voice.

"Help!"

The word came out raw and shrill, tearing from her throat like fishhooks.

There was a loud *thud* as the door rocked in its frame. The white-painted wood cracked as Sharon put her shoulder into it again, trying to break it open.

Meredith reached for the sliding lock again. The snake struck, darting out from under the towel like a whip, its mouth open to reveal nasty-looking hooked fangs. Meredith yanked her hand away, and the snake missed her. It reared back, ready to try again. Just then, the door broke open, slamming into the snake and flinging it across the room to slide under the sink.

The second snake squirmed forward, eager for its own chance to sink its fangs into Meredith. Sharon reached through the doorway, grabbed Meredith's arm, and yanked her out of the bathroom. She slammed the door shut, trapping the snakes inside. Meredith ran for her parents' bedroom, and she and Sharon barricaded themselves behind the door.

"The window!" Meredith said, pointing breathlessly.

The window in the far wall of the bedroom was open to the night. Sharon ran over and closed it. She sat on the floor at the foot of the bed and pulled Meredith to her. For once, Meredith didn't mind Sharon acting like her mother. She huddled against Sharon and let her put her arms around her.

"Are you okay?" Sharon asked. "It didn't bite you, did it?"

"No, I'm okay," Meredith said.

Now that the danger was over, the adrenaline coursing through her body made her shake. She was crying before she knew what was happening. Before, she never wanted to cry in front of Sharon. She didn't want her stepmother to think she was a baby. Now it didn't matter. She let the tears come.

"Are these the same snakes that killed Malachai?" she asked, her breath hitching.

"I don't know," Sharon said. She sounded calm and in control, two things Meredith couldn't imagine feeling right now. "I promise you, I won't let anything happen to you. Your father won't, either. He's out there right now, gathering men to kill the snakes before they hurt anyone else."

Muffled screams came through the thick, weatherproof glass of the window. Footsteps thumped loudly. Shapes passed in the dark, along with the juddering beams of flashlights.

A new panic gripped Meredith. "Is Laura out there, too?"

"I don't know," Sharon said. She held Meredith tighter, as though she understood that Laura meant something special to her.

Meredith pulled away from her. She had to see what was happening outside. She started toward the window, but Sharon clamped a hand around her wrist.

"Don't, it's too dangerous."

Whatever Meredith was going to say in reply, the words caught in her throat. There was a snake on the bed behind Sharon. They hadn't closed the window in time. The snake slithered down the blanket toward the foot of the bed. Its strange, milky eyes were focused on the back of Sharon's head.

"What's the matter, Meredith?" Sharon said.

Meredith's feet were rooted to the floor. None of her limbs worked. All she could do was stare.

Just behind Sharon, the snake opened its mouth. Its long, curved fangs emerged from their pale, fleshy sheaths.

It took everything Meredith had to move. She grabbed Sharon by the hands and hoisted her off the floor just as the snake struck. Its fangs missed her by inches.

Sharon didn't scream. Meredith would have screamed if she were her—in fact, she felt a scream bubbling up inside her right now—but Sharon didn't waste any time. She ran, pulling Meredith toward the bedroom door. But the moment Sharon opened it, Meredith saw the two snakes from the bathroom had gotten out under the door and were coiled in the hallway. They hissed angrily. Sharon slammed the door closed again.

When they turned around, the snake wasn't on the bed anymore. Meredith didn't see it on the floor, either.

"Where did it go?" she shrieked.

"Be careful," Sharon said. "It could be under the bed."

"It could be *anywhere!*" Meredith felt like she was losing her mind.

She scanned the room, taking in every bit of furniture, every possible hiding place—the space under the bed behind the dust ruffle; the bedside tables, each with a small cubby hole at its base filled with books and trinkets; the dark space under the chest of drawers; Sharon's dressing table, with a large mirror a snake could easily hide behind.

"The closet," Sharon whispered.

The sliding door of the closet was slightly open. Wide enough for a snake to pass through.

Cautiously, Sharon started toward it.

"Don't!" Meredith said.

"It's okay. Stay there."

Meredith's heart pounded in her ears. She couldn't catch her breath. She wiped her forehead and was surprised when her hand came away coated with sweat. Sharon inched toward the closet, walking on tiptoes like she didn't want to alert the snake to her presence. Meredith bit her lip to keep from hyperventilating. Finally, after what seemed like an excruciatingly long time, Sharon reached the closet, and with one quick movement, she pushed the sliding door all the way closed. It banged against the doorframe as loud as a bomb going off, and Sharon ran back to Meredith's side. Meredith wrapped her arms around her and held on for dear life.

Something rubbed against Meredith's bare foot.

She barely had time to look down and see the snake on the carpet before Sharon lifted her off the floor and threw her onto the bed. Bouncing on the mattress, Meredith spun around, brushing her wild hair out of her eyes, and saw Sharon kick the snake away. Meredith didn't see exactly where it went—somewhere near the window—but Sharon took off her shoe and stalked after it. She clubbed the snake with it over and over. When she stopped, the sole of the shoe was smeared with dark blood. She dropped it on the floor next to the dead snake.

Still breathing hard, Sharon sat down on the bed next to Meredith. Her hands cradled her pregnant stomach.

"It's dead," Sharon said. "It's dead and everything is going to be okay."

Meredith sensed something was wrong. She'd seen Sharon hold her stomach enough times to know she was holding it differently this time. One hand covered the other. Hiding it.

"Are you okay?" Meredith asked.

Sharon turned to her. "I'm fine, Meredith. Everything is fine. You're safe now."

She reached for Sharon's hands. Sharon shifted, moving them out of Meredith's reach.

"Sharon, show me your hands."

"I'm okay, Meredith."

"Then just show me."

Sharon looked down into her lap. Slowly, she lifted her left hand off of her right. Two puncture marks scarred the back of her right hand. The skin around them looked red and angry.

"It bit you!" Meredith exclaimed.

"It's okay," Sharon said again. With her left hand, she smoothed Meredith's frizzy hair. "You're safe now, and that's all that matters."

"But the man on the couch—"

"I know."

Meredith shook with panic. "Is that—is that going to happen to *you*?"

Sharon looked down at her hand again. "Maybe," she said, but she nodded like she knew it would. "I'm sorry."

Meredith hugged her tight. Why was Sharon sorry? Sharon was bitten while protecting her. Meredith was the one who was sorry. Sorry for every mean thing she'd ever said to her stepmother, every nasty thought she'd allowed into her head about her, every wish she'd made that Sharon would go away forever. She wanted to tell her how sorry she was, but all that came out of her mouth was a desperate whine, followed by convulsive sobs. She hugged Sharon tighter.

Sharon let out a sharp cry. Her body tensed against Meredith's. She rubbed at her hand, which grew discolored with a patch of grayish-brown skin around the bite marks. The same color as the man on the couch. Meredith felt like screaming. She watched Sharon try to flex her stiffening fingers, then Meredith shut her eyes tight, preferring to see nothing.

"There isn't much time," Sharon said. "It all happened very quickly before."

Meredith opened her eyes. "Don't say that!"

Sharon took Meredith by the shoulders. She expected her stepmother to look scared, to be as panicked as she was, but there was no fear in Sharon's face.

"I need you to be strong," Sharon said. A tear rolled down one cheek. She wiped it away quickly, as though it were an annoyance.

"But Sharon—"

"Listen to me, Meredith," she said. "There's something important I have to tell you. It's about your father."

Meredith didn't know how much time passed before she heard her father come home. One hour? Two? She'd spent the time holding Sharon's good hand and trying to comfort her as she died. She stayed brave when Sharon was suffering and crying out, and she stayed brave after Sharon was gone and there was only her stepmother's dead, petrified body on the bed beside her. The stepmother she hated. The stepmother who sacrificed her life to protect her.

She lay curled on her side next to Sharon's body, her hands tucked between her knees. She couldn't bring herself to hold Sharon's hard, stony hand anymore. From the other side of the bedroom door, she heard her father kill the snakes in the hallway with something heavy that shook the floor.

He entered the bedroom with a blood-spattered shovel in his hands.

"Sharon!" He hurried to the bed. When he saw he was too late, he lowered his head and muttered a prayer under his breath.

Meredith sat up. "She killed a snake, but not before it bit her."

She nodded listlessly toward the dead snake on the bedroom floor. The snake that had changed everything.

"Why would Sharon do that?" her father asked. "Why would

she take such a foolish risk in her condition? She should have protected the baby."

Meredith's mouth dropped open in disbelief. Angry tears squeezed from her eyes. "She was protecting *me*, Father!"

"*You* should have protected *her*! And the baby!" he yelled. "Now they're *both* dead!"

Meredith watched through tear-blurred eyes as her father stormed out of the room, the bloody shovel still in his hands.

She told me, Father, Meredith thought angrily. *She told me what you did.*

17

Laura and Chief Morales were hustled into the holy sanctuary along with roughly two dozen other women and girls, all of whom had been too far from their homes when the snakes invaded Valley Grove. The wooden house of worship was enormous, with exposed beams on the ceiling and walls, and a huge pulpit carved to resemble Elijah's chariot from the Bible. Everyone took seats in the pews. Mothers clutched their daughters nervously. Some of them rocked back and forth and sang softly or prayed under their breath. A few of the smaller children were crying in confusion and fear.

Laura noticed two men were stationed outside the door to keep the women safe. Or to keep them from leaving, depending on how you looked at it. She texted Booker to let him know what was happening. He texted back immediately making sure she was okay and promised to let her know the moment he had any new information.

The hours ticked by. Laura chewed her fingernail and kept checking her phone, waiting for a call or text from Booker saying he'd found a match. It wasn't a good sign that it was taking so long. She did an Internet image search on her phone for "snake with red stripes," but none of the pictures that came up looked like the snakes she'd seen slithering out of the lake. With the phone's battery only at 28%, she put it away again to conserve power. This was not the night to be caught without a phone.

Morales sat in the pew in front of her, looking at her own phone. Laura leaned forward.

"We've got to get out of here," she said. "We should be out there helping people, keeping them safe, not stuck in here."

"What exactly do you propose we do?" Morales asked.

"I don't know yet," she said, "but I can't just sit here doing nothing."

Morales smirked. "Why am I not surprised? Going off half-cocked without a plan seems to be your M.O."

"Excuse me?"

"That's your problem, Dr. Powell. You don't think things through. What did you think would happen when you came to Valley Grove against my orders? Did you think I wouldn't find out? Or when I told you to leave this case alone, did you think it was just a friendly suggestion?"

Laura shook her head. "I...*what*? I don't think things through? That's *all* I do."

"Then the only other answer is that you don't respect my authority," Morales said. "So which is it?"

"This is unbelievable," Laura said. "You've had it out for me ever since you got to Sakima, Chief. What is it? Did we get off on the wrong foot somehow? Did I rub you the wrong way? Or do you just hate me?"

She was surprised she blurted it out like that, but what did she have to lose? She was on the verge of being fired anyway.

Morales turned in her pew to face Laura. "Did I ever tell you where I was stationed before I came to Sakima, Dr. Powell?"

The question surprised her. She expected Morales to lay into her, not...whatever this was.

"No," she said. "You never mentioned it."

"I was in Texas, on the border patrol," she said. "My father and grandfather both wore badges. Law enforcement is in my blood. Ever since I was young, I wanted to follow in their footsteps. The border patrol was where I figured I could do the most good. A lot of the officers I worked with didn't speak Spanish. They needed a translator in the interview room, so that's where they put me, talking with the migrants we caught crossing the river, helping to determine who was eligible for asylum and who got sent back."

A dark-haired woman dressed all in white watched them from another pew. Morales stopped talking until the woman looked away, pretending not to eavesdrop.

"I rose up the ranks quickly because I had a skill the others didn't," she continued. "But the border patrol is still mostly men, and still mostly White, and after a while, I guess I rose up too far for their liking. Things changed. People got suspicious. My colleagues started to wonder if I was telling the truth about what the migrants told me in that room, or if I was covering for them because of my Mexican heritage."

Laura was taken aback. "What?"

"Everything turned on a dime," Morales said. "People I had worked with side by side for years, people I considered my friends, started whispering about whose side I was on. A rumor started going around that the migrants were actually from the cartels, sneaking across the border to sell drugs and giving me a cut of the money to lie for them. All the work I'd done for the border patrol, all my years of service—none of it mattered. All that mattered anymore was that I was Mexican."

Morales turned away. She looked at the polished wooden wall for a moment, gathering her thoughts.

"Soon after that," she said, "I wasn't allowed in the interview room anymore. Even though we were told every year that our budget was stretched to the limit, somehow they found the money to hire a new translator to replace me. A new translator who wasn't Mexican. They stuck me at a desk, because if I couldn't be trusted in the interview room, then I certainly couldn't be trusted in the field. I'm surprised they didn't just fire me, but I suppose they didn't want the scandal. Anyway, if they were planning to let me go, I beat them to the punch. When the Sakima position opened up, I jumped at it."

"I'm so sorry that happened," Laura said. "I didn't know."

"It's *still* happening, Dr. Powell." Morales turned to face her again. "It's been an uphill battle in Sakima, too, even if the reasoning is different. The mayor, certain members the city council, even some of the officers under my command are skeptical I can do the job because I'm a woman. My career spans more than thirty years, and I have *never* stopped having to prove myself, either because I'm Mexican or because I'm female. You know as well as I do, Dr. Powell, that if I make a mistake, if I screw up even *once*, I won't just be Sakima's first female chief of police. I'll be the last."

Laura knew the feeling well. How many times had patients questioned her medical advice? How many times had police officers doubted her autopsy findings? She would need more than two hands to count all the instances. The reason was always the same. They didn't trust her expertise because she was a woman.

"You think I'm being hard on you," Morales continued, "but it's not just you. I demand the best from everybody in the department, because I know any failure, at any level, will reflect on *me*. They're looking for any reason to say a woman can't be chief of police, particularly a woman of color, and I'm not about to give them one. So forgive me if I don't take it well when people ignore my authority. I don't have that luxury."

Laura hung her head. She felt mortified. "I'm sorry. You're right. I—I guess I got used to doing things a certain way."

"I know Ralph Gorney was a friend of yours, and he allowed you to do things the way you wanted to," Morales said. "He was a good chief. People at the station speak highly of him. But like it or not, I'm chief now, and I have my own way of doing things. If you're going to continue to work for the Sakima PD, you need to accept that."

"You're not firing me?"

"You sound surprised."

"I was sure you'd already put out the call for a new medical examiner."

"Don't tempt me," Morales said. "Second chances are few and far between in this life, Dr. Powell. Don't make me regret giving you one."

Shouting came from outside, drawing Laura to the window. Through the glass, she saw men hurrying back and forth, hunting snakes by the light of their flashlights and lanterns. They wielded lawn rakes and garden hoes as makeshift snake hooks, and shovels, hammers, and axes as weapons. Women, children, and the elderly had been ordered to stay inside until it was safe again.

"Another one, over here!" someone yelled. A group of men came running with flashlights to dispatch the snake. She heard the clang of a shovel's sharp edge striking pavement. The men danced and shouted in celebration. "God be praised! God be praised!"

One of them reached down toward the snake's remains on the ground.

"Don't touch the head!" Laura yelled.

There was no way they could hear her through the glass from that far away. When the man straightened again, he held the headless body of the snake and joining the others in the celebration. Laura breathed a sigh of relief.

"Why shouldn't they touch the head?" Morales asked.

"A decapitated snake head is still dangerous," she explained. "Severing the head doesn't cause immediate death. Snakes are cold-blooded, which means they don't need as much oxygen to fuel their brains as warm-blooded creatures do. Even if you cut their heads off, the heads can live on for as long as an hour. It can still bite you."

"Is that true?" a woman sitting in a nearby pew asked. She smoothed her blue floral prairie dress with nervous hands.

Laura gave her a reassuring smile. "It's true, but it's nothing you have to worry about. They're not going to let any of the snakes get in here."

Turning back to the window, Laura watched men stalk the streets with their makeshift weapons.

"This is bullshit," she told Morales. "We shouldn't be cooped up in here when we can help."

"I agree," Morales said.

"Language!" a skinny blonde woman snarled. She put her hands over the ears of her daughter.

"Sorry, ma'am," Morales said.

"Let the *men* do their jobs and protect us," the blonde woman continued. "It's the natural order of things. God made them stronger than us for a reason. Our job as women is to be with the children."

Laura held her tongue. It wouldn't do any good to argue the point. The Church of the Divine Chariot had drilled its ideas about strict gender roles into the woman's head for so long she didn't question it. It was doubtful she was the only one. If

Francis wanted to change things around here, he had his work cut out for him.

She looked out the window again. How many snakes had the men killed so far? Had any of the men been bitten? It was impossible to know anything from inside the holy sanctuary. She needed to be out there, but there was no way the men guarding the door would let her leave.

The dark-haired woman who'd been eavesdropping earlier came running up to her. "Miss, please, I—I heard your friend say you're a doctor. Something is wrong with one of the girls in back. I think she's sick. Can you come look at her?"

"Where is she?" Laura asked.

"This way. Hurry!"

Laura and Morales followed the woman to one side of the holy sanctuary, where an aisle ran the length of the wall. They followed it past the pulpit and entered a hallway in the back. Laura didn't see any girls anywhere, let alone a sick one. The woman led them through a door at the end of the hallway and into a storeroom filled with tools and gardening equipment. Still no girls. Laura tensed, wondering if this was some kind of trap.

"I'm sorry for the lie," the woman said. "There are tools in here you can use."

"For what?" Morales asked.

"To kill snakes." She pointed to a door in the back of the storeroom. "That door leads outside. The men in front won't see you."

"Why are you doing this?" Laura asked.

The woman lowered her voice to a whisper. "My husband and I support Elder Francis for Shepherd. We agree with what he has to say about women having a larger role in our community. More people support him than you might think, but it's not safe to do it openly right now. That's why I had to lie to bring you back here. I didn't know who might be listening. If word got back to Shepherd Eliezer that I helped you…"

"I understand," Laura said. "Thank you."

The woman wished them luck and hurried out of the storeroom, closing the door behind her. Laura took a small hatchet and a flashlight off the shelves. Morales grabbed a rake. Together, they sneaked out the back door and into the dark of night.

They walked through the backyards of the houses adjacent to the holy sanctuary. Occasionally, they came across the body of a decapitated snake. They made sure to give the heads a wide berth, just in case. Each house had a concrete garage at the far end of the yard like the one she'd seen behind Eliezer's house. They looked bulky in the darkness, with plenty of shadows for snakes to hide in, waiting to ambush them. Laura stayed on high alert.

"I thought your boyfriend said copperheads weren't aggressive," Morales said. She poked at the grass with the rake as they walked. "From what I've seen, these snakes are aggressive as hell."

"His name's Booker," Laura said, holding the flashlight in one hand and the hatchet in the other. "Obviously, despite the similar markings, these aren't copperheads."

"So what are they?" Morales asked.

"Good question." Laura's phone vibrated in her pocket. She handed the flashlight to Morales and took out her phone. It was a text from Booker. "I think we're about to find out."

She opened the message.

STILL NO LUCK TRACKING DOWN WHAT KIND OF SNAKE IT IS. THOSE HOURGLASS MARKINGS ARE UNIQUE TO COPPERHEADS. NO OTHER SNAKE HAS THEM. THE ONLY ONE THAT COMES CLOSE IS THE EASTERN RATTLESNAKE, BUT THEIR COLORING IS BLACK AND WHITE, NOT BROWN, AND THEIR HEADS ARE A DIFFERENT SHAPE. CAN'T EXPLAIN THOSE RED STRIPES ON THE SIDES EITHER. HAVEN'T FOUND ANY SNAKE THAT MATCHES. WILL KEEP SEARCHING.

"Damn," she said, putting her phone away. "Still nothing."

"Strange. It's like these snakes came out of nowhere."

They passed behind a house where two small children, a boy and a girl, stared at them with their hands and faces pressed against the window glass. They looked frightened. Laura smiled at them to put them at ease. It didn't work, and she immediately felt foolish. Children know when you're lying to them. They know when the danger is real.

"I've been working on a theory," she told Morales.

"And what theory is that?" Morales asked.

They sidestepped around another dead snake.

"I think they're a new breed. Probably a mutation that branched off from copperheads, which would explain why they look so similar. Booker can't identify them with his research, so I'm thinking the mutation must have occurred recently, within one or two copperhead generations."

In the beam of Laura's flashlight, Morales swept the rake through the grass. "It's evolution, then. The next step in snake life, with venom that kills and petrifies its victims, all in about half an hour. Great."

"Not necessarily. Not every new breed succeeds or becomes dominant. There are plenty of blind-alley mutations that don't go anywhere. Aberrations that don't last," Laura said. "Genetic mutations like this don't occur without a mutagen, something that causes it to happen, whether it's an environmental factor or—"

"Watch it!" Morales yelled.

A snake darted toward them across the lawn. It was a big one, made bigger by the shadows cast by the flashlight beam, sidewinding through the grass with shocking speed. Its forked tongue, as red as the stripes on its sides, flicked in and out of its mouth. Its white eyes were iridescent in the light. It opened its mouth and unsheathed its fangs, but before it could strike, Morales slammed the rake on top of it, pinning it. It thrashed angrily, looking for an escape.

Keeping the flashlight beam on the snake, Laura raised the hatchet. At her signal, Morales pulled the rake away quickly. Laura brought the hatchet down, severing the snake's head from the rest of its body. A small puddle of dark blood oozed from the wound. The body twitched and spasmed before growing still. The head continued to snap its jaws at them. Laura hit it with the hatchet again, right between the eyes, putting a stop to it.

"We're not bad at this," Laura said as they walked into the next backyard. "How about we quit the force and become exterminators? It probably pays better."

Morales didn't say anything. Laura wasn't surprised. She didn't seem like the type to enjoy a joke. In the east, a rosy haze appeared at the horizon, the first sign of dawn. Laura kept her flashlight pointed at the ground in front of them. More cheers came from nearby and men shouting, "God be praised! God be praised!" Another snake down, but how many more to go? When she'd seen them come out of the lake, it had looked like there were hundreds of them.

She and Morales moved on, dispatching two more snakes before they heard a faint voice cry out, "Help!"

Laura stopped. "Did you hear that?"

Morales pointed. "It came from over there."

Someone sat slumped with their back against the concrete garage in the next yard over. Laura ran toward the figure, keeping an eye on the ground in front of her for any more snakes hiding in the grass. It was a teenaged boy. His face was flushed. He grimaced in pain as tears squeezed from his tightly shut eyes. Laura knelt down beside him.

"Are you all right?" she asked.

The boy opened his eyes. He couldn't have been more than sixteen years old. "I can't move my left leg. I can't—I can't feel it."

Laura pulled the hem of his left pants leg away from his shoe and rolled down his sock. The leg was already petrified.

"He's been bitten," Laura told Morales.

Morales, coming up behind her, shook her head. "What the hell are you doing out here, kid? Didn't they tell you about the snakes?"

"I—I didn't believe it," he sobbed. "We've had snakes in the village before, and it's never been a big deal. I thought—I thought everyone was overreacting. Please, help me. You have to help me!"

Laura took his hand and held it tight. It was hot from fever. "What's your name?"

"Eddie," he said. "Eddie Gordon."

"I'm so sorry, Eddie," she said. "We don't know how to stop it."

"You have to do *something!*" he yelled, his voice turning

hoarse. "It's getting worse. My stomach, it feels..." He winced and let out a strangled cry.

The petrifaction was spreading up his body, transforming his organs. It wouldn't be long now.

"My family..." Eddie wheezed.

"They're safe." She didn't know that for sure, but it was what he needed to hear.

"I was supposed...to be an Elder one day," he said. His voice grew weaker as the tissue of his lungs began to crystallize. "But I...I didn't stay chaste. I went into the woods with girls. Now I'm going to Hell."

Laura brushed his hair out of his sweaty forehead. "I don't think that's true."

His dry throat making a clicking sound as he swallowed. More tears leaked from his eyes. "I hope...it's not true."

She held his hand until the seizures began. She did her best to keep him steady until they stopped and he fell over onto his side. Through the open collar of Eddie's shirt, she could see his neck begin to change color. She stood up. She didn't want to see the rest of him petrify. She'd seen enough.

Morales looked down at the dead boy and shook her head. "Doesn't get easier, does it, watching someone die?"

"No. Especially when they're so young," Laura said. "It's not how things are supposed to be."

They were interrupted by men's voices in the distance. This time, they weren't cheers of triumph, they were shouts of confusion and alarm.

"What's happening?" Morales asked.

"Look out!" Laura yelled.

A snake came racing toward them through the grass, its iridescent eyes flashing in the light. It was smaller than the last, but no less vicious. Morales trapped it with the rake and Laura chopped its head off with the hatchet. Another snake appeared in the grass, and then another. The lawn around them was alive with snakes. They emerged from trees and bushes, darting quickly across the ground. Laura raised her hatchet...and watched a snake sidewind right past her. All the snakes went right past her. They were heading for the main road on the other side of the houses.

"What the hell is going on?" Morales asked.

"Come on, I want to see where they're going," Laura said.

"Are you sure it's safe?"

"They're not attacking anymore. Something changed. I want to know what."

They hurried to the main road. Groups of men poured into the woods, chasing the snakes through the trees. Morales stopped a young man wielding a garden hoe.

"What's going on?"

"The snakes are leaving!" the young man said happily. "They know they've been beaten!"

Dumbfounded, they watched the young man run into the woods.

"What does he mean, they're *leaving*?" Morales said.

They followed the crowd of men into the forest and once more found themselves on the trail that led to the lakeshore. There, standing by the petrified body of Beth Richter that still lay curled near the water's edge, they watched the snakes slither into the lake and swim away. The men cheered and danced. On the far side of the lake, the dark shape of the Thurmond Biotech plant squatted atop the cliff, its windows reflecting the rising sun in the east.

"Of course." Laura turned to face the crowd. "Listen, everyone! Listen!" She waved her arms. The men quieted and turned to her. "The snakes are nocturnal. They're only active at night. Now that the sun's coming up, they're going back to their den."

The men cheered and hollered. Someone yelled, "It's over!"

"Wait!" Laura shouted, and they quieted again. "This is important. You still need to be careful. Some snakes might have stayed behind. They'll look for places to hide from the sun, under rocks or bushes. They'll be lethargic during the day, but that doesn't make them any less deadly."

"What about tomorrow night?" an older man with silver hair asked. "Will they come back?"

"I don't know," Laura said. "We won't know anything until we know why they came here in the first place."

"I know why they came here." Shepherd Eliezer emerged from the crowd. He held a blood-spattered shovel in his hands like a soldier holding a rifle. The men turned to him, eager for answers from their leader. "The snakes came because God is angry with us. He's angry that we've lost our way. He's angry that we allowed these outsiders, these *women*, to come into our fold to lie to us and pollute our minds with their perversions, so He sent the snakes to punish us."

"Now wait a minute," Laura started to say.

"I was not spared God's wrath," Eliezer interrupted, his voice booming over hers. "In His anger, the Lord punished me, too. My wife Sharon, and the child we were going to have, are both dead. Killed by a snake that got into our home. Our hallowed home."

Laura's stomach dropped. Sharon was dead? What about Meredith? Was the girl all right? She dropped her hatchet and started to run back up the trail toward the village.

Eliezer grabbed her roughly by the arm and pulled her back. "This is your fault. Both you and Chief Morales are to leave Valley Grove immediately."

Laura yanked her arm out of his grasp. "You can't—"

His sharp eyes drilled into her. "You've done enough harm, woman. Go, and don't come back."

A sharp, angry murmur rippled through the crowd of men. "This is *your* fault!" someone yelled. Others followed his lead. "Go home, outsiders!" Laura could feel the hatred and anger coming off the crowd like a wall of heat.

Morales stepped forward. "We'll go. We just have to take custody of Craig Hutsell's body first."

"You'll do no such thing," Eliezer said. "In the Church of the Divine Chariot, the dead remain in their homes for twenty-four hours before burial."

"He wasn't a member of your church," Morales pointed out.

"Nevertheless, he died here," Eliezer said. "Therefore, our customs will be observed. And since there's nothing else to keep you here any longer, it's time for you to leave."

Morales squinted at him, then nodded. "Very well. Twenty-four hours."

She laid down her rake and joined Laura. Together, they left the men at the lakeshore and walked up the path to the village.

"You can't just let him keep Craig's body," Laura said. "It's evidence that what happened to Malachai wasn't a fluke."

"Eliezer isn't going to back down without a warrant for the body," Morales said. "It'll take at least a day to get the warrant anyway. I'm better off just coming back for the body tomorrow, when the twenty-four-hour waiting period is over."

"If it's okay, I'd like to come back with you," Laura said. "I need to make sure my family is all right. And Meredith, too."

"No, I need you in the lab with Dae-jung," Morales said. "I'll check on your people when I come back. I promise, but the best way you can help is for you and Dae-jung to figured out how to counteract the venom before anyone else gets killed."

Laura's first instinct was to argue, to insist that she needed to be here herself, but she knew the chief was right. She could save more lives in the lab, including her family's.

"Okay," she said.

"Good, then I'll see you back in Sakima."

They exited the woods at the top of the trail and parted ways. The street felt unusually quiet after the chaotic snake hunt. The houses were silent. No one had ventured out yet to see if it was safe. They wouldn't until the men returned and gave them the all-clear.

As Chief Morales drove out of Valley Grove in her official Sakima police cruiser, Laura returned to her car to retrieve a plastic evidence bag and a pair of blue nitrile gloves. If she was going to find out how to counteract the venom, she would need to bring one of the dead snakes back to Sakima to perform a necropsy. She didn't have to walk far from her car to find one. The street and lawns were littered with them. She poked the decapitated snake's head with a stick to be certain it was truly dead, then picked it up carefully with one gloved hand and dropped it into the bag. She put the long, limp body in with it and sealed the bag.

When she returned to her car, she tossed the evidence bag onto the passenger seat and stripped off the gloves, which she carefully placed in another bag in case they'd gotten venom on them. Normally, venom needed to be injected into the bloodstream for its toxin to take effect, which made it safe to touch so long as you didn't have any scars or open wounds on your hand. However, if this really was a new mutation, anything was possible. She didn't want to take any chances.

She was about to start the car when Meredith came running out of Eliezer's house. "Laura! Laura!" She was dressed in a fresh prairie dress with pink designs on the skirt. Her cheeks were wet with tears.

The relief at seeing Meredith alive and safe was overwhelming. She opened the door and stepped out of the car. Meredith ran into her embrace.

"I heard about Sharon," Laura said, holding the girl tightly. "I'm so sorry."

Meredith cried into her shoulder. "It's my fault! She was protecting me!"

"It's not your fault. She loved you, and she protected you the way any mother would." She looked Meredith up and down while the girl wiped tears from her eyes. "I'm glad you're all right. You should be safe for now, but it's best you stay inside."

Meredith's face reddened with anger. Her small hands balled into fists.

"I don't want to stay here! I hate it! I should have left with Mal! I would have rather died in the car with him than stay here!"

"You don't mean that," Laura said.

"I do! I wish that snake had bitten *me*, not Sharon!" Meredith burst into tears again and hugged Laura once more. "What am I going to do?"

She held Meredith until the girl stopped crying. She retrieved a pad of sticky notes from the glove compartment of her car. She wrote down her home address and phone number, then peeled off the note and handed it to her.

"If you need help, or if you ever need someplace to stay, for any reason," Laura said. "Any reason at all."

Meredith nodded, holding the paper tight in one hand. "I wish you could take me with you to Sakima."

Laura wished she could, too. The temptation to put Meredith in the car and drive her away from Valley Grove was almost more than she could bear, the law be damned. Instead, her heart breaking, she gave Meredith one last hug and watched her run back home.

18

Laura was bone tired. After staying awake all night, she was tempted to drive straight home to get a few hours' rest. Instead, she drove to Sakima's central police station. She could sleep later. There was too much work to do, and with a good chance that tonight would bring more snakes to Valley Grove, there was no time to waste. She parked in the official lot and called Booker from the car.

"Laura?" he said.

She looked at the clock in the car. It wasn't even seven a.m. yet.

"Sorry, did I wake you?" she asked.

"No, I'm still up. Are you okay? What happened with the snakes?"

"I'm fine. I'm back in Sakima now," she said. "Turns out the snakes were nocturnal. As soon as the sun came up, they went back across the lake. Unfortunately, more people got bitten. I don't know how many."

"I'm sorry," Booker said. "I wish I could have been more helpful. I've been researching snakes all night. I had no idea there were so many species. More than three thousand. Only about two hundred are venomous enough to kill a human being. As far as I can tell, exactly none of them are able to petrify the tissue of their prey."

"I'm not surprised," she said. "I think they're a mutation, a new breed that branched off from the common northern copperhead, probably recently. I'm at the station now. Dae-jung and I are going to perform a necropsy on one of the snakes. Hopefully, we'll know more after that."

"Be careful, all right? Let me know if you need anything."

"I will," she said. "I love you. Get some sleep."

She ended the call and entered the police station. Making her way to the Science Wing in back, she was surprised to find Dae-jung waiting for her in the forensics lab.

"I didn't think you'd be in this early," she said.

"I got an urgent call from Chief Morales," Dae-jung said. "She said she needed me to help you with something important, but she didn't say what."

Laura held up the plastic evidence bag with the decapitated snake inside it. "This."

Dae-jung made a face. "Eww. Is that a snake? What happened to its head?"

"Chopped off."

He looked impressed. "Badass."

"I need your help analyzing its venom," she said. "These snakes are responsible for the petrifaction you saw in Malachai Applewhite's body, and there are hundreds of them living just outside Valley Grove."

Dae-jung stepped closer for a better look at the contents of the evidence bag. "A snake whose venom petrifies its victims? That doesn't make sense. Snakes use venom to kill their prey. How can they eat something that's turned to stone?"

"It's not stone," she reminded him. "But that's an excellent question. I'd like to take another look at Malachai's body. Can you help me get him onto the autopsy table?"

"Sure thing."

Leaving the snake's remains in the forensics lab, they went down the hallway to the morgue. Laura unlocked the door and turned on the overhead fixtures. In the light, the stainless-steel autopsy table gleamed like an unsheathed sword. She put on a pair of nitrile gloves and approached the large, eight-door refrigerator that loomed against the far wall.

"Did you manage to extract his marrow yesterday to check for toxins?" she asked.

Dae-jung put on a pair of gloves, too. "I couldn't, the tools I asked for still haven't arrived. Before Chief Morales left for Valley Grove yesterday, she called me every five minutes about it. With luck, they'll come today. Even knowing about the snake venom now, I'd still like to examine the marrow, just in case there's anything helpful."

Laura opened the morgue refrigerator door where they'd stored Malachai's body and pulled out the telescoping body tray. One look at the sealed black bag told her something was wrong. Malachai had been curled on his side, petrified in an almost fetal position, and it had left the bag bulging so much at the sides that it almost hadn't fit on the tray. Now the bag was wide and flat, and fit the tray perfectly.

"This doesn't look right." She double-checked the tag attached to the zipper pull. It bore Malachai Applewhite's name.

Dae-jung pressed on the bag with one gloved hand. "It doesn't feel right, either. Have you ever touched a waterbed? It feels kind of like that."

"I'm going to open it up and see what's going on," she said.

She unzipped the bag a couple of inches, only intending to look inside, but once it was open, it was like a dam had burst. A cascade of multicolored goo erupted from the opening and splattered onto the floor. Laura and Dae-jung scrambled back before any of it could get on them. The slime continued to flow out of the open body bag like jam from an overturned jar, a swirling mix of dark red and thick yellowish-white. Liquefied tissue and fat, Laura realized. Carried with it were white shapes that she quickly identified as bones. A rib here, a portion of spine there; even the skull slid out and fell to the floor with the rest.

"What the fuck!" Dae-jung tried not to gag.

They backed farther away as the puddle grew larger on the floor. Its frothy edge inched toward them.

"Don't let it touch you," Laura said. "I don't know how toxic it is."

The individual phalanges of Malachai's fingers slid out of the body bag in a waterfall of blood-colored sludge and splashed into the growing pool on the floor.

"Oh, fuck, I'm going to be sick," Dae-jung said and ran out of the morgue.

Laura had no choice but to necropsy the snake in the forensics lab while the morgue was being cleaned and decontaminated by a HAZMAT team. Malachai's remains would be collected for evidence, or as much of his remains as possible, which probably meant just the bones. Somehow, the petrified tissue had broken down into an organic slurry, yet the bones had been left untouched. Dae-jung, who was looking considerably less green now, doubted the marrow would be suitable for testing anymore. Even with the bones still intact, there was no way the marrow inside them was unaffected by whatever chemical process had liquified the soft tissue.

Putting on a fresh pair of nitrile gloves, Laura laid the snake's headless carcass ventral side up on an aluminum dissection tray. Using sharp dissecting scissors, she made a long incision through the skin along the ventral surface, from the cloacal opening to the throat. As she cut, she lifted the skin away from the body to make sure she didn't damage any of the organs underneath. Once the incision was complete, she carefully pulled the skin back and pinned it down on either side. She used a scalpel to cut away the thin membrane that covered the internal organs.

The major organs all looked normal—esophagus, heart, liver, intestines. As with most snakes, there was only a single lung, a long, cylindrical sac about one-third the length of the body. The stomach caught her attention. Normally, a snake's stomach was made from strong elastic tissue, which allowed it to stretch around prey that was swallowed whole. The tissue of this snake's stomach was delicate with no elasticity to it at all.

"Maybe it eats a different diet?" Dae-jung suggested. "Smaller prey?"

"I doubt it. These snakes were going after human beings last night," Laura said. "There's no way they could swallow a full-grown adult whole, and even if they could, the stomach couldn't stretch to accommodate it."

"You don't think that's why Malachai's body…melted, do you?"

She looked up from the dissected snake. "What do you mean?"

"Snakes don't chew their food," he said. "If the stomach can't expand enough for prey that's swallowed whole, maybe it requires a—a liquid diet." His face twisted in disgust. He swallowed hard, but he managed to keep the bile down this time.

Laura thought it over. "The venom petrifies their prey, and the snake comes back later when the prey has liquefied and eats it then. It's not a bad theory, but I don't understand why they would need to petrify their prey first."

"I think I do," he said. "When I was growing up, my older sister, Mi-Sun, used to take food off my dinner plate all the time. It drove me crazy, but she was bigger than me and I couldn't stop her. I knew she hated the taste of ketchup, so, in order to keep her from eating my food night after night, I drenched everything in ketchup. It was no big deal to me, I loved ketchup, but what really mattered was that it kept her away. What if this is the same principle? What if the snakes petrify their prey so nothing else eats it before they can?"

Laura nodded. It was starting to make sense.

"And while the prey is petrified, something in the venom, some chemical or enzyme, breaks down the tissue over time," she said. "Everything except the bones. Why leave the bones?"

Dae-jung grabbed his tablet and did a quick search online. "Snakes can't digest bones. It says here that the bones and hair of their prey are usually compacted into a pellet and regurgitated."

"Okay, so rather than being forced to regurgitate the bones after eating them, the venom cuts out a step by only liquefying the tissue and leaving the bones alone," Laura said. "And the hair. I thought it was odd when I examined Malachai's body that his hair hadn't been affected by the petrifaction. Now I get it. It's a remarkably efficient process when you think about it."

"What if I *don't* want to think about it?" he said.

Laura got back to work. The snake's severed head lay on a separate tray from its body. She made an incision with the scalpel, starting between the nostrils and moving carefully up the head. The scaly skin was dry and hard, like cutting through a fingernail. It would be easier with the scissors, but she needed the precision only a scalpel could give her. Otherwise, she risked piercing the venom glands she was after.

"Copperheads are members of the pit viper family," Dae-jung read off his tablet. "That means they have a heat-sensing organ in the facial pits located on either side of the head between the eye and nostril. This organ helps them locate food in the dark by detecting the body heat of their prey."

She saw the two small pits in the head like extra nostrils. Could the heat given off by the people of Valley Grove be what attracted the snakes? It was possible, but surely they had other, more convenient prey available to them. Booker said copperheads normally waited in the grass to ambush small animals that passed by. Even if these mutations weren't strictly copperheads anymore, why would they go out of their way to cross a lake? And why go after human beings, who were certainly not typical prey?

Laura carefully peeled the skin away from the head and pinned it to the dissection tray. Below the snake's strangely iridescent eyes, she found the venom glands, one on each side, attached by a conducting tube to the venom canal that ran through each fang.

"Copperheads have functional venom glands from birth," Dae-jung read. "Baby copperheads also have yellow tails for the first three years of their lives. They'll sit motionless and shake their tails in a way that makes it look like a caterpillar or insect. Then, when a hungry lizard or frog comes by the eat it, the baby copperhead strikes. It's called caudal luring."

"None of the snakes I saw had yellow tails, and there was no luring involved," Laura said. "They were actively hunting people."

Dae-jung looked up from the tablet. "If copperheads are born with venom, that means they're hunters right from the start. Maybe that instinct was exacerbated by the mutation somehow and made them more aggressive."

She nodded. "Another good theory."

"Gold star for me." He paused. "I, um, I know you were close with the woman who ran the forensics lab before me. I figure that's why we haven't really talked much since I started here."

"You're right. I'm sorry about that," Laura said. "Sofia was a good friend. It's been difficult without her, but I shouldn't have held it against you. It's not your fault."

"I just hope I'll do as good a job as she did."

"You already are."

She began to carefully remove the venom glad from under the snake's left eye, using the tip of the scalpel to sever the far end of the venom-conducting tube from the base of the fang.

"What does that article say about their venom?" she asked.

Dae-jung moved his gloved finger up the tablet's high-touch-sensitivity screen, scrolling farther down the webpage he was looking at. "Copperheads make use of a hemolytic venom to subdue their prey. The venom causes the breakdown of red blood cells, which can be lethal in smaller animals but not usually for larger animals like human beings."

"Hemotoxins do more than just break down blood cells," Laura said. "They break down protein in the region of the bite, which aids in digestion."

"Fuck." Dae-jung looked up from the tablet. "Multiply that by a thousand and could it break down protein in the entire body?"

"On that scale? It's doubtful," she said. "Not by itself, anyway. It would need help. Something a lot stronger."

She removed the venom gland from the head, pinching the end of the conducting tube shut so the contents wouldn't spill out. Dae-jung brought her a metal test tube rack with a single test tube fitted into it. Laura milked the venom, a viscous, yellowish liquid, into the tube. When the gland was empty, she put it on the tray next to the head. Dae-jung fitted a stopper into the top of the test tube.

"How quickly can you analyze it?" Laura said.

"I'll need a few hours," he said. "In the meantime, it occurs to me we can't keep calling these snakes copperheads. They're not copperheads anymore. We need a new name for them, at least a temporary one until someone comes up with something in Latin."

"How about basilisks?"

Dae-jung raised an eyebrow. "Like from mythology?"

"It's something one of the victims said before he died," she explained. "I don't know what he was trying to tell me, but it stuck with me."

Dae-jung did an Internet search for *basilisk* on his tablet. He turned it around so she could see an illustration on the screen. It was a huge snake with a crown-shaped crest upon its head.

"Legend had it the basilisk could kill with a glance, turning its victims to stone," he read from the website. "Commonly known as the King of the Serpents, the basilisk is often pictured with a crown or a crown-like physical feature on its head. Huh. Well, our snakes don't have crowns, but basilisk is as good a name as any. I say we go with it."

Laura covered her mouth as she yawned. "Sorry about that. It's been a long day. A long *two* days, actually."

"You should get some rest. No offense, but you look like you're about to keel over."

The thought of a nap sounded tempting, but she knew she wouldn't be able to sleep, not while she still had so many questions. Instead, she left Dae-jung to his work in the forensics lab and went back down the hall to the morgue. Looking in through the hallway window, she saw two faceless figures in HAZMAT suits moving through the room. One held a large, bright yellow plastic bag marked with the words HAZARDOUS MATERIAL - HANDLE WITH CARE. She could tell from the shapes jutting sharply against the sides that the bag was filled with bones. The second figure hosed frothy red water across the tiles.

Laura watched as the last remaining bits of Malachai Applewhite disappeared down a drain in the floor.

19

The holy sanctuary was the first thing the founders of the Church of the Divine Chariot built when they bought the land that would later be known as Valley Grove from the town of Smithfield, New York, in the 1950s. They'd come across the border from Pennsylvania, nearly a thousand true believers looking to create their own Holy Land where they could live and worship as the Lord instructed them. Before they built their own houses, they slept in cars, tents, and trailers while they worked to erect the enormous wooden monument to their faith.

Shepherd Eliezer, looking out at the nave from where he stood at the pulpit in front, believed their holy sanctuary truly was a monument, with grand exposed beams running along its lofty ceiling and down the walls like the ribs of the whale that swallowed Jonah. The walls were decorated with paintings of the Prophet Elijah. Like Elijah, Shepherd Eliezer and his flock had turned their backs on the corruptions of the modern world and continued to worship the Lord in the true ways of old. And just as Elijah ascended to the Kingdom of Heaven in a burning chariot drawn by fiery horses, so too would the members of the Church of the Divine Chariot ascend to God's glory.

His congregation sat in the wooden pews, their faces turned up to him, listening to his sermon.

"Thus saith the Lord God; Behold, I will take the children of Israel from among the heathen, whither they be gone, and will gather them on every side, and bring them into their own land," he recited from memory. The passage was from Ezekiel 37, the story of the Prophet Ezekiel in the Valley of the Dry Bones. "And I will make them one nation in the land upon the mountains of Israel; and one king shall be king to them all: and they shall be no more two nations, neither shall they be divided into two kingdoms any more at all. Neither shall they defile themselves any more with their idols, nor with their detestable things, nor with any of their transgressions: but I will save them out of all their dwelling places, wherein they have sinned, and will cleanse them: so shall they be my people, and I will be their God."

He paused, letting the words sink in. The holy sanctuary had been built for that original congregation of a thousand, but more than half the pews were empty now. Only two hundred people sat before him. It confounded him that their numbers had shrunk so much over the years. Surely this holy sanctuary, this wooden monument to godliness, should be swollen with people instead. Or did most people no longer wish to enter the Kingdom of Heaven? Perhaps, he thought, the question answered itself.

Some seats in the pews had been left vacant out of respect for those who died when the snakes invaded last night. Eliezer had a list of their names, which he'd solemnly read at the start of this morning's service. Beth Richter. Eddie Gordon. Rich Campbell. Gideon Black. Ira McInerny. Reuben Bailes. Sharon Applewhite, and the child growing inside her. The air in the holy sanctuary was thick with mourning, but prayer was the truest comfort. He was proud his congregation could keep their emotions under control.

The only exception was his own daughter, Meredith. The girl sat next to Sharon's empty spot and wept openly. The hypocrite. She'd hated Sharon from the start, and now here she was, blubbering and brooding in front of everyone in the holy sanctuary. It was sickening. He was certain she was doing it on purpose to make him look like a weak father. A weak Shepherd. It was clear Meredith had too much of her rebellious brother in her. A trip to the Penitence Room would sort her out.

Eliezer had disposed of the dead snakes in the house and moved Sharon's grotesquely petrified body into Malachai's room for the traditional 24-hour waiting period before burial, and all the while he'd been forced to listen to Meredith sobbing in her bedroom. Yet as he lay in his own bed, no tears came to him. He thought of his wife, who had served and obeyed him faithfully, and he thought of his unborn son, who would have become his heir in Malachai's place, and all he felt was anger. A smoldering rage at what had been stolen from him. As he stood before the congregation, he let that anger surge out of him in his words.

"Brothers and sisters, *we* are the people of the Valley of the Dry Bones, raised up by the breath God Himself breathed into us," he said. "Just as the Lord brought the Israelites to the Promised Land so they could worship Him apart from the depraved and perverse world of idolators, Sodomites, and heathens, so He brought us to *our* Promised Land, and for the same reason."

The ten Elders of the Church of the Divine Chariot nodded in agreement as they sat in their own section of the nave. They wore prayer shawls around their shoulders that marked them as Elders, dyed deep red for the divine flames of Elijah's chariot. Eliezer's gaze sought out Elder Francis among them. Francis was his own kind of snake, and after last night, Eliezer knew exactly what to do with snakes.

"But we have failed our Lord," he continued. "More than that, we have angered Him. There are those among us who wish to stray from the path of righteousness, and we have tolerated their wicked dissent for too long. This is why the Lord sent a plague of serpents last night, just as He sent the ten plagues against Egypt, because like Pharaoh, we have *defied* Him!"

A shocked murmur rippled through the congregation.

"Yes, brothers and sisters, we defied the Lord our God, but never again! As you know, my own wife and unborn child were taken from me last night by the plague of serpents." Eliezer closed his eyes and lifted his hands. "I hear you, O Lord! Their deaths were not in vain, for I know they sit by Your side now in the Kingdom of Heaven, while down here, on this flawed and sinful Earth, my ears ring with Your holy message! The Church of the Divine Chariot has thrived for seventy years by adhering to Your principles, and by Your grace we'll thrive for seventy more—for a *hundred* more!"

Congregants cheered and shouted their amens. He had them right where he wanted them. They would eat out of his hand if he asked them to. It was time to bring down the axe.

He opened his eyes and pointed his finger directly at Elder Francis. "It was *you* who brought God's wrath upon us, Elder Francis! Your vain and diabolical ideas will no longer be tolerated! You are *expelled* from this holy sanctuary! Remove the shawl from your shoulders, for you are no longer an Elder of the Church of the Divine Chariot! You will not be welcomed back into this holy sanctuary until you repent your ways!"

Harsh whispers and gasps of shock echoed through the building. Congregants turned to stare at Francis, some angry, others confused. On cue, Fritz and Damien appeared by the pew where Francis sat. They kept their distance for now, but they crossed their arms and glared at him with a clear message: Leave or be dragged out. Seated elsewhere in the holy sanctuary, Francis's daughter Rebecca looked around nervously, hugging herself, wondering what was happening.

"This is outrageous!" Francis said, rising from his seat. "You don't have the right—"

"I am your Shepherd, and God has *given* me the right!" Eliezer yelled, banging his fist on the pulpit. "Now leave this place! If you're wise, you'll spend the rest of the day begging God for forgiveness!"

Several other Elders rose from their seats, voicing their outrage, but Eliezer was gratified to see it was fewer than half of them. The rest of the Elders still supported him.

Congregants rose from their seats, some in disbelief, others pointing and shouting for Francis to leave the holy sanctuary. Fritz and Damien stepped closer, to within a hand's breadth of him.

Eliezer took private pleasure in seeing his daughter look so terrified at what was happening. Meredith's hands were up by her mouth, tears welling in her eyes again. She looked for her friend Rebecca in the pews, but Francis had already pulled Rebecca out of her seat and was starting down the center aisle toward the door. Fritz and Damien followed them up the aisle. The din of angry and upset voices inside the holy sanctuary was deafening. At the door, Francis paused and turned to face Eliezer.

"This is insanity!" he said. "Our numbers are dwindling! We *must* change! If we don't, the Church of the Divine Chariot won't survive!"

"You see how he continues to defy God?" Eliezer called out. "How many more serpents will the Lord send to punish us before Francis Ponder sees the error of his ways?"

Fritz yanked the red prayer shawl off Francis's shoulders. Damien opened the great wooden door of the holy sanctuary. Rebecca held on to her father tightly as she and Francis left. Fritz and Damien closed the doors again with a satisfying, conclusive slam. The congregation turned back to Eliezer in confusion. Some of the Elders were still yelling their complaints.

Eliezer smiled to himself. He'd gotten what he wanted. Nothing else mattered.

After the service, Eliezer walked the road that led from the holy sanctuary to his house with Fritz and Elder Bernard at his side. The cemetery hill behind them cast its shadow across the road like an ink blot—a dark, rugged smear spiked with tombstones like blunt teeth. It was another sweltering day in a summer that was filled with them. Eliezer rubbed his arm across his forehead to wipe away his perspiration.

"Fritz, I want you to keep an eye on Francis's house," he said.

Fritz nodded, scratching his red beard. "You suspect he'll come for you in retaliation?"

"I do, though not in the way you're thinking," Eliezer said. "I know he still has allies among the Elders. They won't be happy he was expelled from the holy sanctuary. If he meets with any of them, I want to know about it."

"Why waste time keeping tabs on him?" Fritz asked, lowering his voice. "Why not just make him and his brat disappear?"

Eliezer looked around the street to make sure no one had heard. At this hour, most of the villagers were in their homes, either schooling their children or preparing midday meals. They could speak freely.

"I would do so happily, Fritz, but right now, I want everyone to see him shunned and shamed. I want them to see him weak. Then his supporters will see how foolish they were to think he could ever be Shepherd in my place."

Eliezer paused, waiting for Elder Bernard to catch up with them. The old man's frail, aged legs carried him slowly.

"Elder Bernard, where do we stand with the other Elders after this morning?" he asked.

"They remain split," Elder Bernard said. He took a moment to brush a few yellowing beard hairs away from his mouth before continuing. "What happened today will not convince those who have concerns about you to join our side."

"They'll come around," Fritz interjected. "They'll see you were right to expel him. You're the Shepherd. What you say goes."

"I agree. Once the congregation falls in line, none of the Elders will dare to move against you," Elder Bernard said. "Give them time. They may be shocked at what happened, but soon enough they'll see there's no path for the Church but the path you're leading us on."

Finally, they reached Eliezer's house. Fritz left to carry out Eliezer's orders, but Elder Bernard lingered.

"I would like to see my future bride," he said with a nicotine-stained smile. "Where is Meredith?"

"Another time, Elder Bernard," Eliezer said. His daughter had gone right home after services without even speaking to him. "After what happened to Sharon last night, I don't think Meredith is in any mood for visitors. Be patient."

Bernard shaded his eyes from the sun with a bony, spotted hand. "I am not a man of infinite patience, Shepherd. Remember our deal. My vote carries weight among the Elders."

Eliezer bristled, but he maintained his composure. As much as he enjoyed imagining throttling the old man's scrawny neck, he needed Elder Bernard happy.

"Of course," he said. "I'll see that you get a chance to visit with Meredith tomorrow."

"Excellent," Elder Bernard said. "There's much she and I need to discuss before the wedding. It's important Meredith knows the ways I like things done around the house."

"Good day to you, Elder Bernard."

"Good day to you, Shepherd. Or should I say father-in-law?"

The old man tittered and shuffled off.

Inside the house, Eliezer half expected to hear Sharon greet him, or the clatter of dishes in the kitchen as she prepared lunch. Instead, the house was eerie in its silence. Behind the sitting room door was the dead body of an outsider, a man he didn't know. Behind Malachai's bedroom door was the body of his wife and, within her, the corpse of his second son. It was a house of the dead.

He'd planned to name his son Solomon, after his own father. There was so much promise in that name. It was the name of a king and prophet, of the builder of the First Temple in Jerusalem. Now that promise would never be fulfilled. The thought of it fanned the embers of his rage.

He threw open the door to Meredith's bedroom. She was lying on the bed, her face still stained with tears, looking at a yellow sticky note. She sat up quickly when she saw him and hid the note behind her back.

"You're supposed to knock!" she said.

He stepped into the room. "Guests knock. This house belongs to me."

Her shoulders slumped. "What do you want, Father?"

"Sit up straight," he told her. With a heavy sigh she squared her shoulders. "I've had enough of your attitude. Your shameful behavior at the service this morning was the last straw."

"What behavior?"

"Who did you think you were fooling with those crocodile tears?" He circled the bed. She turned to face him, keeping the yellow note hidden from him behind her back. "Was it your intention to make me look like a fool in front of everyone in the holy sanctuary? To make everyone think I have no control over my own daughter?"

"What are you talking about?"

"What's that behind your back?"

The color drained out of her face. "Nothing."

"Show me."

"It's nothing," she insisted.

He grabbed her arm and wrenched it out from behind her back. He snatched the yellow sticky note from her hand.

"That's mine! Give it back!" she yelled.

Meredith stood up to try and take it from him, but he shoved her back onto the bed. On the note was written Dr. Laura Powell's name, followed by a phone number and an address in Sakima.

His blood ran hot. "What is this?"

"It's mine," she protested. "She gave it to me."

Eliezer crumpled the note into a ball. "Why?"

She stayed silent, fuming, eyes downcast.

"*Why* would she give this to you, Meredith?" he demanded.

"Because I hate it here!" she erupted, springing off the bed. "I hate you and I hate Elder Bernard! I don't want to marry him! I don't want to have children! I don't want any of this! That's why Laura gave me her phone number, so I can go stay with her when I finally leave this awful place behind—"

His struck her across the face with the back of his hand. She flinched but didn't fall. She wiped away a trickle of blood from the corner of her mouth and laughed bitterly.

"Is that supposed to make me change my mind?" she said.

"*She* put these thoughts in your head, didn't she?" Eliezer waved the crumpled sticky note in front of her. "*She* filled your mind with this filth!"

"You'd really like to believe that, wouldn't you?" she said. "That would make it so much easier."

"Shut your mouth," he warned her.

"I know why you promised me to Elder Bernard, Father," she said. "You're scared of losing your position in the Church."

"I said that's enough!"

"You're scared that Elder Francis's ideas are catching on."

He grabbed her by the wrist and yanked her toward the bedroom door.

"Ow, my arm! You're hurting me!" she said. "What are you doing?"

"Your disobedience shames you in the eyes of God," he told her. "Some time in the Penitence Room will set you right."

"No!"

She held on to the door frame as he dragged her out of her bedroom. With one strong tug, he pulled her free and carried her down the hall. She thrashed and screamed like a demon.

"Let me go!"

With his free hand, he opened the door in the kitchen and then hauled her into the backyard. She screamed in his ear and hit him ineffectually with her small fists. He brought her to the concrete garage behind the house, unconcerned that anyone might hear her cries. He was the Shepherd. They would trust he was doing what needed to be done.

The garage was mostly used for storage. As Shepherd, he had no need for a car, as he rarely left Valley Grove. The few times he did, one of his congregants was always happy to drive him. He pulled Meredith inside. She tried to dig the heels of her shoes into the cement floor, but he dragged her between the stacks of boxes filled with prayer books and the shelves of preserves Sharon had made. A metal trap door waited in the floor.

"Stop, please!" Meredith begged. "I didn't mean it! I'm sorry!"

He ignored her pleas. Her words couldn't be trusted; the Devil had taken control of her tongue. He threw her to the floor beside the trap door.

"Open it," he ordered.

She looked up at him, tears glistening in her eyes. Her frizzy red hair had come loose from its ribbon and stuck out in all directions like hay from a bale.

"Please, Father!"

"Do it."

Whimpering, she slid the thick metal bolt to one side, unlocking the door. She looked up at him again but was met only with his merciless glower. She pulled the trap door open. Underneath, a ladder led downward into pitch darkness.

"Climb down into the Penitence Room," he told her.

"Father..."

"Go!"

He drew back his arm as if to hit her again. She quickly scampered onto the ladder without looking at him again. He closed the trap door over her and slid the bolt back into place, sealing her in the darkness below.

Next, he went to find Fritz. He found him standing across the street from Francis's house, watching as he'd been instructed to.

"No one has come to see him yet," Fritz reported, squinting in the sun. "I haven't heard his phone ring, either, but I've no idea if he's made any outgoing calls."

"Get Damien to take your place here," Eliezer said. "I have a new task for you."

He handed Fritz the crumpled sticky note with Laura's address on it. Fritz looked at it and raised an eyebrow.

"The woman who was here yesterday?"

"I want her gone," Eliezer said. "It can't be traced back to me or to Valley Grove. It has to look like an accident."

Then, because it tickled him, he added, "An act of God."

20

L aura and Chief Morales looked over Dae-jung's shoulder as he sat before his laptop in the forensics lab. The monitor showed row after row of structural formulae, each line representing a different chemical compound. A plastic hood was attached to the top of the monitor to shield the screen from the lab's bright overhead lights.

"Snake venom is made of a complex mixture of various molecules," Dae-jung said, pointing to different rows on the screen. "Proteins, lipids, peptides, amino acids, carbohydrates, nucleosides..."

"I'm not going to pretend I know what half of that is," Morales said.

"Well, nucleosides are structural subunits of nucleic acids," Dae-jung said, adjusting his wire-rimmed glasses. "Molecules of sugar are linked to nitrogen-containing organic ring compounds—"

She put up one hand to stop him from going any further. "Please just continue with your report, Mr. Park."

Morales was wearing fresh clothes, something Laura found herself inordinately jealous of. Still in the same clothes she'd worn yesterday, she felt filthy, certain every inch of her was coated in a layer of dried sweat. She could only imagine how awful she must smell, especially standing so close to Morales and Dae-jung.

"All the expected molecules are present in the venom I analyzed," Dae-jung went on. "However, I also found a few molecules that *shouldn't* be there. Chemical compounds you wouldn't normally find in snake venom."

"Such as?" Morales asked.

Laura leaned forward. It felt like they were finally getting somewhere.

"Calcium chloride for one, an enormous amount of it," Dae-jung said. "Small quantities of calcium chloride are perfectly safe for the human body, but at the level I detected in the venom, it would act as a—well, as a kind of desiccant. You know how kelp is sometimes dried with calcium chloride to become the inorganic crystalline compound sodium carbonate?"

Morales said, "Let just assume we're not as up to speed on our chemical compounds as you are."

"Right. Anyway," he said. "What I'm getting at is that once this venom is injected into the bloodstream, the calcium chloride completely dehydrates and crystallizes the victim's cells. Connective tissue, epithelial tissue, muscle tissue, nervous tissue—all of it is affected."

"But the victims don't *look* desiccated," Laura said. "The flesh isn't withered, the eyes aren't sunken into the skull..."

"That could be because of what else I found." Dae-jung pointed to the next chemical compound on the screen. "Mercuric bichloride. Unlike calcium chloride, mercuric bichloride is toxic to humans in any amount. It's a chemical reagent that's usually used for creating amalgams, alloys of mercury and other metals. Mercuric bichloride is what bonds the two metals together. In this case, it bonds the crystallized cells together into a hard, stonelike substance."

"Petrifying them," Laura said.

"Precisely." Dae-jung turned to her in his desk chair. "The more I think about it, the more your mutation theory makes sense. This can't the result of natural evolution. These chemicals have no business being in snake venom. Something happened to the basilisks. Something *made* them this way."

"Can you explain what happened to Malachai Applewhite's body?" Morales asked. "That doesn't sound natural, either. What could have caused it to turn into slush like that?"

"I still don't know," Dae-jung replied. He pointed at the two rows at the bottom of the laptop screen. "These are chemical compounds in the venom I haven't been able to identify yet. I'm thinking they might be what causes the crystalized cells to rehydrate again and break down."

Morales nodded. "Okay. At least I finally have something I can tell Mayor Sutherland. Email me your report so I can show it to him."

She left the lab. Dae-jung stared after her in the humming quiet of the forensics lab.

"A simple 'good work, Dae-jung' wouldn't have hurt," he said.

"Get used to it. Positive reinforcement isn't in her vocabulary," Laura said. "Now that we know what's causing the petrifaction, is there a way to stop it?"

"Honestly, I don't think there is. From what you told me, the victims die within roughly thirty minutes of the venom entering their bloodstream. The amount of hydration needed to counteract the calcium chloride, not to mention the amount of chelating agent needed to remove the mercuric bichloride from the body, would be so massive there's no way either could be applied in time."

"If there's no antidote, how can we keep people safe?"

Dae-jung sighed, folded the hood over the monitor, and closed the laptop. "There's only one way. The basilisks have to be destroyed."

Laura winced.

"You don't like that plan?" he asked.

"I know it has to be done. The basilisks are a danger, not just to the people of Valley Grove but to any community they wander into or set up a den in."

"But?"

Laura sighed. "They're a completely new species of snake. A species no one has ever seen before. Destroying them seems like such a wasted opportunity compared to how much more there is to learn about them."

Dae-jung got up from his chair. "I know, but what choice do we have? They're only going to kill more people."

She nodded. "So how do we do it?"

"The best way would be to get them all at once in their den," he said. "Typically, a calcium cyanide gas is used to fumigate a snake den, but there are three big problems with this approach. First, it's a deadly poison. Using it outside, the gas can drift on the wind and kill other animals and even small children nearby. Second, copperheads den socially in a large space. Since the basilisks are an offshoot of copperheads, we can assume for now that they do the same. That kind of den makes it difficult to judge exactly how much calcium cyanide would be needed. Too little and the basilisks survive; too much and you risk the gas leaking out and drifting on the wind as I mentioned. Third, it takes about thirty to forty-five minutes to work, and if the basilisks are as aggressive as you say they are, that's way too long. During the interval, it's inevitable they'll vacate the den to attack, which would render the fumigation process useless. In my opinion, it's just not worth the risk."

"Then we're back to square one," Laura said.

"Not necessarily. I have an idea. You know the chrysanthemum flower?"

She raised her eyebrows. "You want to kill the basilisks with flowers?"

"With something *extracted* from them," he said. "A chemical compound called pyrethrin. The chrysanthemum uses pyrethrin as a natural defense against insects and other pests. It happens to be highly toxic to snakes. With an aerosolized version, you wouldn't have to worry about it drifting like poison gas would. It could be sprayed directly on them, ensuring that they die."

"How far away can it be sprayed from?" she asked.

"That's the problem," he said. "It's not long-range like the fumigating gas. Whoever does the spraying would have to be closer."

"How much closer?"

"Within striking distance."

Laura sat down on the computer desk chair. "Shit. But it'll work?"

"It'll work," he said.

"How soon can you get some for me?"

"What do you mean, for *you*?" he said. "You're not thinking of doing this yourself, are you? Why not contact the Department of Environmental Conservation? They're the ones who deal with wildlife issues."

"The DEC takes a couple of weeks to process a request. That's two weeks of basilisks coming back to Valley Grove night after night. We can't wait that long. It has to be done quickly, which means doing it myself."

"Are you going to tell Chief Morales?"

"No. She'd only order me not to do it."

"Maybe she would be right."

"Not for the people of Valley Grove," she said.

Dae-jung sighed and flapped his arms in resignation. "Well, if you're going to do it, the best way would still be to get them while they're all in one place."

"The den," Laura said.

"You said they're nocturnal. If you go to the den in the daytime, they should be asleep."

"That means Valley Grove will still be in danger tonight."

"Unfortunately, yes. But you won't be able to go tonight anyway. I don't have the pyrethrin yet."

Laura gripped the silver heart pendant around her neck. She had to warn Francis and Rebecca to stay inside with the doors and windows closed once the sun went down. It didn't feel like enough, but it was something, and it would keep them safe.

"How soon can you get it?" she asked.

"Pyrethrin's not hard to find," he said. "It's present in any number of over-the-counter pest control products. It's lethal to snakes even in low doses, but I don't want to take any chances. I'll put together something more powerful for you and have it ready for tomorrow. The only question is, do you know where the den is?"

She thought back to what Craig Hutsell told her.

The cave under Thurmond Biotech...Malachai saw...saw them hiding something in the cave. Something that shouldn't be there.

"Yes, I think I do," she said.

21

When Laura returned home, she dropped onto the living room couch, found the folded piece of paper with Francis's phone number on it, and dialed. While it rang, she looked up at the antique, cherrywood clock mounted over the doorway to the dining room, the only thing she owned that had belonged to her mother. The hands read a little past four p.m. Where had the day gone?

"Hello?" a female voice said in her ear.

"Rebecca? It's Laura."

"Cousin Laura!" Rebecca said excitedly. "Are you still in Valley Grove?"

"No, I'm back home in Sakima now," she said. "Are you and your father okay after last night?"

"Yes, we're fine. It was scary, but we stayed inside."

Laura breathed a sigh of relief. Not knowing if they were all right had been weighing on her all day.

"It's just as well you're not here, Cousin Laura. Things are really bad."

"How so?"

"During services this morning, Shepherd Eliezer blamed Father for the snakes. He called it God's punishment because we want to change things, and he kicked Father out of the holy sanctuary. The whole thing was really scary. They even stripped him of his prayer shawl. I don't think he's an Elder anymore."

"What the hell?"

"Please don't use that word, Cousin Laura."

"Sorry," she said with a wince. "I'm just surprised, that's all. Can Eliezer really do that?"

"He's the Shepherd," Rebecca said, as if that were enough to explain it all. "Damien Acker is watching our house right now. He's across the street trying to stay hidden, but he's not very good at it. Father and I are just staying inside."

"That's for the best," Laura said. "I'm sorry about what happened, but I need you to listen very carefully, okay? There's a good chance the snakes will come back tonight. I want you to stay inside just like you are now. Keep the windows and doors closed tight so they can't get in."

"Are you sure they'll be back?" Rebecca asked nervously.

"It's how they hunt," she said. "They kill their prey with venom, and then they come back later to eat them, but they only do these things at night. Promise me you and your father will stay inside again tonight."

"I promise," Rebecca said. "I don't think Father is in much of a mood to leave the house anyway."

"I'll be back tomorrow," Laura told her. "I'll stop in to see you and your father then."

"I'd like that, Cousin Laura, but from what I heard, the Shepherd told you never to come back. I don't want you to get in any more trouble."

"I'm not scared of the Shepherd, or the Order of the Faith," she said. "You're my family, Rebecca, and that means more to me than anything else."

"Me too," Rebecca said. "Are you wearing the necklace I gave you?"

Laura touched the pendant around her neck and smiled. "Yes, I am."

"Good," Rebecca said. "Maybe it will bring you luck."

She hoped so. She could use all the luck she could get tomorrow.

After the call, Laura went upstairs to take a shower. She stripped off her dirty clothes and gave serious thought to burning them rather than throwing them in the hamper. She stood under the hot water, letting it wash off the grime and unknot the muscles in her back. She stood there for so long she lost track of time. The swirl of soapy water circling the drain reminded her of Malachai Applewhite's gory remains being hosed down the drain in the morgue, and she turned away. Just a moment's peace, that was all she wanted. She'd been running on adrenaline since yesterday and now, in the comforting heat of the shower, it finally sank in just how tired she was. Afterward, she toweled off and put on her pajamas. There was no point in changing into fresh clothes. She didn't plan on being awake much longer.

She went back downstairs to put on the kettle for a cup of herbal tea before bed. The doorbell rang before she reached the kitchen. She went to the front door and looked through the peephole. Then, with a chuckle, she opened the door.

Booker stood on her doorstep holding a plastic bag with the name GOLDEN CHOPSTICKS emblazoned across the side. "I thought you could use some dinner."

Laura waved him in. He stepped through the doorway, kissed her hello, and went into the kitchen. She locked the door and followed him in.

"This is very sweet of you, but I was about to go to bed," she said. "I'm exhausted."

"I'm sure you are, but you need to eat," Booker said, putting the bag on the kitchen counter. "When was the last time you ate something?"

She shrugged. "Yesterday?"

"I thought so." He pulled a couple of takeout containers from the bag. "I got your favorite, shrimp fried rice."

"You spoil me."

She brought two bowls from the cupboard over to the counter. He scooped the rice into both bowls, and then they brought them into the dining room and sat. Laura speared a plump shrimp with her fork and popped it in her mouth. It was delicious, firm enough to snap when she bit into it and richly flavored by the spices in the rice. Her stomach rumbled to let her know it was grateful to no longer be ignored. She took a few more forkfuls.

"Honestly, I'm just glad to see you're okay after last night," he said.

"You should have seen it, Booker," she said, patting her lips with a napkin. "There were hundreds of basilisks in Valley Grove. The village was completely overrun."

"Basilisks?"

"It's something Craig Hutsell said before he died. The name stuck." She shook her head. "All it took was a single bite, and the victims petrified just like Malachai. I did what I could to help, but I haven't been that scared in a long time."

"It's strange. Snakes might den together, but they don't hunt together. They're solitary predators. I've never heard of snakes hunting in a group before. If you think of it like a wolf pack, there would have to be an alpha. Who's giving the orders? Who's telling them what to do?"

She didn't have an answer for that, but the idea burrowed into her mind and stayed there, gestating.

"I don't blame you for being scared," he said. "I would be, too."

"You?" She scoffed. "I didn't think anything scared you."

She was well aware she was changing the subject away from herself. She didn't like feeling vulnerable. Booker played along.

"That's not true," he said. "You want to know what scared me the most as a kid?"

"Desperately."

He put down his fork. "Strange matter. The stuff that's at the core of neutron stars."

"Oh, come on." She took another bite of fried rice.

"It's true. I was a lonely kid, I didn't have a lot of friends. I had weird hobbies instead, like reading about strange matter."

"Why did it scare you?"

"Because strange matter breaks the rules of the universe," he said. "Its atoms are different from anything else in existence. Normal atoms have protons and neutrons, held together by quarks, but strange matter doesn't have protons *or* neutrons. It's *all* quarks. That makes it dense, all but indestructible, and more stable than any other matter in the universe. It remains unchanged even if it comes into contact with other atoms. If another atom collides with strange matter, its protons and neutrons are stripped away, leaving just the quarks. Think about that. Anything that touches strange matter *becomes* strange matter. If even one tiny bit of it were to reach Earth, the whole planet would be transformed. You, me, everything.

One little atom of strange matter is all it would take to end the world."

"But you said it only exists in the core of neutron stars," she said. "There's no way it could come into contact with the Earth."

"Unfortunately, there is," he said. "When neutron stars collide with other neutron stars, they spew out everything in their cores, including particles of strange matter. I used to lie awake at night and scare myself thinking about how much strange matter was shooting all over the universe like stray bullets, and how it was only a matter of time before some of it reached Earth."

"*That's* what scared you as a kid?"

"Honestly, it still does sometimes."

Laura shook her head. "You're so weird."

Booker grinned. "You're just figuring that out now?"

They ate some more in silence before she finally told him what she'd been dreading to tell him.

"We discovered there's no antidote for the venom. The only way to keep people safe is to destroy the basilisks."

"How?"

"Dae-jung figured out a way to poison them, so tomorrow I'm going to find their den and put an end to this."

His eyes widened in surprise. "You're not going alone, are you?"

She nodded.

"That scares me more than strange matter does," he said. "Let me come with you."

"No, Booker."

"You need someone to watch your back," he said. "You've seen firsthand how deadly these snakes are."

"I'll be fine," she said. "I'll wear protective gear, and I'm going during the day. The basilisks will either be asleep or lethargic and slow. I'll be in and out in no time."

"Laura—"

"I have to do this, Booker. I can't let the snakes keep killing people."

He sighed and leaned back in his chair. "If I didn't love you, I'd call you a fool for doing this alone."

"But since you do love me?"

"Since I do," he said, "I'll just keep it to myself."

"Smart man," she said, and took another bite of her rice.

Booker wanted to stay the night, but she sent him home after dinner. All she wanted to do was sleep. She crawled into bed, turned off the bedside lamp, and was out before she knew it.

22

Down in the dark of the Penitence Room, sitting on the hard concrete floor, Meredith closed her eyes—she didn't need them in the darkness anyway—and went deep into herself. In her mind, she pictured her mother. Her birth mother. A feeling of warmth flooded through her, of safety and comfort. Sometimes it seemed like her mother was the only blood relative who'd ever truly loved her. Her father didn't. That much she knew for a fact. He saw her as a means to an end, a gift he could give to Elder Bernard in return for power. Even Mal, who'd been so much more than a brother, who'd been an ally and a confidant, had eventually abandoned her. Only her mother had truly loved her, and only cancer had been strong enough to separate them. Even then, her mother had hung on longer than anyone thought. Meredith was sure she lived as long as she did just for her.

Meredith hadn't been sent to the Penitence Room as often as Mal, not nearly as often, but she knew one important thing about it. One thing that kept her from losing her mind in the cold and dark. She groped along the wall until she found the letters carved into the cement, letters that spelled out Malachai's name. He'd scratched them there himself. She traced the letters with her finger, and for a moment it felt like Mal was there with her in the dark, comforting her. Tears welled in her eyes, and she let out a sob. Of course her brother had loved her. How could she ever think he hadn't? She missed him so much it felt like her heart would shatter.

She remained in the Penitence Room until dinnertime, when her father finally let her out and brought her back to the house. He heated up soup for both of them. She was angry and wanted to punish him by not eating, but she was starving after not eating all day and couldn't resist. She ate the soup silently. She hoped that was enough to let him know how mad she was.

Sharon's empty chair kept drawing her eye. Meredith was only just getting used to Mal's empty chair, and now there were two at the table. She glared at her father while he slurped his soup. She wondered what he'd done with the paper that had Laura's address and phone on it. He'd probably thrown it away where she couldn't find it. Or maybe he burned it. It didn't matter. Leaving Valley Grove to live with Laura in Sakima was nothing but wishful thinking anyway. It would never happen. Her fate was laid out for her. She would marry Elder Bernard and bear the old man's children, and then, if she was lucky, maybe she would get cancer like her mother and die before the last remaining spark of herself was stamped out.

After dinner, she went to her bedroom, closed the door, and threw herself onto the bed. She cried angrily until she fell asleep.

Sometime later, she was awakened by raised voices outside. She went to her window to see what was happening. In the dark of night, the street looked like it was alive, writhing and undulating with dark, sinuous shapes. Strange, opalescent eyes reflected the light of the moon. The snakes covered the village like a living, squirming carpet. Screams came from nearby homes. The silhouettes of men moved between the houses bearing tools as weapons.

A serpent appeared at the bottom of her window and began to crawl up the glass. The overlapping scales of its belly bunched and pushed as it moved upward. Its head reared back, and then it lunged at her, banging its head into the glass over and over as it tried to bite her. Meredith backed away from the window in horror. Finally, the snake lost its grip on the glass and fell away.

Her skin crawled. Thank God she wasn't outside.

But…what about Rebecca? Her best friend could be out there right now! Meredith had to make sure she was okay.

She hurried out of her bedroom and down the hall to the kitchen as quietly as she could. The last thing she wanted was for her father to hear her. He would never let her call Rebecca, especially after exiling Rebecca's father from the holy sanctuary. She stopped when she heard voices coming from the dining room. Her father had company. Who would come here on a night like this, when it was so dangerous to be outside? She peeked through the dining room door.

Her father and Elder Bernard sat at the dining room table. Their expressions were bitter and stern. Her father fidgeted in a way she only saw him do when he was deeply frustrated.

"The scales have tipped," Elder Bernard said. He clasped his frail, age-spotted hands on the table before him. "The Elders are now evenly split between favoring you and favoring Francis. Your foolish outburst in the holy sanctuary did you no favors."

"And what about you?" her father asked.

"You still have my vote, as long as I get what I want in return," Elder Bernard said.

Meredith shuddered. She knew what he wanted.

"In the meantime," Elder Bernard went on, "if you wish to remain Shepherd, you'd be wise to find a way to take Francis out of the running."

The old man rose from the table. Meredith shrank back from the doorway, but it was too late. Elder Bernard spotted her.

"Meredith," he called. "How nice to see you. Come here, child."

She inched forward into the dining room. Elder Bernard smiled at her through the nicotine-yellow hairs of his beard. His teeth were as discolored as ancient ivory. He caressed her cheek with one hand, his thumb straying close to her mouth. She felt his dry, rough skin at the corner of her lips.

"The bloom of youth," he said. "Don't ever get old. Don't ever change from the way you are now."

Meredith looked to her father, but no help came from him. Why would it? This was his doing. She wished her father was dead. It wasn't the first time she'd wished it, but she'd never felt it with such rage before. Elder Bernard removed his hand. She wanted to scrub her cheek in a hot shower until it bled.

"I look forward to starting our life together, Meredith. I have no doubt you will bear many beautiful children," he said. "Goodbye, Shepherd Eliezer. Think about what I said."

Elder Bernard left the house. Before the door closed, she caught a glimpse of men waiting outside for him, armed with hatchets and shovels to escort him home safe from the snakes. She turned to her father again, but he was already on his feet and heading into the kitchen, where he dialed the phone.

"I have a very important task for you, Damien," he said into the handset. "I need you to catch one of the snakes and bring it to me. No, Fritz can't do it. He's doing something else for me at the moment. The less you know, the better. Just do as I say and bring it here. No, it can't be dead. I need it alive."

One of the snakes? What would her father want with one of those awful creatures? Was he planning to keep it in the house?

Her thoughts were interrupted by the sound of something wet and heavy falling loudly to the floor. She looked around the dining room, but nothing was out of place. She heard it again, a wet slap, and realized it was coming from the sitting room. She walked down the hallway and opened the sitting room door. The lamps were off inside, but the light that spilled in from the hallway illuminated the couch and the lump under the blanket where the dead man lay. Something on the floor glistened. She reached into the room and flicked on the light switch for a better look.

Meredith gasped and covered her mouth.

A puddle of something thick and frothy lay on the floor. Some of it was as red as blood, and some of it was a putrid yellow. More of the syrupy liquid oozed out from under the blanket on the couch. A viscous globule fell into the puddle with a sickening slap. Meredith thought she was going to be sick.

Her father grabbed her roughly by the arm and pulled her out of the sitting room. He slammed the door shut.

"You see?" he said. "That's what happens to non-believers, Meredith. They are corrupt even in death. Is that what you want for yourself?"

Meredith yanked her arm out of his hand and glared at him.

"The snakes are bringing divine justice to all who turn their backs on the Church and challenge our ways," he said. "Think on that before you decide to disobey me again."

Meredith stomped back toward her bedroom, all thoughts of calling Rebecca gone from her mind. What her father said wasn't true. It couldn't be. After all, a snake had bitten Sharon, and Sharon would never turn her back on the Church.

The dead man in the sitting room was melting like ice cream on a hot day. Did it have something to do with the snake bite? Did that mean the same thing was happening to Sharon's body? She paused outside the door to Mal's bedroom, where her father had put Sharon's body until she could be buried. Meredith tried the door, but her father had locked it. She knelt and peered through the keyhole. She only saw a corner of the bed and a bit of the sheet he'd put over Sharon. Maybe it wasn't happening to her. Meredith sighed with relief. She didn't want to think of Sharon like that. It was too disturbing. Too awful.

From inside the room came the sound of something wet and heavy falling to the floor. Meredith ran into her bedroom and slammed the door.

23

Fritz Ruggen watched Laura's house from inside his car. He'd been parked across the street all day, waiting for her to come home, obsessively going over the details of his plan. The items he'd brought with him waited in the trunk, more patient than he was. He wanted to get on with it. Not because he wanted it over with. Quite the opposite. He was going to relish eliminating this bothersome woman.

There was an angel inside him, a righteous burning angel like the one that guarded Eden after Adam and Eve were expelled. It yearned to be let out. Fritz had let it out on occasion when he was young, to let it feed on wood and tinder, but he learned quickly that it was best to keep the angel hidden. Other people didn't understand. They couldn't, because unlike him, they were empty inside. Their bellies were cold ovens, while his burned with holy fire. The Shepherd was the only one who understood. It was why he'd recruited Fritz into the Order of the Faith. The Shepherd gave Fritz permission to let the angel out, to let its divine burning light engulf the sinners and heretics the Shepherd unleashed him upon.

Laura's house was dark. The Black man had left over an hour ago. Fritz didn't know who the man was and was angry that his unexpected appearance pushed back his timetable. Probably, she and the Black man had been fornicating. The thought disgusted him. All the more reason to let the angel loose upon her.

The thought of them fornicating had another effect on him as well, one that shamed him. He clasped his hands into fists until it went away. When he loosened his fingers again, both his palms were adorned with red crescent moons where his nails had dug into the flesh. The pain focused him. It was important he remain alert, undistracted by sinful thoughts.

It was time. He glanced up and down the street. Lights were turning off in all the houses. Fritz got out of his car and opened the trunk. Inside were two plastic gas cans, each holding two gallons of gasoline. Taking one in each hand, he hurried across the darkened street and around to the back of the house. As he expected, there was a back door. Through the door's window, he could see a darkened kitchen with empty Chinese food takeout containers on the counter. He tried the doorknob. It was locked.

Smart woman. How many houses had he entered where the owner had foolishly left the doors unlocked? It was almost as if they'd invited him in. This woman was no fool, but the angel would not be denied its chance to shine.

Fritz took off his shirt, exposing a patch of burn-scarred skin on his bare chest. A remnant of his first communion with the angel. He folded the shirt into a thick square and placed it over the door's window. Then he drove his elbow into it, breaking the glass while the shirt muffled the sound of the impact. Glass shards tinkled to the floor inside. He froze and waited for a sound or light from inside the house. When none came, he moved quickly, using the shirt to safely brush away any sharp bits of glass that remained in the window frame. He reached through and unlocked the door from the inside.

He slipped his shirt back on and brought the two gas cans into the house. It didn't take long to find the stairs to the second floor. He left the gas cans at the base of the stairs and made his way up quietly, testing each step for noise before putting his full weight on it. On the second floor, the door to the bedroom was open. Laura lay curled on her side on top of the covers. The sound of her breathing told him she was fast asleep.

He stood next to her bed and gazed down at her sleeping form. It would be so easy to strangle her in her sleep. She wouldn't even be aware until his hands were crushing her throat. The thought excited him. It wouldn't be the first time he'd strangled someone, but it would be the first time he'd strangled a woman, and that excited him in a different way. His gaze moved over her body. The curve of her hip. The soft swell of her breasts beneath her pajama top. The hint of cleavage visible in her neckline.

Shame flooded through him. He clenched his hands into tight fists again, feeling his nails dig into the tender skin of his palm, until the thoughts went away.

Shepherd Eliezer had instructed him to make it look like an accident. Strangling her—or doing anything else to her—would endanger that. It was best to stick with the original plan.

Outside the bedroom, Fritz spotted the smoke alarm on the ceiling. He climbed nimbly onto the stairway railing, pulled a flathead screwdriver from his back pocket, and jammed it into the smoke alarm in the way he'd learned long ago would quickly and silently disable it.

He disabled the smoke alarms downstairs the same way. Then, taking his time to avoid excessive noise, he poured out the contents of the gas cans all over the first floor—the living room, the dining room, the kitchen, the bottom stairs, even the coat closet. The smell of gasoline was overwhelming. He tied a bandana he'd brought with him over his nose and mouth, and paused occasionally to listen for any sign that the smell had woken up Laura. So far, so good. She slept like the dead.

When he was done, he brought the empty cans out into the cricket-filled stillness of the backyard. His fingerprints were all over them, and since Shepherd didn't want anything to be traced back to Valley Grove, he would have to take the cans with him. The fire would look like an accident so long as there was no investigation to find traces of the gasoline. But why would they investigate? Houses burned all the time, especially here in Sakima, where dozens of them had gone up in flames last year. The Shepherd would be pleased.

Fritz returned to the kitchen and took a book of matches from his pocket. He lit one and watched it flare to life. Deep within him. the eyes of the angel opened. He touched the lit match to the others in the book. They erupted into glorious flame. He tossed the book to the gasoline-soaked floor and left.

He threw the empty gas cans into the trunk of his car and drove away. In the rearview mirror, he saw the angel's flickering form dance in the windows. Free from its shackles, it cleansed everything it touched with its divine fire.

"God be praised," Fritz said.

24

The smell of smoke caused Laura to stir in her bed. Her mind, still half asleep, told her it was nothing to worry about. It was winter, and she'd fallen asleep with the bedroom window cracked, letting in the smoke from a neighbor's chimney. If it were an emergency, surely the smoke alarms would go off...

Another, more urgent part of her mind countered that it wasn't winter but the thick of summer, and none of her neighbors had a fire going. Laura's eyes snapped open. Dark, formless phantoms moved in the hallway outside her bedroom door. As her eyes adjusted, she saw it was smoke, billowing heavy and dark from downstairs. She leapt off the bed and ran to the bedroom door. Flickering orange flames burned at the foot of the steps. Waves of heat blasted up at her, hot enough to push her back. The smoke thickened by the second.

Shit!

What happened to the smoke alarms? She looked up at the ceiling. The small green light that indicated the smoke alarm outside her bedroom was operational was out. The pipes in the walls rattled as the sprinklers suddenly burst into life, dousing her in a blast of cold water.

The sprinklers wouldn't be enough to stop the fire. She had to get out of the house while she still could. Going downstairs was out of the question. She ran back into her bedroom, yanked her phone off the charger, and hit the Emergency Call button that connected directly to 911. She held the phone in the crook of her neck and worked to unlock the bedroom window. More smoke drifted the room, burning her eyes and lungs.

"911, what's your emergency?" a female operator's voice said.

"There's a fire. My house is on fire." She struggled to stay calm and get the words out.

She got the window open, the fresh air giving her a momentary reprieve from the thick smoke. She glanced back to the bedroom doorway. The fire was already halfway up the stairs, burning its way toward her like a relentless assassin.

"There's a fire in your house, is that correct?" the operator asked.

"Yes, please hurry!"

Laura climbed out the window onto the shingled roof of the verandah. It was a warm night, but she shivered in her water-soaked pajamas. The operator asked for her address and assured her the fire department was on its way.

"Would you like me to stay on the line with you until they get there?" the operator asked.

"I'm not going to be able to stay on the line. Just make sure they get here fast!"

Laura ended the call and tucked the cell phone into the elastic waistband of her pajama bottoms. She made her way carefully toward the edge of the verandah roof, but one wet, bare foot slipped out from under her. She regained her balance quickly, but her foot dislodged one of the wooden shingles. It tumbled to the lawn below with a disquieting thud.

Okay, she thought, trying to keep herself calm, *it's not that far down and the grass is soft.*

That was a lie. How many broken ankles and legs had she set where the patient thought grass was enough to safely break their fall? She shook her head, silencing the thought. It wasn't helpful.

Her chest felt like someone was sitting on it. Behind her, the fire had reached the door of her bedroom. Adrenaline spiked through her system. It was now or never.

Just focus on getting to the ground. Forget everything else. You've got to keep it together.

She took a deep breath to calm herself, but the smoke billowing out of the window made her cough. She sat and dangled her legs over the edge. She'd read somewhere that when you fell from a distance, you were supposed to relax your body and bend your knees slightly to better absorb the impact. Land on the balls of your feet, it said, and when the downward momentum carries you, try to fall to your side instead of on your back. Don't roll, just fall, or you could injure your spine. It all sounded easier said than done.

The flames crackled behind her. She was out of time.

Here goes nothing, she thought, and pushed off. She plummeted through the air for only a second before her feet struck the ground, a jarring impact that made her jaw click shut. She let herself fall to her right side on the grass. Her right knee and shoulder ached, but she was alive and no bones were broken. She couldn't ask for more than that.

She stood and looked at the house she'd called home for years; the house she'd so proudly purchased for herself with money she'd made from her medical practice. Now, all she could see through the windows was fire. The antique cherrywood clock—the only thing of her mother's Laura still owned—was gone, eaten by the fire. Laura's chin quivered. Her eyes stung. An intense heat radiated from the glass. At any moment, the thermal stress could cause them to break.

You need to get away from the house. Keep it together. Now's not the time to lose it.

Laura retreated to the street. In the distance, she heard approaching sirens. Lights snapped on in some her neighbors' houses. She pulled the phone from her waistband, relieved to see it had survived the fall about as well as she had, and called Booker.

There was a part of her that wanted to rage, to cry, to scream, but she held it all in check. *Now isn't the time*, she told herself again, but as soon as Booker picked up and she heard his voice, she finally let herself break down.

"We're going to get to the bottom of this, I promise you, Dr. Powell," Chief Morales said. The lights from the fire trucks flashed against one side of her face. "We're going to find out exactly what happened."

"Thank you," Laura said.

Booker had his arm around her, and she leaned into him

for comfort. They stood on the lawn across the street while the firefighters blasted her house with water. The fire was still burning, but not as strongly, and it had already been extinguished in some spots. What she could see of the interior now wasn't as bad as she'd imagined. There was fire damage, but her home wasn't the smoldering pile of ashes she'd expected. The house was still standing. That was something, at least.

Her neighbors stood on their lawns to watch the spectacle. Laura felt strangely embarrassed, as if it were her fault all this commotion had come to their quiet street in the middle of the night. Part of her expected to get a handwritten note from her busybody neighbor Melanie Elster, reminding her that raging house fires were frowned upon by the Homeowners Association— but she reminded herself Melanie died last year during the spore outbreak. Christ, Laura's house had survived the fires back then only to burn now, stupidly, when the danger was long gone. Heartbroken, she turned her face to Booker's chest.

"I've got you," he said.

"Does she have a place to stay tonight?" Morales asked him.

"She can stay with me," Booker said. He looked down at Laura. "Does that sound okay?"

Laura nodded. She wiped the tears from her face. "I've got some things there I can wear."

"Try to get some rest," Morales said. "I'll get in touch tomorrow, and we'll send a report to your insurance company."

Insurance. Laura couldn't even imagine handling something like that right now. She just wanted everything back the way it was. She wanted to wake up in her bed and discover it was all a bad dream, but as she rode silent and dazed in Booker's car to his house, she kept not waking up.

It was real. It was all real. She'd lost her home.

When they got to his house, he sat her down on the living room couch, wrapped a throw blanket around her shoulders, and made a cup of peppermint tea to soothe her nerves. In the safety of his house, with warm tea in her stomach, she finally stopped shaking and felt more like herself.

Booker sat next to her and put his arm around her again. "You're sure you're okay?"

"I'm sure."

He was sweet for being so worried about her, but she didn't want to talk about it. It was too new, too raw. She couldn't find the words to describe everything she felt. None of the words felt big enough, or painful enough. She took a sip of tea from the mug and wished it were whiskey instead.

Booker's laptop was open on the coffee table. A webpage on the monitor showed a shallow opening in some rocks. Within the opening was a tangled mass of copperheads.

"What's this?" Laura asked, putting down her mug to bring the laptop closer.

"Just more research," he said. "We don't need to talk about it now."

"No, it's okay. I need something to take my mind off the fire."

"Well, I found out that while most snakes lay eggs, copperheads give live birth to their young," he said. "Females give birth communally in special places in or near the den called birthing rookeries."

Laura looked at the picture again. The copperheads in the rocks looked swollen in their lower halves. Pregnant.

"Honestly, I don't know if this is helpful, or if I was just trying to keep busy." Booker looked at the picture and shook his head. "I can only imagine what happened to the nest after the first batch of basilisks were born."

"What do you mean?"

"Mother snakes don't take care of their young," he said. "The snakelets are on their own to find food from day one. I suspect the first prey the basilisks killed were the original copperheads themselves."

"They...ate their mothers?" The thought was horrifying.

"Unfortunately, it's not that unusual in evolution for a new species to eliminate the old," he said. "Anthropologists think there used to be as many as nine distinct human species on Earth. Now there's only one. The prevailing theory is that *Homo sapiens* came along and killed the rest."

She didn't want to think about it. She couldn't think about anything right now, not the fire, not this. It was all too much. She felt full up, and any new bit of information bounced off her. She finished her tea, and they climbed the stairs to Booker's bedroom. There, she had the surprising presence of mind to change into the fresh pajamas she kept there so she wouldn't have to spend the rest of the night in wet ones that smelled of smoke. In bed, Booker held her as she tried to relax enough to sleep, but even after he drifted off, she was still wide awake and staring into the blackness of the room.

Her mind fired into overdrive, reviewing every cause of house fires she could think of, trying to piece together what could have happened. She hadn't turned on the oven or any other heating appliance; Booker had brought takeout for dinner. She certainly hadn't made a fire in her fireplace in this sweltering summer weather. There was no faulty wiring in her house. She wasn't a smoker, and she hadn't left any candles burning.

Then there was the matter of the smoke alarms. What were the odds the alarms—*all* of them—would suddenly stop working the night a fire broke out?

25

Laura got out of bed early. She showered, dressed, and was eating breakfast by the time Booker limped his way gingerly down the stairs. She was too on edge to sit at the breakfast table, so she ate a bowl of muesli while standing at the kitchen counter.

"Morning," Booker said. He was still in the sweats and t-shirt he'd slept in. "How long have you been awake? I didn't hear you get up."

"I never fell asleep," she said, putting the empty bowl in the sink. "I've already called Dae-jung. He'll be here in a few minutes."

Booker poured himself a cup of coffee from the pot she'd made. "Dae-jung? Why?"

"I told you, I'm going back to kill the basilisks. He has the pyrethrin for me."

He put the mug down. "You're still going through with it after what happened last night?"

She'd spent much of her sleepless night asking herself that same question. After the fire, part of her wanted to curl into a ball and ignore everything else until she could process what happened, but her thoughts kept turning back to Rebecca and Francis, even Meredith. Laura had come to care about all of them. Leaving them at the mercy of the basilisks for a third night was unthinkable.

"I have to," she said. "I have family in Valley Grove, and they need my help. It has to be today, and it has to be during the daytime, when the basilisks are asleep. If I put it off any longer, more people could die."

"Laura, *you* almost died. Let someone else do this."

"There's no one else," she said. "I've thought this through, Booker. It's up to me."

Booker sighed and turned away from her to retrieve his coffee mug. She knew what he was thinking. She didn't need to see his face to know.

"You think I'm being stubborn," she said.

He took a sip of coffee and turned to her. "I think you've just been through a huge, traumatic event, and I'm worried that you're not thinking clearly."

"I am, I promise you," she said. "I've gone over it again and again in my head. I can't put this off."

"Then I'm coming with you."

"No," she said. "Your leg still isn't fully healed, and I don't want you anywhere near the basilisks if you can't move quickly."

"That's not fair."

"But it's true," she said. "I couldn't forgive myself if anything happened to you."

"Funny, I was going to say the same thing about you."

The doorbell rang.

"That'll be him," Laura said.

Booker sighed again and went to open it. Dae-jung stood on the doorstep with two large plastic backpacks by his feet. The backpacks were covered in knobs and dials, and each had a long metal wand attached by a vinyl hose holstered to its side.

"You must be Booker," he said, adjusting his wire-rimmed glasses. "I'm Park Dae-jung. I work with Laura. It's nice to finally meet you."

Booker shook his hand. "Don't take this the wrong way, but I wish you weren't here."

Dae-jung nodded. "I hear you. I have my concerns about this, too."

Laura leaned against the kitchen doorframe and crossed her arms. "You're both very sweet, but there's nothing to worry about."

"Hey, Laura." Dae-jung waved from the doorway. "I'm so sorry about the fire. Are you all right?"

"I'm fine." She wished everyone would stop asking her that.

Booker invited him inside. Dae-jung picked up the two backpacks and carried them in. Liquid sloshed noisily inside them as he set them down again in the living room.

"So that's the pyrethrin, huh?" Booker asked.

"It's extremely poisonous to snakes," Dae-jung explained. "Hit them with the spray and they'll die almost immediately."

"*Almost* immediately?" Booker said.

Laura ignored his comment and knelt in front of the backpacks for a closer look. "Show me how it works."

"These are top-of-the-line fumigation sprayers. Each one holds three gallons of a pyrethrin solution. See this?" Dae-jung pointed to a covered compartment on the face of the backpack. "That's an eighteen-volt lithium-ion battery, which means you can set the sprayer on an automatic spray instead of having to constantly manually pull the trigger. I've made sure it's fully charged. Now, this is the wand." He pulled the wand free of the side holster to show her the trigger at the opposite end from the nozzle. "It's got an adjustable pressure control that gives you a range of anywhere from eight to one hundred and fifteen psi. If you're spraying on low pressure, the battery can last up to three hours on a single charge. On high pressure, the spray can reach over thirty feet away, but of course that'll eat up the battery life."

"They look heavy," Booker said.

Laura raised an eyebrow at him. He was still hoping she would change her mind, but if he thought heavy equipment would be the reason, he was wrong.

"It's about twenty pounds fully loaded, but it's got a lot of padding that makes it easy to wear," Dae-jung said.

She looked over the second backpack, which was identical to the first. "Do you think I'll need both of them?"

"No," Dae-jung said. "One of them is for me. I'm coming with you."

She stood up. "What? No. I can't ask you to do this, Dae-jung."

"Then it's a good thing you didn't," he said.

"Dae-jung—"

"Hey, we're taking my car, aren't we?" he said. "If I'm driving, I'm going the whole nine yards. You didn't expect me to wait in the car, did you?"

"Yes, I did," she said.

"Fat chance."

"I like this guy already," Booker said. "Thanks, Dae-jung. She wouldn't let me go with her. I feel a lot better knowing she's not doing this alone."

"She's definitely *not* doing this alone."

Laura let out an exasperated sigh. Now she was getting it from both of them.

"Fine," she said. "With two of us, it'll get the job done faster anyway."

"Great," Dae-jung said. "I've got N95 respirators and safety goggles in the car. It's best not to inhale the pyrethrin or get it in your eyes."

"When can we go?" Laura asked.

"No time like the present," Dae-jung said. "The more daylight that's available to us, the better."

"Hold on," Booker said. "Before you go, I think I've got something that can help you."

He went to the coat closet and dug around on the floor, tossing boots and shoes aside. He returned with four thick sleeves of brown fabric, each about a foot long.

"What are these?" Dae-jung asked.

"Snake gaiters," he said. "They cover your feet and lower legs to protect you from snake bites. I used to take a lot of long nature hikes in California. You can never be too careful with the rattlesnakes out there." He handed them over. "Any basilisk that tries to bite you will get a mouthful of high-strength ballistic fiber instead."

"Thanks, Booker," Laura said. She stood on her toes and kissed him. "I know this is hard for you. I appreciate it."

"Check in with me," he said. "I'll keep my phone on me. You do the same. And be careful, both of you."

"I will be."

"Me too," Dae-jung said.

While she and Dae-jung fastened the gaiters over their legs, tightening the straps for a snug fit, Booker asked, "What do I tell Chief Morales? She said she's coming by with your insurance paperwork today."

"If she asks where I am, there's no point in lying to her," Laura said.

"Feel free to lie about *me*, though," Dae-jung added. "I'm not ready to update my résumé again."

"I'll take care of the paperwork when I'm back," Laura said.

"You *better* come back."

She kissed him again. "I promise."

In the car, Dae-jung drove eastward out of Sakima while Laura fidgeted in the passenger seat. She hoped she was right about the basilisks being nocturnal. The hypothesis had only been an educated guess based on circumstance. What if she was wrong? She chewed her fingernail and tried not to think about it. Unfortunately, putting it out of her mind only made room for new questions about last night's fire. She couldn't win.

Dae-jung interrupted her maelstrom of thoughts. "Remember those chemical compounds I couldn't identify in the snake venom?"

"Yes," she said, grateful for the distraction.

"It turns out there's a good reason I couldn't," he said. "They're artificial."

"Artificial?"

"Those compounds don't exist in nature."

"Then where did they come from?"

"I don't know," he said. "Even if they started out as naturally occurring chemicals, something tainted them. Turned them *un*natural."

"What could do that?"

He shrugged. "I don't know that, either. It would have to be potent. Strong enough to force chemicals together that normally wouldn't cooperate. Only, I can't think of anything in nature that could do that."

"What about something manmade?"

"Like what?" he asked.

"Like genetic modification?"

Dae-jung glanced at her. "It's possible, but I'm having a hard time imagining the religious zealots of Valley Grove messing around with something like that."

"They're not," she said. "Thurmond Biotech is."

26

They parked behind the abandoned gas station on the old road that led to Thurmond Biotech. Retrieving their equipment from the trunk, Laura tucked her N95 respirator into her pocket and hung the safety goggles around her neck. She wrapped an LED rechargeable headlamp around her forehead and hoisted her fumigation sprayer onto her back. It was heavy, but the padded shoulder straps and extra cushioning against her back made it tolerable. The pyrethrin solution sloshed noisily inside it.

"We're going to have to go the rest of the way on foot," she said.

"You're sure we can't just ask them to let us onto their property?" Dae-jung asked, putting on an LED headlamp identical to hers.

"Trust me, they won't unless we have a warrant," she said.

He strapped on his fumigation sprayer. Wearing their oversized backpacks with attached wands, she thought the two of them looked like something out of a cheap *Ghostbusters* knockoff.

She unhooked the wand from the side of her backpack and examined the grip and the trigger. "You're sure this stuff will work?"

"It has to," he said. "I've never heard of a snake that can survive pyrethrin."

"These aren't normal snakes," she reminded him.

"It's still our best shot at taking out the den."

She replaced the wand on her backpack. "We have to kill them all. If any of them get away and reproduce..."

"I know," he said. "I saw what happened to Malachai

Applewhite, before *and* after. I know what's riding on this."

She took a deep breath. "All right. Let's go."

They walked, keeping to the woods so they wouldn't be spotted by any passing cars. The heavy weight on their backs didn't make it easy. Neither did the heat. By the time they reached the chain link fence that surrounded Thurmond Biotech's property, Laura's face was dripping with sweat. She wiped an arm across her forehead and got her bearings.

They were facing the back of the plant. Through the fence she saw the cliff below the building and the lake with Valley Grove on the far side. She searched the rocky face of the cliff for the entrance to the cave Craig Hutsell said were there, but she couldn't see anything from this far away. They needed to get closer, but with the heavy fumigation sprayers on their backs, climbing the fence wasn't an option. She followed the fence with her eyes all the way to the lake, where the posts went into the water. They grew successively shorter in size until the fence ultimately ended about ten feet from the shore. That was their way in.

"Hold it," Dae-jung whispered.

On the other side of the fence, a procession of five men descended the grassy, weed-covered slope toward the lakeshore. Four of them were security guards—three walking with their hands on the butts of their holstered guns, the fourth pushing a hand truck that was loaded with something large covered in a tarp.

The fifth man in the group was Hugh Robertson, president of Thurmond Biotech. His white hair looked even whiter in the sun. He had to be the one Malachai saw hiding something in the cave, and from the looks of it, he was about to do it again.

Hugh led the guards to the base of the cliff. They stopped halfway across. The guard with the hand truck wheeled it toward the cliff before disappearing from view into the cave.

Hugh pulled a pen out of his suit blazer and wrote something on a clipboard. The three remaining guards outside the cave looked around to make sure they weren't being observed. Laura ducked into a crouch behind a tree. They couldn't get caught now. If they did, it was over. Even if she tried to explain about the basilisks to Hugh, he wouldn't care. He'd have them thrown in jail before he let anyone see what he was hiding in the cave.

And she had a pretty good idea of what he was hiding in there.

The guard returned, his hand truck empty now and the tarp folded neatly under one arm. Hugh led them back up the hill. Once they were gone from sight, Laura and Dae-jung sprang to their feet. They moved quickly toward the lake and waded out to the end of the fence, the water a shock of cold on a hot day. The lake wasn't deep; ten feet from the shore, it only reached her knees. They rounded the fence and hurried back to the shore on the other side, moving as quickly as the waterlogged snake gaiters on their legs allowed. Between the gaiters and the fumigation sprayer on her back, she was winded when they reached dry land, but there was no time to rest. The guards could return at any time.

They followed the footprints in the wet earth to where Hugh and his men had stopped in front of the cliff. There, partially obscured by an outcropping, she found the cave mouth, narrow and slanted like a jagged lightning bolt etched into the stone. It opened into darkness like a gaping throat.

Dae-jung swallowed nervously. "You're sure the den is in there?"

"I'm sure," she said. "Copperheads like to den in enclosed spots near water. This would suit them perfectly."

She switched on her headlamp and shone it into the cave mouth. The beam split the dark but didn't penetrate more than a few feet. She saw rocks, muddy soil, and a few clusters of weeds, but no snakes. The den itself would most likely be much farther back, where it remained cool and dark.

"Are you ready?" she asked.

"Not really," he said, "but I don't think I'll be any more ready if you ask me later."

They took a moment to put on their N95 respirators and adjust them for a proper fit, then their safety goggles. They entered the cave. Laura led the way, keeping her light aimed at the ground in front of her in case any basilisks appeared. Dae-jung used his headlamp to help illuminate their surroundings.

The muddy ground sucked at their shoes. The air was cooler inside the cave but sticky with humidity. Dark, dry pellets dotted the ground.

"Snake droppings," she said, grateful she couldn't smell anything through the N95. "We're definitely in the right place."

"Hooray for us," Dae-jung said flatly. "I read that sometimes copperheads share their dens with other snakes. We should be on the lookout."

"If there *were* other snakes here, they're dead now. The basilisks eat everything. Look."

She pointed her headlamp at a cluster of small white bones on the ground. They belonged to a small animal, a mouse or a rabbit. A dark stain blotted the mud under the bones where the animal's flesh had liquefied for the basilisks to ingest. She shone her light ahead and saw the ground was littered with bones from all manner of animals unlucky enough to venture into the cave. At one time, petrified animals must have lined the cave floor like the shores of Lake Natron at low tide.

She thought about the sheer number of snakes that had attacked Valley Grove. It wouldn't have taken long for that many of them to exhaust their natural prey on this side of the lake. No wonder they swam across at night. They were desperate for a new source of food.

The cave widened the deeper they walked. The number of bones on the ground increased, as did the amount of snake droppings. She could see where the guard's feet and the wheels of the hand truck had crushed the fragile bones and left prints in the mud.

Something up ahead glinted like metal in the beam of her headlamp. As they got closer, she saw a collection of 55-gallon industrial steel drums. It wasn't a stretch to conclude that one of these drums had been under the tarp on the hand truck. This was what Malachai Applewhite saw Hugh Robertson hide in the cave. She could guess what was in them. Hugh had already told her when she asked about the anti-aging drug Thurmond Biotech was working on.

Genetically modified biological substances.

Mother Nature always has the answer, Dr. Powell, but sometimes you just need to give her a little push.

Dae-jung took photos with his phone for evidence. Some of the drums looked considerably older than the others, partially buried in the mud and spotted with rust. Thurmond Biotech's illegal dumping had been going on for some time. The oldest drums had rusted through and were leaking their contents into the mud in toxic pools and streams, a dull red in color like old blood. The same color as the stripes on the sides of the basilisks.

Dae-jung took pictures of the spill. He lowered his phone and pointed at one of the drums.

"What does that writing on the side say?"

Laura walked over to the drum he pointed at. Stenciled on the side was the name Thurmond Biotech had given to the genetically modified biological substance inside: BSLSK-168.

"Oh my God," Laura said, finally understanding what Craig Hutsell had told her. *"Basilisk."*

27

Booker was so worried he could barely taste his breakfast. After Laura and Dae-jung left, he'd showered, dressed, and tried to eat something, but his mind kept torturing him with images of Laura dead and petrified on the ground like a grotesque toppled statue, her features obscured by writhing snakes. He trusted her, he knew she could handle the task at hand and wouldn't take any unnecessary risks, but that didn't quell his fears. He looked at the muesli in his bowl and decided there was no point in trying to finish.

When the doorbell rang, it was a welcome distraction. He opened it to find Chief Morales on his doorstep, her eyes hidden behind mirrored sunglasses. She had a manila folder tucked under one arm. Though she'd been the chief of police for the better part of a year now, last night at Laura's house was the first time he'd actually met her. She didn't strike him as someone who made a lot of small talk. Even now, she got right to business.

"Good morning, Mr. Coates," she said. "Can I speak to Dr. Powell?"

"Laura's not here," he told her. "She and Dae-jung went to find the snake den. Apparently, they figured out how to kill them. Some kind of chemical spray."

"You're kidding me." Chief Morales took off her sunglasses and rubbed the bridge of her nose. "I can't believe she went back. She's a damned fool. They both are."

"Nothing I said could change their minds." He nodded at the folder under her arm. "Are those the insurance papers? I can give them to her when she gets back."

"Yes, thank you." Morales handed the folder to him. "It's

the preliminary report on the damage of the house. The investigation is still ongoing, but this should get the ball rolling with her insurance company."

"Thanks for staying on top of this," Booker said. "It means a lot to both of us."

"I intend to make sure Dr. Powell gets answers," Morales said. "Provided she doesn't get herself killed first. You'd think she'd want to stay as far away from those damned snakes as possible."

"You don't know her very well, do you?"

"I'm starting to."

Over Morales's shoulder, Booker saw a small truck with a square, boxy cargo container in back parked at the curb. The words SAKIMA POLICE DEPARTMENT were written along the side, and underneath that, REFRIGERATED HAZARDOUS MATERIALS TRANSPORT.

"You drove here in that?"

"I'm on my way back to Valley Grove to pick up a body," she said.

"Craig Hutsell's body?" he asked. When she raised an eyebrow, he added, "Laura told me what happened."

Morales nodded. "Officer Rosenberg was supposed to assist me, but he was called away at the last minute, so I'm on my own."

"How about I go with you?" Booker said. "You'll need a hand transporting the body and I wouldn't mind an opportunity to make sure Laura's okay. Two birds and all that."

"I appreciate the offer, Mr. Coates, but you're a civilian and it really ought to be an official member of the police department."

"Then I guess you'll just have to deputize me."

Booker tossed the file onto the living room couch, stepped outside next to Morales, closed the door behind him, and started walking to the truck. Morales put her sunglasses back on and followed him.

"Mr. Coates," she said, but when he didn't stop, she let out an annoyed grunt. "Now I know where Laura gets it from."

"Actually, I learned it from her," he said, opening the passenger-side door and getting in.

"It figures." Morales got in the driver's seat and turned the key in the ignition. As the engine rumbled to life, she said, "I never agreed to this, you know."

"And yet you started the truck anyway."

Chief Morales grunted again and pulled into the street. As they drove to Valley Grove, Booker tried to strike up a conversation.

"So how are you liking Sakima?" he asked.

"It's fine," Morales said.

He nodded, waiting, but no more words came.

"I grew up in Sakima," he said. "I spent a few years in California, then came back last year. I'm at the high school now. I teach science."

"Uh huh," Morales said.

"My degree is in botany, but I have experience with just about every branch of science."

"Uh huh."

"You're...not interested in talking, are you?"

"Nope."

They rode the rest of the way in silence.

When they arrived in Valley Grove, Booker was surprised at how quaint the village looked. He wasn't sure what he'd been expecting—a compound like the Branch Davidians? Lopsided shanties like the backwoods polygamists? The modest houses and neatly trimmed yards looked like something out of a magazine. In the distance was a large hill dotted with gravestones, and at the foot of the hill stood a large, barn-like wooden structure that he took to be their church. Morales parked the truck in front of a house on the main road.

Villagers on the sidewalks and lawns stopped what they were doing and stared as he and Morales got out of the truck. More people emerged from their houses to see what was going on. No doubt they were curious about the truck, particularly the signage on the side that identified it as belonging to the Sakima PD, but it wasn't just that. It wasn't lost on Booker that every face he saw was Caucasian. Their community was insular in the extreme, all but ignoring the world beyond the village borders. It wouldn't surprise him if he was the first Black man any of them had seen.

Morales knocked on the door. A young teenage girl with frizzy red hair and freckles opened it.

"Hello," Morales said. "May I speak to Shepherd Eliezer?"

"He's not here," the girl said.

"You're his daughter, aren't you? Meredith, right?"

The girl nodded.

"Meredith, can you tell me when he'll be back?"

She shrugged. "I don't even know where he went. I haven't seen him since this morning's services."

"He left you home alone?"

She shrugged again. "I'm supposed to be at Bible study, but I don't even care. I'm not going anymore."

She noticed Booker standing behind Morales, and her big brown eyes got even bigger.

"Hey, you're Laura's boyfriend, aren't you?" she said. "She showed me a picture of you!"

That surprised him. "You met Laura?"

Meredith nodded happily. "She's my friend."

"Have you seen her today?" he asked.

"No, is she here?" Meredith poked her head out the door and looked to either side, as if she might spot Laura walking by.

"If you don't mind," Morales interrupted. "We're here on official business. We've come to collect Craig Hutsell's body. I have a warrant from a New York State judge if you want to see it."

Meredith shrugged once more and opened the door wider to let them into the house. The girl led them down a short hallway to a closed, white-painted door. She put her hand on the knob and paused.

"Is it okay if I don't look?" she asked. "I saw it last night, and I don't want to see it again."

"You mean the body?" Morales said.

"No," Meredith said. "I mean this."

She opened the door and turned away quickly. Booker and Morales stepped into the sitting room. It smelled awful, much worse than he expected a day-old body to smell. Only, there was no body, just a large, gooey, reddish stain on the floor in which floated a collection of slimy white bones. On the couch above it was a wet disheveled blanket, more of the red, frothy sludge, and a few additional bones, including an overturned skull. Booker's stomach flipped and he looked away. Morales simply shook her head and sighed.

"We're too late," she said. "I was hoping we'd get here in time to contain the body before it broke down. I'll have to notify Mr. Hutsell's next of kin that there's no body to bury."

"I think the same thing happened to my stepmother," Meredith said, still with her back to the room.

They joined her in the hallway. Meredith closed the door quickly, making sure not to look inside.

"It's because of the snakes, isn't it?" the girl asked.

"Yes," Morales said. "We think there's something in the venom that breaks down the tissue after a certain amount of time."

Meredith thought a moment. "That means my father's wrong. It's not because they were bad people, or that God was angry with them."

Booker was taken aback. "Your father said that?"

The girl's face darkened. "I don't care what he says anymore. He may be the Shepherd, but he's wrong about everything. Other people got bitten by the snakes, and I bet their bodies are all melted now, too, and they were *good* people."

"You're sure you don't know where your father is now?" Morales asked.

Meredith shook her head, her mouth squeezed into a hard, flat line. "I hope he's dead."

28

Laura and Dae-jung walked deeper into the cave. The dirt floor slanted gently downward as they went. Thin, dull red streams of the leaked substance flowed along the cracks and fissures at their feet like blood through veins. Following the streams led them to a small nook in the stone wall, inside of which several basilisks lay in a pool of the liquid. They were bloated and swollen, just like the pregnant snakes Laura saw on Booker's laptop. Their iridescent eyes glowed and seemed to change colors in the beam from her headlamp. The basilisks hissed a warning to stay away.

"It's the birthing rookery," Laura said.

Soon, these pregnant basilisks would give birth to live young. The toxic pool they were lying in—comprised of Thurmond Biotech's BSLSK-168—was undoubtedly the mutagen she was looking for, the cause of the new breed of copperheads that killed Malachai Applewhite, Craig Hutsell, Sharon Applewhite, and so many others. It was possible the leaked substance was creating new and worse mutations even now, *in utero*.

"Anything that touches strange matter becomes strange matter," she murmured.

"What?" Dae-jung asked.

"It's something Booker said." In the light of her headlamp, the basilisks hissed another warning and thrashed in the dull red liquid. "Those compounds you couldn't identify in the venom, I think they're from genetically modified substance in those drums. Snake skin is hygroscopic, it absorbs moisture from the air. Only, here in the rookery it's absorbing the substance, too. It's being absorbed by the mothers and passed onto the young, where it becomes part of their venom."

"The part that breaks the victims down into slush," Dae-jung said. "It's awful."

"Thurmond Biotech was looking for a way to slow the aging process," she said. "They wanted to enhance cells' immune function, but the experiment failed. What they developed crystallized the cells instead. Except it wasn't stable, and the cells broke down."

Dae-jung drew the wand from the fumigation sprayer on his back. Done with giving warnings, one basilisk in the birthing rookery lunged at him with its mouth open and its fangs glistening. Startled, Dae-jung stepped back, just out of the basilisk's reach. He didn't wait for it to try again. He engaged the trigger on the wand and sprayed pyrethrin over birthing rookery. Laura drew her wand, too. The trigger was more like that of a gas pump than a gun, but when she squeezed it, the result was no less lethal. The battery-operated mechanism in the pack whirred to life and sent out a steady stream of pyrethrin from the wand's nozzle. The basilisks in the rookery seized and suffocated with their mouths open, struggling to breathe. A few seconds later, they stopped writhing and lay as limp as cut rope.

Laura stowed her wand again, her heart heavy. She hated to see any living thing suffer, even the basilisks. None of this was their fault. As aggressive as they were, the basilisks weren't evil. They were just trying to survive. Hunting, mating, reproducing—it's what every animal on Earth did.

The real evil here was Thurmond Biotech. Illegally storing a toxic substance in the cave was directly responsible for the creation of the basilisks, and every death the basilisks caused.

She had no doubt the leaking drums kept so close to the lake had contaminated Valley Grove's water, too. It was likely the cause of the cancer that had killed so many in the village, including Meredith's birth mother and Laura's own aunt Gwen. All those deaths, too, could be laid at Thurmond Biotech's feet.

She was determined to see them pay for it.

29

Rebecca Ponder kneaded dough in a bowl the way her mother had taught her. He father searched for the bag of caraway seeds in the kitchen cupboards when the front door crashed open.

"Francis Ponder!" a voice called out angrily.

It sounded like the Shepherd, and from the sound of multiple footsteps in the hall, he'd brought the Order of the Faith with him. Rebecca froze, frightened, her hands still in the bowl. After the confrontation in the holy sanctuary yesterday, things had reached a boiling point between her father and the Shepherd. If the Shepherd was here now with his men, it wasn't for anything good.

"Stay here," her father said.

"Father…"

"Just stay here."

He left the kitchen. Rebecca grabbed a dish towel off the counter and wiped the flour from her hands, straining to listen. She needn't have tried so hard. The Shepherd shouted her father's name again, as loud as a thunderclap.

"I'm here," she heard her father reply. "What do you want, Eliezer?"

"*Shepherd*," Eliezer corrected him. "You hear how he disrespects the Church? He's learned nothing. Take him."

There was the sound of a struggle, shoes scuffing on the wooden floor, and her father's indignant voice. "What's the meaning of this? Let me go!"

Rebecca pushed down the dread that crept over her and quietly sneaked into the dining room. From there, she could look into the living room, where the men were. She crawled under the dining room table and let the long tablecloth hide her, the way she used to when she was little and played hide-and-seek with her parents. She peeked out from under the tablecloth and saw Fritz and Damien restraining her father by the arms. Shepherd Eliezer faced him with a triumphant smirk.

"You are a plague upon the Church of the Divine Chariot, Francis Ponder," the Shepherd said. "Your foolishness has brought the serpents upon us as punishment."

"Even you don't believe that," Francis said.

"Luckily, God has revealed to me what's needed to bring this plague to an end," the Shepherd continued. "As it was with Abraham and Isaac, there must be a sacrifice."

Francis laughed bitterly. "You never did understand the story of Abraham. It's not about God demanding a sacrifice, Eliezer. It's about His mercy in staying Abraham's hand."

Rebecca's heart swelled with pride for her father, but she was scared for him, too. She was used to him being at odds with the Shepherd, but nothing like this had ever happened before. All this talk about sacrifice put a bad feeling in her stomach.

"How far you've fallen, Francis," the Shepherd said. "Praise God your wife isn't still alive to see it."

Hearing him talk about her mother made Rebecca so mad she wanted to run out from under the table and punch him. Instead, though she was fuming with anger, she stayed where she was. Her father had told her to stay away for a reason.

"Gwen hated you, Eliezer," Francis said. "She hated how you act like a king and treat the rest of us like your subjects. And you know what? She was right. Look at you. Look what you've become. Do you even know anymore if you're the Shepherd or the wolf?"

Eliezer's face twisted in anger. "Get him out of here!"

Damien dragged her father toward the door. The more he tried to pull away, the rougher Damien was with him, grabbing him by the scruff of the neck like he was a misbehaving animal. Rebecca had to bite her lip to keep from crying at the sight of her father's anguished face. During the scuffle, the wooden chair next to the front door was knocked over, and the loud crash of it on the hardwood floor set every nerve in her body on edge. Finally, Damien muscled her father out of the house. Fritz remained behind with the Shepherd. She hated that red-bearded psychopath. The fact that he was still in her house was the only thing that kept her from running after her father.

"What about the girl?" Fritz asked.

Rebecca's stomach clenched. He was talking about *her*. What would Fritz do if he found her? Would he make her disappear like he did to everyone else who crossed the Shepherd?

"Never mind about Rebecca. She won't be a problem once we deal with Francis," the Shepherd said. "It's time that girl was matched to someone, anyway. It's time you were, too, my friend. Perhaps we can kill two birds with one stone."

Rebecca thought she was going to be sick. Married to Fritz? She'd sooner die.

The two men left. Rebecca stayed under the table, her heart pounding in her ears. She counted to fifty to be sure they didn't come back, then crawled out and went to the front door. She opened it slowly and peeked outside. Her father and the others were nowhere to be seen. Where had they taken him? What were they going to do to him?

She needed help. She ran to Meredith's house, knowing it was unlikely the Shepherd would be going there. Whatever he was planning to do to her father, whatever awful thing he meant by "sacrifice," she doubted it was anything he wanted to be out in the open.

When she got to the house, she banged on the front door with her palm and yelled, "Help! Meredith, help!"

Meredith opened the door. "Rebecca, what is it?"

"It's my father," she said. "They took my father!"

30

A sound reverberated through the dark of the cave that was unlike anything Laura had heard before. It was a low, eerie hum, almost a rumble. It reminded her of thunder, but it was constant, unceasing, like some kind of machine. She walked toward the sound.

"What *is* that?" Dae-jung said.

He swept his headlamp beam in front of them, looking for the source of the sound, but the pitch-black darkness ate the light after only a few feet. Laura paused and put one hand on the cave floor. The loose dirt didn't vibrate. Not a machine, then. Something else.

"It reminds me of the sound my cat makes when she purrs," Dae-jung said. "But this would have to be one hell of a big cat."

Laura kept walking. The sound grew louder as the light from her headlamp disappeared into a wider space. A cavernous hollow opened up at the rear of the cave. The floor sloped gently downward into a large crater-like basin. Probably, there'd been a subterranean lake here once, maybe even part of the lake outside, but it had dried up long ago. She shone her headlamp into the basin and gasped. They'd found the den.

It was like nothing Laura had seen in her research. Within the basin was an extensive knot of basilisks. The drone was deafening now and emanated from the snakes.

"What are they doing? Sleeping?" she asked.

"Copperheads don't sleep communally like this," Dae-jung said. "Maybe it's some new characteristic of the mutation?"

Laura shone her light over the scaly, sinuous shapes. There were so many of them. The droning continued. Listening to it now, it was more complicated than she'd first thought. There were higher notes and lower notes, some louder and some quieter, all integrated into the overall sound. It reminded her of a choir, and she realized suddenly that she had it all wrong.

"They're not sleeping," she said. "They're communicating with each other."

"I thought snakes communicated with pheromones," Dae-jung said.

"Not these," she said. "They're a brand-new species, remember?"

Joined together into a single mass, the basilisks were communicating through sound. Snakes couldn't hear airborne sounds very well, but their inner ears were attuned to picking up vibrations in the ground. And now, vibrations in each other's bodies, too. It was remarkable. The basilisks had developed a completely new form of communication. Once more, she felt a pang of regret that they had to be destroyed. There was so much to be learned from them.

A sudden light from behind her made her shadow stretch across the basin. She turned around. The coating of her safety goggles refracted the light into dizzying rainbow stars. She shielded her eyes with one hand and saw a figure coming toward them with a flashlight.

"Uh oh," Dae-jung mumbled. "We're busted."

"Hold it right there!" a voice echoed through the cave. "This is private property! You can't be here!"

It was one of the uniformed guards she'd seen earlier, a beefy man with round cheeks and a bushy moustache. She guessed he'd come back on a routine security sweep, spotted their footprints, and followed them into the cave. The guard shone his flashlight in her face, momentarily blinding her. When he moved the light off her to Dae-jung, she saw the guard had drawn his gun.

"What's with the masks?" the guard said. "Take those down. Let me see your faces."

They pulled down their N95s.

"You don't understand, we—" Laura started.

"Save it. Mr. Robertson will want a word with you."

Hugh Robertson would either have them escorted from the

premises or arrested. Either way, they'd never get back into the cave to finish the job. It would mean another night of terror for Valley Grove. Another night in which more people would die.

"If you'd just let us explain," she said.

"You can explain it to Mr. Robertson, or you can explain it to the police. Me? I don't really give a damn what you have to say. Now, let's go."

He waved them forward with the gun. They walked to him with their hands in the air. The loud drone from the den behind them stopped. The basilisks were finished communicating. She didn't like what that might mean.

"You have to get out of here," Laura told the guard.

"That's my line, lady." He used his gun to wave them on toward the cave entrance, then turned and followed them. He jumped suddenly. "Ow! What the fuck...?"

The guard pointed his flashlight at the floor and stared in disbelief at a basilisk hissing next to his foot. He raised his foot to flatten its head, but another basilisk lunged out of the darkness. Its eyes eerily reflected the light as it sank its fangs into his other ankle.

"Ah! God damn it!"

The guard tried to club the second basilisk with his flashlight, but more of them attacked from the darkness. A wave of snakes latched onto his legs and his batting arms. His gun went off, and the bullet ricocheted off the floor. Laura and Dae-jung ducked. The guard crumpled, and the basilisks went for his face and throat. He reared up again, screaming. Snakes dangled from him in writhing coils.

Dae-jung grabbed Laura by the arm. "Run!"

She hesitated, her training insisting she help the guard. The venom from the multiple bites he'd sustained would be coursing through his body already, dehydrating and crystalizing his internal organs and tissues, petrifying him even as she watched. There was nothing she could do. She sprinted away, following Dae-jung as fast as the heavy tank on her back would allow. Another gunshot rang out. She stopped, glanced over her shoulder, and saw the guard fall into a twisting, undulating mass of snakes. She ran. The basilisks swarmed over the guard's body and chased after her.

Dae-jung stopped as she caught up to him. Breathing hard, he pulled the wand from his fumigation sprayer. "It's now or never."

He was right. They wouldn't get another chance. She put her N95 respirator back on and yanked the wand off her backpack. The basilisks rushed toward them in a tumbling wave, eyes glowing in the beams of their headlamps. Laura squeezed the trigger, spraying a thin stream of pyrethrin into the oncoming horde. The mechanism whirred at her back. Basilisks spasmed and suffocated under the deadly spray, but for every one she and Dae-jung killed, there were dozens more that struck at the gaiters protecting their legs.

Laura moved the switch on her fumigation sprayer from low speed to high. She backed up and kept spraying. The mechanism whirred faster as the pressure and reach of the spray increased, killing more basilisks.

Still, they kept coming, their forked tongues lashing the air, their iridescent eyes shining. There were so many of them pouring out of the darkness that even with the pyrethrin giving them an advantage, Laura and Dae-jung were vastly outnumbered.

31

"What do you mean, someone took your father?" Booker said.

The dark-haired girl who'd burst into the house stared at him and Chief Morales, confused by their presence. Meredith took her hand.

"It's okay, Rebecca," she said. "They're with the police. They can help."

Rebecca's blue eyes welled with panic. "It was the Order of the Faith! They came and took him away!"

"Who are the Order of the Faith?" Chief Morales asked.

"The Shepherd's men," Rebecca said. "Damien Acker and Fritz Ruggen."

"My father's minions," Meredith said, her features darkening with anger. "Rebecca, I'm so sorry."

"Your father was with them," Rebecca said.

"Wait, the Shepherd *helped* take your father?" Morales asked. "Why?"

"My father challenged him for the Shepherdom," Rebecca said.

"And *my* father doesn't like being challenged," Meredith added.

Booker remembered Laura had nothing good to say about Shepherd Eliezer Applewhite. She'd called him controlling, domineering, power-hungry, and a few other words he wouldn't repeat around girls this young.

"When did this happen?" Morales pressed.

"Just now," Rebecca said. "We were at home and they barged right in!"

"Can you take us there?"

Rebecca led them outside. She and Meredith both hurried down the main road away from the Applewhite house. Booker's leg gave him trouble keeping up. Morales hung back with him.

"I'll be fine," he told her. "Don't lose the girls."

Morales sped up to join them as they got to Rebecca's house. As Booker limped closer, he saw the name PONDER written on the mailbox and the pieces slotted into place. Rebecca was the young cousin Laura told him about. That meant her father, Francis Ponder—Laura's uncle—was the one the Shepherd and his men had taken.

Laura needed to know. He called her, but it went to right to voicemail. That worried him.

"Laura, it's me. I'm in Valley Grove. I came to give Chief Morales a hand picking up Craig Hutsell's body, but something's happened. Francis Ponder has been taken away by the Shepherd. I'm with your cousin Rebecca now and heading over to her house. Call me as soon as you get this."

He hung up, hoping Laura was all right. When he joined the others inside Rebecca's house, Morales was inspecting scuff marks on the hardwood floor. Beside her was an overturned wooden chair.

"Looks like a struggle," Booker said.

Morales nodded. "He didn't go easy."

"They *dragged* him out of here," Rebecca said. "Do you think he's still okay, Meredith?"

Meredith hugged her. "Yes. I'm sure he is. I think my father is just trying to scare him. He wouldn't really hurt him," she said, but she didn't look too sure.

"Rebecca, your father is Francis, right?" Booker asked.

"Yes, how did you know?" Rebecca asked.

"I know our cousin Laura," he said. "I'm Booker."

Rebecca nodded. "Laura told me about you. She said she hoped we would meet someday, but I didn't want it to be like this. Will you help me find my father?"

"Of course I will."

The scrape of a shoe on the hardwood floor came from somewhere deeper the house. Booker froze.

"Is someone else here?" he whispered.

"There shouldn't be," Rebecca whispered back. She glanced around nervously. "I think it came from the kitchen."

"Wait here," Morales said.

She moved carefully toward the kitchen with one hand on her holstered gun. A moment after she disappeared through the kitchen door, there was the unmistakable sound of something heavy hitting the floor.

"Chief?' Booker called. There was no answer. "Chief, you all right?"

Something wasn't right. The girls felt it, too. Meredith and Rebecca stared wildly at him.

"I want you both to go outside," he told them.

Rebecca clung anxiously to Meredith. "But…"

"Please, just do it. If everything's okay, I'll come get you."

"What if everything *isn't* okay?" Meredith asked.

"Then I want you to find help. Now go."

The girls darted out the front door. Booker edged toward the kitchen. His knee gave a dull, annoying throb, angry at him for the amount of walking he was doing. He did his best to ignore it and opened the kitchen door.

A cardboard box had been overturned on top of the kitchen table, spilling out a heap of paper pamphlets. Next to the table, Morales lay face down on the floor. Her gun was missing from its holster.

"Chief!" Booker rushed into the kitchen.

A sharp pain blossomed in his skull as something hard struck him behind the ear. He fell, cursing himself for being stupid enough to miss someone hiding behind the door. The side of Booker's head hit the floor. Everything went dim and blurry. A dark pair of men's shoes appeared in front of him, followed by a second pair. Booker struggled to stay conscious. He felt like he was being pulled down into quicksand. He hoped Meredith and Rebecca would run. He hoped they were running already.

One of the men collected the spilled pamphlets and dumped them back into the box. He picked it up and carried it toward the kitchen door.

"You going to burn those yourself, Fritz?" the other man said. His voice sounded miles away.

"Why? You want to watch?"

The other man scoffed. "I don't get my kicks from fire the way you do."

"Whatever, Damien. We got what we came for. Let's go."

"Hang on, Fritz. What should we do with these two?"

Booker slipped into a numb darkness before he heard the answer.

32

Laura took a step back, then another step, all the while spraying pyrethrin at the oncoming horde. The mechanism inside the tank on her back whirred as loudly and quickly as helicopter blades. Beside her, Dae-jung sprayed furiously in wide arcs. The basilisks were undeterred, slithering and sidewinding over their dead kin in front of them. The problem wasn't just that they were aggressive; they were also starving. They'd exhausted their natural prey in the area. It was why they'd attacked Valley Grove, and why they kept surging forward now, mindlessly, fearlessly, hungrily.

In her mind, flames raged up the stairs toward her again, as hungry and relentless as the basilisks. She started hyperventilating behind her N95. She hadn't had time to process the fear she'd felt when her house was burning, and now it came blasting back at her like a hurricane, causing her throat to tighten. Booker was right to worry about her. She'd been a fool to attempt this so soon after the fire. She froze. The basilisks came at her, but it was a wall of fire she saw rushing toward her—

"Laura!" Dae-jung shouted. "Laura, are you all right?"

That was enough to snap her out of it. She forced herself to focus and continued her retreat. She swung the wand from side to side to spray as many of them as she could. She was hopelessly outnumbered. When she sprayed to one side, basilisks from the other side got too close. When she whipped the wand back again, basilisks on the first side took advantage. They were drawing closer by the moment. She and Dae-jung were forced backward. They were losing the battle.

Something hit her shin, hard as a punch. A basilisk with

its fangs bared struck at the gaiter over her leg. She sprayed it and kicked it away, reminding herself to thank Booker for the gaiters when she got the chance.

If she got the chance. It wasn't looking good.

More basilisks struck at her from the ground. She kept spraying, kept backing up.

"How many of these damned things are there?" Dae-jung yelled.

She wished she knew. Looking at the carpet of dead snakes that stretched all the way back into the darkness, she would have thought they'd killed most of them by now. Yet there always seemed to be more. The cave floor was a sea of iridescent eyes reflecting the light back at her.

Another basilisk struck her gaiter. She blasted it with pyrethrin. How much longer could this go on? Her goal to wipe out the basilisks entirely was starting to look impossible. Maybe if it wasn't just the two of them, maybe if they had help, a large team of people armed with pyrethrin sprayers, it would be different, but it *was* just the two of them. Her own stubborn refusal to be talked out of coming here had seen to that. Now it was going to get her and Dae-jung killed.

She took another step back. Her backpack hit stone. *Shit.* Somehow, they'd backed up against the cave wall. There was no place left to retreat. She and Dae-jung moved their wands back and forth frantically, the spray forming a chaotic mist in the light of their headlamps. More basilisks died. More slithered forward. It was an endless cycle.

Laura sprayed and sprayed until the mechanical whirring in her tank slowed, and then stopped. The high-pressure spray of pyrethrin from her wand trickled away to nothing.

"No, no, no!" she said, shaking the wand. "Come on!"

It was no use. The battery in her fumigation sprayer was dead.

The basilisks surged forward.

33

Booker woke up in absolute darkness. The back of his head ached where he'd been hit. When he touched it, he only felt a sore bump. No blood. *Thank God for small miracles*, he thought. He shivered in the unexpectedly cold air. Where was he? The sound of someone else's breathing came to him in the dark. He wasn't alone.

Booker pulled out his phone and activated the flashlight app. When the bright light snapped on, he saw he was in a small, square room with cement walls. There were no windows or doors. He was sitting on a hard cement floor, along with two other people: Chief Morales and a man Booker had never seen before. He was tall, in his fifties, with dark hair that turned silver at the temples. His face was bruised, and he had one black eye. Spots of dried blood dotted the front of his white dress shirt.

"Chief, are you all right?" Booker asked.

"I've been better," Morales grunted. She noticed the other man with them and said, "Elder Francis, I presume?"

"It's just Francis now," the man replied. "Shepherd Eliezer stripped me of my position. I guess he didn't like what I had to say."

He chuckled, then stopped with a wince. He touched his bruised face gently.

"You're Rebecca's father?" Booker asked.

Francis perked up. "Have you seen her? Is she safe?"

"She's with Meredith," Booker told him. "That's all I know."

"Please God, keep her safe." Francis leaned his head back gently against the cement wall. "And who are you, friend? I haven't seen you around here before. What did you do to get on the Shepherd's bad side?"

"My name's Booker. I came looking for Laura. I'm concerned about her. She's…we're together."

"You're with Laura?" Francis said. "Yes, that would definitely do it. He hates her, too."

"What is this place?" Morales asked.

Booker shone the light from his phone across the small room. A rusty iron ladder was bolted to the middle of the floor, leading up to a wooden trap door in the ceiling eight feet above them.

"It's cold in here. I'm guessing that means we're underground," he said. "Whoever knocked us out must have put us down here."

"The Order of the Faith," Francis said. "On the Shepherd's orders, I'm sure."

"They did that to you, too?" Morales asked. "Your face…?"

Francis nodded. "I'd say they got overzealous, but I'm pretty sure the Shepherd told them to rough me up. I've caused him a lot of aggravation. I suppose he wanted to return the favor."

Morales stood, wincing and rubbing the back of her neck. She climbed up the ladder and pushed on the trap door, but it didn't budge. Gritting her teeth with effort, she put her shoulder against it and pushed against the ladder with her feet, but the door stayed closed.

"It's no use, I already tried," Francis said. "It's locked from the other side."

"Of course it is." Morales sighed and climbed down again. "So how the hell do we get out of here?"

Booker shone his light around the room again, looking for a way out he might have missed. The walls were solid, but the light showed him something he hadn't before. A word was etched into the wall in rough, irregular letters.

MALACHAI

The Shepherd's son. The one whose petrified body had wound up on Laura's autopsy table. He'd been down here too, in this very room, and left his mark. Something for others to remember him by, or perhaps something to remind himself who he was when he was locked down here. From everything Booker had heard, he wouldn't put it past the Shepherd to shut his own son inside this tiny, dark cement room.

Some of the letters had dark blotches of dried blood inside them. A chip of broken cement stuck out from the final I. When he pulled it out of the wall, he saw it wasn't cement after all, but a piece of broken fingernail. Malachai had etched his name into the cement with his fingernail. It must have taken ages to do. Booker could only imagine how many times Malachai must have been locked down here.

"Does your phone have a signal?" Morales asked.

"No," he said. "The cement must be blocking it."

Francis pointed toward a dark lump in the far corner. "Friends, I don't mean to alarm you, but what is that?"

Booker shone his light in the corner. A canvas bag sat on the cement floor. The bag shifted suddenly as something moved inside it. The large, triangular head of a snake poked out of the bag's opening. Milky iridescent eyes with black vertical pupils glowed in the light. The snake tasted the air with its forked tongue and then slithered out.

34

Laura tried the trigger on her wand again, but it was no good. No more of the pyrethrin would come out. Her fumigation sprayer was useless.

Dae-jung sprayed pyrethrin in a wide arc, killing the basilisks that came too close. Then he quickly removed his backpack fumigation sprayer.

"What are you doing?" Laura said.

"There are too many of them, and your battery is dead," he said. "If we're going to get out of here alive, we need to think outside the box."

He twisted off the cap at the top of the tank and yanked out the intake filter. More basilisks came writhing over the carpet of the dead. Holding the tank by its backpack straps, Dae-jung swung it forward. The pyrethrin splashed over the approaching basilisks. They coiled and twisted as the deadly solution washed over them and put them into instant respiratory failure. He continued splashing more and more of it, creating a wide pool that spread across the cave floor, killing every basilisk it touched.

Laura removed her tank, opened it, and started splashing her remaining pyrethrin the same way. It killed basilisks by the dozens, its efficiency the difference between a six-shooter and a machine gun. She wished they'd done this from the start, just poured their full tanks of pyrethrin into the basin when the basilisks were gathered there and kill them all in one fell swoop. It took another fifteen minutes of splashing before nothing else moved in the darkness. Her arms ached from swinging the tank.

They dropped their empty tanks to the cave floor. Before

them was a sea of dead snakes, their iridescent eyes still eerily reflecting the light from her headlamp. They waited to make sure no more arrived, then started walking. There were so many dead basilisks, particularly near the spot where they'd cornered themselves, that the carcasses came up to their shins in places. They waded through the limp and tangled remains, stepping carefully. If any of them were still alive, they could strike without warning.

"We need to go back to the basin," Laura said. "We have to make sure we got them all."

"I was afraid you'd say that," Dae-jung replied. "Can't we just get out of here? I've had my fill of snakes for one day. Hell, I've had my fill for a *lifetime*."

"We have to be sure."

Walking through the cave was like wading through a bowl of thick, oversized noodles. More than once, her heart fluttered with panic as she felt a snake move against her leg, only to discover it was just a carcass shifting in the pile.

Soon the carpet of dead basilisks thinned. She found the dead body of the guard. He was contorted from the pain and already fully petrified. She picked up his gun.

"Just in case we find any more basilisks," she said.

When they reached the cavern in back, she looked down into the basin and saw it wasn't empty. There was a lone shape all the way at the bottom. From where Laura stood at the edge, it didn't look like a snake. It was fat and tubular, like the stub of a giant cigar.

"What is that?" Dae-jung said.

"I don't know."

They walked carefully down the slope to it. As they approached, Laura began to feel dizzy. Pain throbbed in her head. It was so strong, she had to pause a moment for fear that she would pass out.

Dae-jung felt it, too. He put a hand to his head. "What—what's happening?"

"I don't know," she said.

The cave swam around her. She concentrated on the ground in front of her and continued slowly down the slope toward the strange object at the bottom. The closer she got, the more powerful the feeling became, washing over her in pulsing waves. There was no doubt where it was coming from.

Close up, it looked almost like an earthworm, except it was nine feet long and thick as a tree trunk. It had the same coloring and hourglass markings as the basilisks, even the stripe of red scales on both sides, but those were its only features. She couldn't tell which end was which. It didn't appear to have a head. It was alive, twitching and shuddering, but it gave no indication that it was aware of them.

"What is this thing?" Dae-jung asked. A splotch of red grew on his N95 respirator.

"You're bleeding," she said.

Dae jung lifted his respirator. Beneath it, blood trickled from his nose. He wiped it away.

"I don't understand." He rubbed his head. "This headache, it's—it's worse than any I've had before."

The organism didn't look like it could move, at least not quickly. She figured it must have been at the bottom of the basin the whole time, beneath the mass of basilisks. That strange vibrating drone...she'd thought it was the basilisks communicating with each other. What if they were communicating with this organism instead? Or was *it* communicating with *them*?

She got as close as she could, but the thrumming waves of pain behind her eyes were almost too much for her. It felt like the blood in her head was boiling. Something hot and slick trickled from her nose. The organism's bloated midsection was actually a massive, squirming embryonic sac. Within it, something big twisted and writhed. She could just make out its serpentine shape through the thin membrane of the sac, and what looked like a crown-shaped crest upon its head.

Laura emptied the security guard's gun into the huge wormlike organism. She sent the last bullet into the creature that was growing inside it. Blood and amniotic fluid dribbled from the bullet hole. Her headache stopped instantly.

She dropped the empty gun to the cave floor. Neither the organism nor the creature inside it moved again.

35

"Get back!" Booker shouted.

The basilisk inched its way toward them. The black slit pupils in its eerily iridescent eyes fixed on them as they pressed themselves against the far wall. It wouldn't do any good. There was no place to hide, and not much space to put between themselves and the basilisk.

Morales reached for her holster only to find it empty. "Shit, they took my gun. Don't let that thing bite you. If it does, you'll be dead and petrified in half an hour."

"Great," Booker said. "Do you have any more uplifting news for us?"

"There's no antidote, either."

The basilisk slid toward them on its belly. It coiled its lengthy body, then lunged at Booker's leg. He darted out of the way. The basilisk missed him and collided with the concrete wall. He hoped the impact would break its fangs and render the snake harmless, but that was wishful thinking. The basilisk appeared only mildly dazed. Its fangs intact, it went after Francis next.

Francis jumped out of its path. Morales leapt nimbly over the basilisk, grabbed hold of the ladder, and scrambled to the top. The basilisk struck at Francis again. He darted aside and hurried up the ladder after Morales. Booker grabbed the rungs and went up next. All three of them crowded together at the top of the ladder. Morales tried to open the trap door in the ceiling again, but it was still locked from the other side. Francis and Booker joined in, pushing with everything they had, hoping the break the lock. It refused to give.

Morales glanced down. "The snake!"

The basilisk was starting to wind its way up the ladder's

side rail. Even at the top of the ladder they weren't safe.

"Take this and keep the light on the snake." Booker handed his cell phone to Francis. "Both of you stay here."

He let go of the ladder and dropped to the floor. A dull pain stabbed through his injured leg, bad enough to trip him up. He pushed himself as far from the ladder as he could. As he'd hoped, his presence drew the basilisk's attention away from the others. It slithered down off the ladder and belly-crawled toward him.

Booker backed away from it, circling the small room. He removed one shoe and held it in front of him. It wasn't the most efficient weapon, but the heel was made of solid wood. He could use it like a hammer to crush the basilisk's head. The only problem was getting close enough to do it without getting bitten.

"Booker, catch!" Morales called from the top of the ladder.

She took a small cylinder off her belt and dropped it down into his waiting hand. A can of pepper spray. He pointed it at the basilisk and pressed the button on top. A thin, powerful spray of concentrated capsaicin hit the basilisk in the face. It reared back, momentarily blinded, hissing and striking at the air.

Booker brought the shoe down toward its head. The basilisk darted aside at the last moment, and the heel caught it in the midsection. The basilisk hissed and struck at him.

Booker leaped back. The fangs missed him by centimeters.

"Shit," he said.

All he'd done was make the damned thing angry.

36

Walking out of the cave into the bright sunlight, Laura pulled the N95 respirator off her face, happy to breathe in fresh air again. Squinting against the bright light of day, she hung her safety goggles around her neck and took off her headlamp. Her thoughts went back to the bizarre organism they'd found at the bottom of the basin. Its coloring and the pattern of its scales marked it as a basilisk like the others, yet its mutation was far beyond theirs. Was it the next step in their evolution, spurred by the genetically modified mutagen, or was it something else? How had it grown so large? And that thing inside its embryonic sac…

"Do you think we got them all?" Dae-jung asked, pulling her from her thoughts.

They started walking. "We searched the cave. There aren't any left."

"There could be stragglers," he pointed out. "Out in the woods, or somewhere by the lake."

"I think they were all in that basin," she said. "Whatever was happening in there, it seemed…important. I think they all came back for it."

What had called them there? The organism? Was it possible?

Booker's words came back to her.

I've never heard of snakes working in a group before. If you think of it like a wolf pack, there would have to be an alpha. Who's giving the orders? Who's telling them what to do?

Dae-jung looked back at the cave mouth. "You still think it was some kind of communion?"

She knew he didn't mean it in a religious way, but she wondered if maybe it was. Could the strange, pregnant organism the basilisks had heaped themselves upon as they droned in unison be something they considered divine? Normally, the question would strike her as ridiculous. There was no indication snakes had the kind of intelligence necessary for complex concepts like religion. Yet she'd seen enough lately to wonder if it might be time for humankind to expand its definition of intelligence to something beyond a reflection of itself.

"I don't know what it was," she admitted.

"That crown," Dae-jung said. "You saw it too, didn't you? It was just like the picture on the website. What does it mean?"

Commonly known as the King of the Serpents, the basilisk is often pictured with a crown or a crown-like physical feature on its head.

"I don't know." She sounded like a broken record, but there were no answers to be had. The organism couldn't be removed for examination. With the amount of toxic material present in the cave, its remains had to be considered toxic, too.

"Hey, you!" a voice cried out. "Hold it right there!"

Another Thurmond Biotech security guard came running down the hill toward them, one hand on his holstered gun. Laura and Dae-jung broke into a run. The guard sprinted after them. When they reached the chain link fence, they scrambled up and over it, then dropped down into the woods on the other side. Laura looked over her shoulder as she kept running. Frustrated at their escape, the guard banged a fist against the fence and ran back up the hill, presumably to fetch his colleagues.

They hurried through the woods. Once they reached the access road, they continued to stay hidden among the trees. A Thurmond Biotech security jeep roared past them as they ducked behind a red maple. As soon as the jeep was out of sight, they continued carefully through the forest to the abandoned gas station. Circling around behind the building, Laura was relieved to see Dae-jung's car was still there. They got in quickly and drove away. Dae-jung kept their speed within the limit so they wouldn't attract any attention.

Finally, he let out a laugh and hit one palm joyously against the steering wheel.

"Sorry. It's the adrenaline," he said.

"First time running from security guards?" she asked.

He smirked. "First time since college."

Laura's phone buzzed in her pocket. She pulled it out and saw she'd missed a call from Booker while she'd been inside the cave without a signal. She put the phone to her ear and listened to his message.

"Laura, it's me. I'm in Valley Grove. I came to give Chief Morales a hand picking up Craig Hutsell's body, but something's happened. Francis Ponder has been taken away by the Shepherd. I'm with your cousin Rebecca now and heading over to her house. Call me as soon as you get this."

She called Booker. It rang and rang until finally his voicemail picked up.

"Booker, call me right away. Let me know what's going on," she said. She ended the call and chewed her fingernail. Shepherd Eliezer had taken Francis? Where? What was he planning to do with him?

"Everything okay?" Dae-jung asked.

"I think something's wrong," she said. "I need you to drop me off in Valley Grove."

"Sure, okay."

"While I'm there, I want you to drive back to Sakima and call the EPA and any other agencies that need to know about those drums of hazardous material Thurmond Biotech hid in the cave."

"Are you sure you don't need me in Valley Grove? If something's wrong…"

"No, I need you on this," she said. "We can't let Thurmond Biotech get away with what they did."

Dae-jung nodded. "Damn right, and I've got the pictures to prove everything."

When they reached Valley Grove, she had Dae-jung drop her off in front of Francis's house. Booker had said he was coming here, but that was more than an hour ago. He could be anywhere now. As Dae-jung drove off, Laura dialed Booker's number again.

It rang again without being answered, but this time, she heard his ringtone, the opening drum beat and funky clavinet riff of Stevie Wonder's "Superstition." It came from inside the house. Why wasn't he picking up?

She knocked on the door and was greeted with silence. Trying the handle, she found it unlocked and let herself in. She followed the sound of the ringtone into the kitchen. Booker's phone was on the floor. She ended her call and picked it up. Booker wasn't the type to just leave his phone lying around. Something wasn't right.

"Laura!"

Meredith came running into the kitchen with Rebecca at her side. They both looked pale and distraught, their eyes puffy from crying.

"Meredith? Rebecca? What are you doing here?" she said.

"Oh, Cousin Laura, the Shepherd took them!" Rebecca said, running to her and hugging her tightly. "He took my father, and then he took the others, too!"

"Fritz and Damien attacked Booker and Chief Morales. They knocked them out and dragged them away," Meredith said. "We saw it happen."

"We were hiding. They didn't catch us," Rebecca said, letting go of Laura. "We didn't know what to do. If we told anyone, they could hand us over to the Shepherd. We didn't know who we could trust."

"I'm calling the police," Laura said, taking out her phone again. As she dialed 911, she asked, "Where did the Shepherd take them?"

"I don't know," Rebecca said.

"I think I do," Meredith said. "The Penitence Room."

37

They ran back up the street to Meredith's house, skirting around it toward the concrete garage in back. They didn't make it that far. Shepherd Eliezer and the Order of the Faith burst out of the house and intercepted them. Eliezer grabbed his daughter in a bear hug around the waist, nearly lifting her off the ground. Damien caught Rebecca by the arm, twisting it hard and making the girl cry out in pain. Fritz seized Laura.

He put one arm around Laura's neck, the crook of his elbow at her throat. He squeezed his arm for a moment, choking her just to show that her life was in his hands, then loosened up as she gasped for air. He breathed hard in her ear, his red beard inches from her face.

"I don't know how you managed to crawl out of Hell, woman, but you made a mistake coming back here."

She had no idea what he was talking about, but the threat was clear. He wasn't going to let her leave Valley Grove alive.

"Stop squirming, child!" Eliezer bellowed as Meredith tried to break free of his grasp. "You'll be punished for this insolence!"

"Sharon told me what you did, *Father*." She spat the word like it left a bad taste in her mouth. "Before she died, she told me you stopped her from calling for an ambulance when that man was dying on our couch."

Laura's jaw dropped. "You did *what*?"

Meredith's face darkened with anger. "She said it was like the scales fell from her eyes and she finally saw you for the monster you are!"

"None of that means anything now," Eliezer said. "The man is dead. So are Sharon and the baby she carried, your brother, Meredith. They're dead because of you."

"It means you're a murderer!" Meredith said. "You know what else she said, Father? She gave me her blessing to follow my heart the way Mal did, even if it means leaving the Church of the Divine Chariot and Valley Grove behind. Even if it means leaving *you* behind. And that's exactly what I'm going to do!"

She kicked backward, ramming her foot into her father's knee. He howled in pain, releasing her. Meredith bolted for the garage. Damien threw Rebecca aside and darted after Meredith. Meredith got the garage door open just as Damien grabbed her.

Laura bit Fritz's arm hard enough to break the skin and taste copper on her tongue. He cried out, and while he was distracted, she broke away from him, spitting his blood on the ground. As Damien tried to drag Meredith away from the garage, Laura barreled her shoulder into him, catching him in the ribs. He spun off Meredith and lurched for Laura's throat. She grabbed him by the shoulders and drove her knee into his groin. Damien doubled over, coughing with his hands between his legs.

Laura ran into the garage with Meredith. The girl made a beeline for a trap door in the floor. She pulled back the bolt and threw open the door.

Fritz came up behind Laura. He turned her roughly toward him and punched her in the face. His knuckles caught her on the cheek, and she spun from the force of the blow before falling to the cement floor. She didn't know which hurt more, her face or the heels of her hands from trying to break her fall. She turned onto her back on the floor, dazed and shaking. Fritz loomed above her, his eyes blazing with an insane rage. He drew back his arm for another punch. She squeezed her eyes closed and put up her hands to block it.

The blow never landed.

She opened her eyes to see Booker had caught Fritz's arm. He drove his fist into Fritz's midsection, and the red-bearded man doubled over. With the wind knocked out of him, he stumbled out of the garage. Booker reached down and helped Laura to her feet.

"I'm here to rescue you," she told him.

"My hero," he said. "Are you okay?"

She touched her face. There would be a bruise, but no bones were broken. "Yes, are you?"

"Just barely. That crazy son of a bitch locked us down there with a basilisk."

She looked over at the trap door and saw Francis and Chief Morales climb out.

"So that's the Penitence Room," she said. "My God, he really is a madman. Where's the basilisk now?"

"It's still down there, I think," he said. "I tried to kill it, but you'd be surprised how fast those things move."

"Believe me, I know."

She hugged him, relieved he was all right. Sirens approached and flashing red and blue lights painted the interior wall of the garage, announcing the police had arrived. Morales went out to greet them. It was bad enough Shepherd Eliezer and his men had kidnapped and endangered the lives of civilians, but they'd kidnapped a police chief, too. They would get serious jail time for that. Laura was more than willing to testify at the trial to make sure they did.

She and Booker walked out of the garage into the flashing lights of the police cars parked at the house.

Rebecca ran to embrace Francis. "Father!"

"Rebecca," he laughed, scooping the girl up in his arms.

Laura smiled at the sight. An unfamiliar warmth spread over her. She never thought she would have family again, short of getting married and starting her own, but seeing her young cousin and her uncle locked in a joyous embrace left her feeling like she was part of something bigger than herself, something more important. Something lasting.

Uniformed officers led Damien Acker in handcuffs to the waiting police cars. Laura looked around the yard.

"Where are Eliezer and Fritz?" she asked.

Morales shook her head. "Gone."

38

Eliezer limped through the woods. His knee flared with pain from the kick his traitorous, ungrateful daughter had given him. He never should have let her out of the Penitence Room. He should have left her down there to rot. Or put a snake down there with her like he had with Francis and the others. She'd ruined everything, her and that outsider Laura. He'd been so close to eliminating the thorn in his side that was Francis. So close.

The pain in his knee grew sharper with each step. Finally, he stopped and leaned against a tree. "I have to rest. Just for a moment."

Fritz looked back in the direction they'd come. "We're not far enough away yet. They could still find us."

"I said I have to rest!" Eliezer growled. "Do not question my decisions, Fritz! I'm still your Shepherd!"

Fritz nodded. "Yes, Shepherd."

"How was Laura there?" he demanded. "I thought you told me that bitch was dead."

"I thought she was. I saw the angel myself."

Eliezer squinted at him. "The what?"

"I saw the *fire* myself," Fritz corrected himself quickly. "I saw her house burn."

"Obviously, she escaped," Eliezer said. "Your incompetence has cost us dearly, Fritz."

"Forgive me, Shepherd. The angel has never let me down before."

"Have you lost your mind, Fritz? What angel? What are you—"

A sharp pain stabbed his ankle. He looked down in shock, just in time to see a snake slither away. Apparently, he and Fritz weren't the only ones who'd escaped unseen. The snake from the Penitence Room had as well. It must have climbed up the ladder, then slipped out of the garage and into the woods, only to bite him now instead of its intended targets. Eliezer laughed at the irony, but the laughter ended quickly when he remembered what happened to those the snakes bit.

With an angry cry, Fritz crushed the snake's head with a stone. He knelt at Eliezer's side as the Shepherd collapsed to the forest floor.

"Fritz, you need to go," Eliezer said. "Leave me. I'll be dead soon."

"No," Fritz said. "No, that's not right, you're the Shepherd. I couldn't..."

"Enough, Fritz. Listen to me." Eliezer could feel the venom spreading up his leg from the bite wound. It felt like a hot, rising tide. Sweat beaded his forehead. Was this what Malachai had felt the day he died? "I don't have much time. There's something important you have to do. One last mission for me."

"Anything, Shepherd. You know that."

Eliezer winced as a strange, prickling pain overtook his leg. If he reached down and felt it, he was sure he'd discover his leg was already petrifying.

"I was chosen by God to be Shepherd," he said. "Only me. No one else."

Fritz nodded. "Only you, Shepherd."

"I would rather see the end of the Church of the Divine Chariot itself than allow an imposter to become Shepherd in my place," he said. "After this, the Elders will move to elevate Francis to the Shepherdom, I'm sure of it. You can't let it happen."

"But I'm not an Elder," Fritz said. "I won't have a vote."

Eliezer looked into his eyes. "You *can't* let it happen. Do you understand what I'm saying, Fritz?"

Fritz nodded. A slight smile of anticipation twisted the corners of his mouth. "Yes. I understand."

"Then go see to it," Eliezer said. "Don't let them catch you."

"Yes, Shepherd. Godspeed to you, until we meet again in the Kingdom of Heaven."

Fritz ran deeper into the woods. Eliezer stared up at the sky as his body slowly petrified. The pain was agonizing, almost exquisite, like the pain of the martyrs, but he refused to cry out. This was a test, God was testing him, and he refused to fail. Surely the Lord would see what a faithful servant he was. Surely He had reserved a seat for Eliezer Applewhite at His side in the Kingdom of Heaven. Surely this pain, this suffering, this ignoble death on the filthy forest floor was all part of His Divine Plan.

"And the Lord said unto Satan, Hast thou considered my servant Job, that there is none like him in the earth," Eliezer whispered as his insides crystallized and hardened.

If this were a service in the holy sanctuary, his congregation would have responded in unison with, "A perfect and an upright man, one that feareth God, and escheweth evil." Instead, the forest remained silent.

Soon, his soul would be free. Perhaps Elijah's burning chariot itself would appear, drawn by fiery horses to carry him to glory. But no chariot came. Staring up into the sky, Shepherd Eliezer saw only infinite emptiness, until finally his eyes saw nothing else.

39

Later that day, as the sun sank lazily toward the horizon, Laura and Booker stood with the two girls, Meredith and Rebecca, outside the holy sanctuary. The massive wooden building was abuzz with activity. Shepherd Eliezer's body had been discovered in the woods earlier, and word had spread quickly about how he'd kidnapped and tried to kill Francis—or *Elder* Francis, as he was once again known after having his position in the Church restored. Fritz remained at large. Chief Morales had returned to Sakima, but she vowed to come back and help the local police for as long as it took. She wouldn't rest until Fritz was captured.

With Eliezer dead, it was like a smothering lid had been lifted from the community. Some spoke without fear about how they'd always been aware of Eliezer's corruption. Others finally began to voice their suspicions out loud about the disappearances of those who'd defied the Shepherd. The shock of it had turned the Church of the Divine Chariot upside down. As Laura understood it, the Elders had called an emergency meeting of the entire congregation to address how they would move forward.

"Father says the Elders have agreed to name him Shepherd tonight," Rebecca said. "He's already inside, talking with them. They all agree that naming a new Shepherd will help us heal."

"And the reforms you two have been pushing for?" Laura asked.

"It's all going to happen. As soon as he's Shepherd, Father's going to announce that there will be a place for women in Church leadership." Rebecca put a hand on Meredith's shoulder. "He's also going to put an end to arranged marriages."

"Oh, thank God," Meredith said with relief.

"Poor Elder Bernard," Rebecca teased. "Without you, who will make mashed potatoes for him every night? It's the only thing he can eat without his dentures!"

Meredith poked Rebecca in the ribs, and the two girls laughed. Laura smiled. This was how it was supposed to be. A girl Meredith's age ought to be goofing around with her best friend, not preparing to marry a man old enough to be her grandfather.

"I should go find Father," Rebecca said. "Cousin Laura, Booker, are you sure you won't stay for the ceremony? You're welcome to. You're family, after all."

"Thank you, but I think we should go," Laura said. "We're still outsiders here."

"Not to me, you aren't," Rebecca said. She hugged Laura tightly.

"I'll be in touch," Laura said. "Please give Uncle Francis my congratulations."

"Goodbye, Cousin Laura. Thank you for everything." Rebecca hugged Booker, too, surprising him. He put his arms gently around her. "Goodbye, Booker. Take care of Cousin Laura. She's very special to me."

"She is to me, too," he said.

"I'll see you inside, Meredith," Rebecca said. She ran into the holy sanctuary with the last of the arriving congregants.

Rebecca weaved her way through the crowd of people milling about in the central aisle of the nave. Everyone was still in shock and needed to talk to each other about what happened. She wished they'd seen Shepherd Eliezer's true face sooner, the way she and her father always had. Some of them had been blinded by faith, firm in their belief that God would never allow a bad man to become Shepherd; others had kept silent out of fear of reprisal. All of that would change now. This was a new beginning for the Church of the Divine Chariot. No one had to live in fear anymore.

She spotted her father near the pulpit, once again wearing the red shawl that marked him as an Elder. He was deep in conversation with the other Elders. She didn't see Elder Bernard among them. She hoped he was off somewhere hanging his head in shame for being Shepherd Eliezer's ally. As far as she was concerned, the old man deserved to be stripped of his position as an Elder, but she knew her father wouldn't do that. He wasn't vindictive like Eliezer.

She was proud of her father. She'd always been proud of him, but she didn't think she'd even been as proud as she was now. She only wished her mother could be here to see him named Shepherd. Perhaps she *was* here, watching from Heaven and feeling just as proud.

The conversation the Elders were having looked important, so she decided not to interrupt. Rebecca turned to look at the congregation gathering in the holy sanctuary—and froze. Was that Fritz she saw in the back of the crowd? It couldn't be, and yet, she was certain she'd seen his unmistakable red beard. It was only a glimpse. Now she didn't see him anywhere.

Her eyes were probably playing tricks on her, but she had to be sure. She pushed her way through the crowd toward where she thought she'd seen him. He wasn't there, but a strange odor lingered in the air, sharp yet sweet. It emanated from a trail of clear liquid that ran along the base of the wall. No one else had noticed it yet. She followed the trail along the wall, trying to identify the odor that was at once familiar and peculiar.

She followed it down the length of the building, all the way past the pulpit to a hallway in the back. At the end of the hall, the door to the storeroom was open, and there was Fritz, surrounded by tools and paint cans. He was facing away from her, but his red hair was unmistakable. So were the empty plastic gas cans on the floor.

Now she knew why the odor was so familiar. It was gasoline.

Another shape appeared in the storeroom. It was Elder Bernard, jabbing a bony finger angrily into Fritz's chest. "Stop this at once, Fritz! It's madness!"

Fritz pushed Elder Bernard back, and the frail old man fell against the shelves. Fritz pulled a book of matches from his pocket. Elder Bernard hissed in pain from the fall but struggled back to his feet.

"You're insane," Elder Bernard said. "I'm an Elder of the Church! You will listen to me when I tell you to stop!"

He grabbed for the matchbook but only managed to knock it out of Fritz's grasp. Fritz had his hands around the old man's neck before he could make another move. Bernard scratched at Fritz's hands and slapped at his face, but Fritz kept throttling him, refusing to let go. Rebecca was rooted in place with fear, unable to move. She watched, terrified, as Elder Bernard sank to the floor, his face turning red, his neck muscles straining under Fritz's hands.

"The angel will not be denied," Fritz said through gritted teeth.

He let go and straightened again. Rebecca stared in horror at Elder Bernard's dead body on the floor.

Fritz picked up the book of matches, then turned suddenly and saw her standing outside the room. Rebecca's paralysis broke and she ran, screaming for her father, but no one heard her over the din of loud, excited voices. Fritz ran after her. He grabbed the collar of her dress from behind and slammed her against the hard wooden wall. Her head hit it with enough force that she heard her skull crack before she fell unconscious to the floor.

Outside the holy sanctuary, Laura hugged Meredith goodbye. "You sure you're going to be all right?"

Meredith tucked a strand of frizzy red hair behind her ear. "As long as I don't have to marry anyone."

"Francis and Rebecca have agreed to let you stay with them," Laura said. "And remember, I'm only a phone call away."

"Do you think I could come visit you in Sakima someday?" Meredith asked. "I want to see what it's like. When I'm old enough, I want to follow in Mal's footsteps and leave Valley Grove. He didn't get to live the life he wanted. Maybe I can do it for both of us."

"Anytime," Laura said.

From the corner of her eye, she saw the holy sanctuary's

door being pulled closed from the inside. When she looked up, she saw Fritz's face just before it shut.

"No!" She ran to the door and tried to pull it open, but it was locked from the inside. She banged on it with her palms. "Open the door! Hey, open the door!"

Booker ran up to her. "What is it?"

"It's Fritz. He's inside. He's locked us out."

"How did he get past us?"

"He must have been hiding in there this whole time."

She ran to the closest window. Through the glass, she saw a fire breaking out inside the building. It seemed to be everywhere at once, spreading quickly through the wooden structure. The flames blocked her view, but she heard screams and a frantic banging on the door from inside. Laura ran back to the door and tried to pull it open again, but it still wouldn't budge. Fritz hadn't just locked it, he'd barricaded it from the inside as well. No one could get out.

"Rebecca!" Meredith screamed as thick black smoke billowed out of the roof.

Booker ran around to a window on the side of the building. He drove his elbow into the glass, shattering it. Instantly, flames leapt out at him, driving him back.

"Rebecca!" Meredith screamed again, tears streaming down her face.

The back door—Laura had almost forgotten about it! She ran around the back of the building, waving away the smoke that roiled in her face and ignoring the growing heat. Somewhere behind her, she heard Booker on the phone with 911. She found the door in back and threw it open. The storeroom wasn't burning. The first thing she saw was Elder Bernard's crumpled body on the floor. His eyes were still open, the whites spotted red with the petechial hemorrhaging that came from being strangled. The next thing she saw were the empty gas cans. Cursing Fritz, she ran for the closed door that led to the interior of the holy sanctuary.

As soon as she yanked it open, thick black smoke rushed at her, along with a jarring blast of heat. Her eyes stung. She put her arm over her nose and mouth as she stepped inside. Even just crossing the threshold, the heat increased dramatically. She could still hear screams coming from the main part of the holy sanctuary. She squinted, trying to see anything in front of her, but all she got was a face full of caustic, blinding smoke. The air was thin as the fire devoured the oxygen. Every instinct told her to turn back. Instead, she pushed forward.

Something moved ahead of her. A shape parted the billowing smoke and came into the light. It was Francis. He had burns on one arm and half his face. He coughed heavily from the smoke. In his arms he carried Rebecca's limp form. Laura cried out with relief. Removing her arm from across her face, she held her breath against the smoke and took Rebecca from him. The girl wasn't badly burned, but she was unconscious and there was blood on her scalp.

She carried Rebecca back toward the door. She glanced behind her to make sure Francis was coming and saw another shape spring like a demon from the roiling smoke. It was Fritz. His clothes were a shroud of fire, yet somehow he was still standing. He wrapped a burning arm around Francis's neck and pulled him back into the smoke.

Laura's lungs ached for air. She had to get Rebecca out of the building before the smoke suffocated them both. She hurried out of the building just as Booker came running toward the back door to find her.

"Take her," Laura said, handing Rebecca off to him. Then she ran back inside.

"No! Laura!" Booker yelled after her.

She ran through the storeroom again and into the holy sanctuary. She couldn't see anything but smoke.

"Francis!" she yelled. The smoke bullied its way into her nose and mouth, hot embers burning her throat. She doubled over and coughed. "Francis!" she yelled again, but her hoarse voice would barely carry.

A thick, burning beam from the ceiling fell directly in front of her. The blast of heat that washed over her was so intense she could smell her own hair burning. Strong arms wrapped around her from behind as Booker pulled her out of the building.

"No!" she yelled, coughing. "Francis is still in there!"

"He's gone!" he said. "They're all gone!"

She realized then that the screaming had stopped. There was no more banging on the doors and windows. The only sound was the hungry roar of the fire.

A moment later, it was joined by the sound of sirens in the distance. Booker brought Laura across the street from the burning building. Meredith was already there on the grass, sobbing with relief and gratitude as she knelt over Rebecca's unconscious body.

40

The small hospital room in the Hudson Valley Medical Center was quiet except for the steady beeping of the heart monitor. *At least Rebecca's heart is strong*, Laura told herself, sitting in one of the room's two visitor chairs. Rebecca looked so small and frail in the bed. An IV drip was attached to her arm, and a big, chunky pulse oximeter was clipped to her finger. An oxygen mask had been secured over her mouth and nose. Laura knew oxygen was the best treatment for smoke inhalation. There was nothing else she or the doctors at the hospital could do but wait and monitor her progress. It didn't make things any easier.

Miraculously, Rebecca only suffered minor burns, which were being treated with topical antibiotics and bandages. However, she'd breathed in a lot of smoke. They found soot in her nostrils and throat, and her chest X-rays revealed swelling in the bronchial passages. They were thinking about prescribing a bronchodilator medication to widen the airways but hadn't decided yet. Her blood test revealed an elevated red blood cell count, but Laura was assured that was to be expected with smoke inhalation, and the count was still within a safe range. The results for her arterial blood gas test also had them optimistic, but they couldn't say for sure yet if her brain had been starved of oxygen long enough to cause permanent damage. They needed her to be awake to test her cognitive functions, but so far, Rebecca still hadn't regained consciousness. The doctors tiptoed around the word coma.

Rebecca also had a concussion, which the doctors thought might be delaying her recovery. They thought she might have passed out from the smoke and hit her head when she fell.

Laura, knowing Fritz had been inside the holy sanctuary with Rebecca, had different ideas about what might have happened. But Fritz was dead now. He died in the fire of his own making.

Francis was dead, too. His body had been recovered with the rest. The uncle she'd only just met, the man who'd loved and married her aunt Gwen, was gone. With Rebecca still in the hospital, Laura barely had time to process the loss, but she knew it would hit her soon. When it did, it would hit hard.

She dreaded breaking the news to Rebecca when she woke up that her father was dead. That everyone she knew in Valley Grove was dead.

If she woke up.

Not everyone was dead. Meredith was still with them. Two orphaned girls, the only survivors of a fundamentalist religious sect. Laura wanted to take care of them both, but the thought was too overwhelming. Booker had asked Sam Templeton, the ex-member of the Church of the Divine Chariot whom Malachai was on his way to see when he died, to take Meredith in temporarily until something else could be arranged.

Days bled by unacknowledged as Laura sat with Rebecca. Meal times came and went unnoticed. At some point, Dae-jung came to see her in the hospital room.

"Are you all right?" he asked, sitting in the other visitor chair.

"They checked me out. Minor smoke inhalation. They gave me an inhaler to use for the next week. It's nothing to worry about."

"That's not what I meant."

"I know," Laura said. "I'm hanging in there."

He looked at Rebecca's unconscious form in the bed. "It looks like she is, too. She's a fighter."

It runs in the family, Laura thought. Rebecca had Gwen's stubbornness and tenacity. If anything would help her pull through, it was that.

"I have an update for you about Thurmond Biotech," Dae-jung said. "There's good news and bad news. Which do you want to hear first?"

Laura shrugged. That kind of decision was way beyond her right now.

"The good news is, the EPA is holding them accountable for illegally storing hazardous materials on their premises," he said. "The bad news is, they're being fined. No one is being charged with a crime."

Laura nodded numbly. She wasn't surprised. The government would rather pull in revenue from fines than put business owners, many of whom were big political donors, behind bars. It was a slap in the face to everyone who'd died.

Dae-jung stood up and put a hand on her shoulder. "Hey, it's still a win."

Laura put her hand over his. "Thanks, Dae-jung."

He smiled kindly. "Try to get some rest. I'll see you at the station when you're ready to come back."

Chief Morales had told Laura to take all the time she needed. It was unusually nice of her.

Dae-jung left. The heart monitor kept beeping. The oxygen concentrator kept humming in the background like white noise. When visiting hours were over, Laura went back to Booker's house. He got her to eat a little dinner, then held her all night. She cried once. The rest of the time, she lay in bed and stared out the window, waiting for the sun to rise. In the morning, she went back to sit in Rebecca's hospital room. The nurse on duty, a tall, pretty woman named Blanca, informed her there'd been no change overnight. Rebecca still hadn't woken up. The doctors were less reluctant to use the word coma now.

At some point in the afternoon, there was a knock at the door. Booker came in with Meredith. It was a shock to see the girl in jeans and a t-shirt instead of her prairie dress. Her frizzy red hair had been fashioned into a long braid. Apparently, she was adjusting well to life in the outside world.

"Are you sure this is a good idea?" Laura said, getting up from the chair. "I didn't want her to see Rebecca like this."

"She wanted to come," Booker explained.

"It's okay, Laura," Meredith said, circling around to the far side of the bed. "I thought maybe if I was here, it would help Rebecca wake up."

Laura looked at Booker, who shrugged.

"I didn't think it was right to keep her from seeing her friend," he said.

Laura sighed. Maybe Booker was right. She thought she was protecting Meredith, but it was clear Meredith could handle it. The girl was stronger than she thought someone her age would be. Both girls were.

Meredith took Rebecca's limp hand in hers. "Rebecca, can you hear me? It's Meredith."

Booker put his arm around Laura. She leaned into him.

"You're exhausted," he said. "Why don't you go back and get some sleep? Let me take over for a while."

"No, I want to be here," she said. "I wouldn't be able to sleep anyway."

Meredith rubbed Rebecca's hand gently. "You're not alone, Rebecca. I'm here, too. Please wake up."

"What are we going to do with her?" Laura asked. "With either of them?"

"Sam's happy to give Meredith a place to stay, but it's only temporary," Booker said. "At some point, we're going to have to call Children's Services."

"They'll put her in a foster home," Laura said. "If Rebecca pulls through—"

"*When* she pulls through," Booker said. "She will."

Laura wished she shared his confidence, but she was afraid to let herself hope for the best. It felt safer to shield herself for the worst.

"They'll put Rebecca in a foster home, too," she said. "There's a good chance the two of them will be separated. Look at them, Booker. There's a strong bond there. I don't want them to be separated."

"I don't either." He pulled her away from the bed for more privacy. "Look, please don't freak out about this, but I've been thinking about it a lot. What if we adopted them?"

Laura looked up at him. "What?"

"You're Rebecca's cousin, and probably her last living relative," he said. "Meredith is going to need a legal guardian, and she already knows us. Plus, they're as close as sisters already, and we both don't want them separated. Adopting them makes sense."

She watched Meredith bend down to kiss Rebecca on the forehead.

"Please wake up, Rebecca," Meredith said. "It's safe now. We're both safe."

"If we *did* adopt them," Laura said, "we'd need a bigger place to live."

"True."

"Your house isn't big enough for four of us, and my house..." She trailed off. She could only handle one tragedy at a time. "If we're serious about this, we have to figure everything out first."

"To be honest, this wasn't how I pictured asking you to move in with me," Booker said. "I had wine, candles, and a nice dinner in mind, not a hospital room and two teenage girls to consider. But I know someplace we can live that has enough room for all of us."

"It'll be expensive."

"Nah," he said. "It won't cost us a thing."

She looked up at him again. "What are you talking about?"

"Victor's house," he said. "I decided not to sell it. It'll need fixing up, of course. There's a lot of junk to clean out. Weapons, too. He had guns stashed all over that house."

"And the drugs," Laura added.

"The house has three bedrooms," Booker said. "Plus, it's located far enough from the center of town that it might help the girls adjust at their own pace. What do you think?"

Beside the hospital bed, Meredith held Rebecca's hand again. "You have to wake up, Rebecca. If you don't, I'll be all alone."

Laura's heart, already broken, managed to break again.

"Okay," she said. "Let's do it."

There was a knock at the door behind her. Chief Morales came into the room.

"Sorry," Morales said. "I didn't realize you had company."

"It's all right," Laura said, pulling away from Booker. "It's nice of you to come by."

"Is there someplace we speak in private, Dr. Powell?" Morales asked.

"Sure, there's a visitors' lounge on this floor. No one is ever in there."

She and Morales went into the hallway outside, where the hum of voices and the beeping of equipment was louder. A nurse wheeled a portable blood pressure machine past them on her way to another room. Laura led the way to the lounge at the other end of the floor, just past the nurses' station, weaving around staff and visitors walking in both directions. *Lounge* was an overstatement. It was a small, stuffy room with a few chairs and tables, a vending machine, and a water fountain. As she'd expected, it was empty. Laura took a seat while Morales closed the door for privacy.

"The fire investigators found something at your house," Morales said, sitting down across the table from her. "There were traces of gasoline."

Laura stiffened. "The fire wasn't an accident? Someone set it?"

"That's not all," Morales said. "Traces of gasoline were also found in the remains of the church in Valley Grove as well. I don't think that's a coincidence."

"You think Fritz set both fires?" She paused as the implication hit her. "He was *in my house* that night?"

Her skin crawled at the thought of Fritz breaking into her home while she slept. Had he come upstairs? Had he been in her bedroom while she slept? She shuddered thinking about how vulnerable she was. What he could have done to her.

"Using an accelerant like gasoline is part of his M.O.," Morales said. "Turns out Fritz Ruggen had a record. He had a stint in juvie for being quite the firebug in his youth."

"Fritz was Eliezer's right-hand man," Laura said. "He wouldn't have done this on his own."

Morales leaned forward in her chair. "You think Eliezer sent him to kill you?"

"I can't think of any other reason Fritz would leave Valley Grove and come all the way to Sakima," Laura said. "I gave my address to Meredith. Eliezer must have found it and told Fritz where I live."

"Why?"

"I was an outsider and a woman. He didn't like me putting my nose where he thought it didn't belong."

"I'm almost sorry one of the snakes got that bastard before I could," Morales said. "I would have loved to put him behind bars myself."

The door to the lounge burst open, and Booker ran into the room.

"Laura, come quick! She's awake!"

She ran back to Rebecca's room with Booker. Her heart was in her throat. When she got there, she saw Meredith leaning over Rebecca's prone form and hugging her. Rebecca's arms were around Meredith. Her eyes were open.

"I knew it," Meredith said. "I knew you could hear my voice!"

Tears of relief streamed down Laura's cheeks. Rebecca turned her head, saw her, and smiled.

"Cousin Laura!" she said. She was pale, and her voice sounded hoarse and weak through the oxygen mask. She let go of Meredith and opened her arms to Laura.

Laura ran to the bed to embrace her.

Sometime later, Nurse Blanca came in and asked Laura to stop hugging Rebecca so she could take the girl's vitals, but Laura just needed another minute.

41

Mateo Linares had been on an EPA cleanup team for the past fifteen years. Having worked on Superfund sites up and down the East Coast, he'd seen things most people wouldn't believe. He'd pulled an antique car out of a TCE-contaminated leech field in Rhode Island, and a human skeleton out of the Gowanus Canal in Brooklyn. He'd seen an abandoned petroleum refinery in Pennsylvania where the walls were covered in toxic, bioluminescent mold, and a landfill in New Jersey where they'd discovered dozens of coffins from a cemetery that had supposedly been moved to make way for a new highway. None of it spooked him as much as the cave full of dead snakes did.

Moving through the dark in their stark-white HAZMAT suits, Mateo's teammates looked like ghosts as they removed the drums of hazardous material and carried them out to the disposal trucks. More of the material had spilled onto the cave floor and would take a lot longer to deal with than the drums. They would probably have to excavate, maybe even seal off the cave.

Then there were all the goddamned dead snakes.

They were everywhere, hundreds of them. The carcasses would have to be incinerated because of their proximity to the toxic material. Mateo figured he must have been a real bastard in a previous life because for some reason he was stuck on the snake collection team. It was the first time in his career he would have rather handled drums full of toxic sludge.

He used stainless-steel claw grippers to pick up the snakes and drop them into one-gallon plastic hazardous material bags. His bag was already getting full and the team had barely made a dent. There were places in the cave where the dead snakes were still so thick you couldn't even see the ground.

"Yo, Mateo!" Iris Caldwell said, hustling over to him.

He'd worked with Iris for most of his time with the EPA. She was the one who found the coffins in Jersey. Nothing fazed her.

"You gotta see this!" She sounded excited.

Mateo dropped a dead snake into his bag. "What did you find this time?"

"I don't know what the hell it is." Under the clear plastic face plate of her hood, the lines around her eyes deepened with excitement. "Come see, huh? Maybe you can tell me what the fuck it is."

He tied up his hazardous materials bag, left his claw grabber beside it, and followed her deeper into the cave. The rest of the snake collection team shot him dirty looks as he passed, envious that he was taking an unauthorized break. They'd give him an earful about it later, maybe even prank him to get even. He'd probably find a rubber snake waiting for him in his locker.

"It's back here," Iris said.

She led him into an open cavern at the rear of the cave, where there was a crater-sized recess in the floor. At the bottom was something that looked like a length of sewer pipe, only the work lights showed it was covered with snake scales.

"Tell me what the fuck that is," Iris said.

"You got me." Mateo started down the incline toward it. "It's not alive, is it?"

"I don't think so," Iris said, walking down with him. "It hasn't moved at all, thank God."

"Jesus," Mateo said. "*Could* this thing move? Look at the size of it."

"You know what really freaks me out?" Iris said. "It doesn't have eyes. Or a mouth. So what the fuck is it?"

Mateo shrugged. "Gonna have to burn it later along with the snakes."

"I'll gladly burn this shit right now, before the fucking thing gives me nightmares," Iris said.

Mateo circled it. On the other side, he discovered a part of the creature where its hide looked thinner, like the membrane between a hard-boiled egg and its shell. The skin there was torn open. The floor was still sticky from some kind of fluid that had spilled out.

"Oh fuck, I think it was a mama," Iris said.

Mateo examined the ruptured sac again. It looked like it had been broken open from the inside, as if something had pushed its way out. He shuddered.

"Where's the baby?" he asked.

He looked around himself nervously. A wet, sticky trail led from the dead creature into the darkness beyond the work lights.

Whatever it had given birth to was long gone.

AFTERWORD

In the immortal words of Indiana Jones, "Snakes? Why did it have to be snakes?"

That pretty much sums up how I feel about them. I know there are people out there who love snakes, and some who even find snakes to be very affectionate companions. Believe me, I've seen them proudly carrying their pet boas across their shoulders in Central Park, a sight that never fails to make my chest tighten with apprehension. *What if it decides to strangle its owner? What if it decides to strangle ME?*

I'm well aware that my fear of snakes is primal, not rational. They're animals like any other and generally won't bother you if given space and treated with respect. I think the fear that I and so many others have about snakes stems from the fact that they're so unlike us. They have scales instead of soft skin and hair. We can't read emotion in their eyes or faces. Perhaps most alarmingly, they don't have any limbs. To see these legless creatures move by bending their spines into coils and pushing off of surfaces, or by violently sidewinding, or by gripping the ground with their wide belly scales while pushing forward with other scales is, for some of us, like witnessing something out of a nightmare. It's not the snake's fault. They have their own reasons for evolving to look and act the way they do. Still, this fear dates back to humankind's earliest days. We've been wary of snakes for a long time. It's no wonder the Bible makes the snake the bad guy.

Of course, the reason this ancient fear developed—and a much more rational reason to be afraid of them—is that some snakes are venomous. As with the previous Dr. Laura Powell novel, *The Hungry Earth*, I tried to keep the science in

The Stone Serpent as accurate as possible. When Laura assures poor, doomed Craig Hutsell that a copperhead's venom is the least toxic of all of the venomous snakes in the United States, she's not lying. Copperheads don't pose much of a threat to humans, provided you seek medical help after getting bitten. An estimated 2,900 people are bitten by copperheads every year, but the fatality rate is approximately 0.01%. The only reason there are so many bites per year is because copperheads like to be near water and forests, which unfortunately is also where most humans like to be. Copperheads enjoy taking shelter from the sun under fallen leaves, and they're perfectly camouflaged to do so. The problem is that those leaves are often in people's yards.

They also like to shelter from the sun in piles of toys left outside, or under porches and sheds, or in woodpiles. Without intending to, people create very attractive shelters for copperheads, so who can blame them for taking advantage? Unfortunately, this is why most copperhead bites happen. The snakes are startled by people accidentally stepping on them or coming too close, and they strike in self-defense. They're not aggressive, just scared that you're a predator out to get them, which is why I was pleased to discover in the course of my research that most experts urge people not to kill copperheads and instead either leave them be (and tread carefully during the warm months when they're out of their dens), or take away the items in your yard in which they might be tempted to curl up for a midday nap.

The most fun part of writing these novels is the research phase. It's when I get to learn all kinds of fascinating things. For instance, the story of Peng Fan, a chef in the Guangdong province of China. Back in 2014, he decided to make snake soup, which is a delicacy in the region. He wanted to use only fresh snake meat, so he had a live spitting cobra sent to his kitchen. He cut off the cobra's head, and then spent the next twenty minutes or so deboning the body and dicing up the snake meat for the soup. When he was done, he went to throw away the head—and it bit him! Unfortunately, help didn't reach him in time, and Peng Fan died from the venom.

Now, you might be thinking it was just a reflex or he accidentally pricked his finger on a fang, but no, the snake head actually bit him. What Peng Fan didn't know was that after decapitation, a snake's head can live on for up to an hour. So here's this decapitated cobra head, still alive and forced to watch the chef cut up its body right in front of it. As soon as it has the chance, it takes its final act of revenge and bites him.

Pyrethrin, a naturally occurring chemical compound found in chrysanthemum flowers and often used as a pesticide, really is fatal to snakes, even in low doses. However, for the sake of the narrative, I may have stretched things a bit by using a pyrethrin spray to take out an entire massive snake den. Don't try it at home.

As interesting as researching snakes was, taking a deep dive into the science of petrifaction was even more compelling. Using petrified wood as my jumping-off point, I wondered how and why a human body might become similarly petrified, and if it could be done in a matter of minutes instead of taking centuries. That question led me to some truly amazing discoveries.

The art installation Laura and Booker visit at Storm King Arts Center at the beginning of the novel, in which simulated human organs are grown with crystals, is based on a real installation at Washington, D.C.'s Industry Gallery in 2013 called *The Invisible Human* by a group of British artists from Studio Tobias Klein and Ordinary Ltd. When I read about *The Invisible Human*, it helped spark my imagination and I knew I had to pay homage to it in the book.

The story of poor Stuckie the dog is, unfortunately, a true one, and the pictures I found online are just as sad and chilling as I described in the novel. As a dog lover, the thought of this unfortunate pooch getting stuck in a hollow tree and dying from dehydration broke my heart.

Unfortunately, *Corpus Delecti: The Journal of Death Studies* isn't a real journal—how cool would that be?—but the story Laura reads in it about nineteenth-century Italian scientists artificially petrifying cadavers is true, much to my morbid excitement. The scientist Paolo Gorini (1813-1881) petrified hundreds of cadavers during his career by injecting them with a chemical formula he created that combined mercuric bichloride and calcium chloride. I borrowed that same formula for the basilisks' venom. I hope Paolo Gorini won't mind.

Also shockingly real is Lake Natron, with its morbid underwater statue garden of petrified birds. Its reputation as the deadliest lake in the world continues to this day. Unless you're a flamingo, apparently.

Many thanks to my incredible agent, Richard Curtis, who is definitely a resilient flamingo in the deadly lake of publishing. Thanks once again to David Niall Wilson and David Dodd at Crossroad Press for giving Dr. Laura Powell a home for her adventures. Thanks to All That's Interesting, Bob Ferguson's Fascinature, Cambridge University's "NakedScientists," Centers for Disease Control and Prevention, Fast Company, Home Science Tools, How It's Made, the Jewish Chronicle, the Journal of the American Academy of Dermatology, Live Science, Mayo Clinic, National Science Foundation, Nature, Origins Explained, Sharecare, Smithsonian Magazine, Smithsonian's National Zoo & Conservation Biology Institute, ThoughtCo, Underknown's What If, Wikipedia, WSILTV, and Vice for being invaluable research resources.

As always, special enormous thanks to my wife, Alexa Antopol, for her love and support, and for her belief in me on the days when nothing seems to go right.

About the Author

Nicholas Kaufmann is the Bram Stoker Award-nominated, Thriller Award-nominated, Shirley Jackson Award-nominated, and Dragon Award-nominated author of eight novels, including the bestsellers *100 Fathoms Below* and *The Hungry Earth*. His short fiction has appeared in *Cemetery Dance*, *Black Static*, *Nightmare Magazine*, *Interzone*, and others. In addition to his own original work, he has also written for such properties as *Zombies vs. Robots*, *The Rocketeer*, and *Warhammer*. He lives in Brooklyn, NY.

Bibliography

100 Fathoms Below (with Steven L. Kent)

Chasing the Dragon

Die and Stay Dead

Dying Is My Business

General Slocum's Gold

The Hungry Earth

Hunt at World's End

In the Shadow of the Axe

Still Life: Nine Stories

The Stone Serpent

Walk in Shadows

Curious about other Crossroad Press books?
Stop by our site:
http://store.crossroadpress.com
We offer quality writing
in digital, audio, and print formats.

www.ingramcontent.com/pod-product-compliance
Lightning Source LLC
Chambersburg PA
CBHW030404020726
47493CB00003B/943